MW01128287

ALSO BY BEN MONOPOLI

The Painting of Porcupine City: A Novel

The Cranberry Hush

a novel

Ben Monopoli

For Josh and Ethan

The Cranberry Hush

FRIDAY
February 4, 2005

I had a feeling when I looked outside that morning that something cool was going to happen. Maybe it was the snow, so clean and blank and ready for anything—and still coming down. Through the night the wind howled and slammed against my windows and the clanking storm door in the garage. Now it was windless and quiet—flakes came straight down, thick and heavy, making the backyard sparkle in the weak morning sun. Judging by the vague white hump I knew to be the picnic table, there was well over a foot already, maybe even closer to two.

Something cool was definitely going to happen. How could it not? Maybe today was the day I'd tell Zane I loved him. Maybe I'd just get a snow-day.

I heard a voice mumbling out of the phone so I put it back to my ear.

"—ince. You there?" The voice belonged to Simon, my boss at Golden Age Comics. He'd scrambled away mid-conversation to let in his new wife's yipping dog.

"Get her?" I said.

"I had to go way the hell out. She sunk in a drift." He chuckled, or maybe he was huffing a bit. "I swear—that dog."

"Pretty deep, huh?"

"I'll say. You don't have a yardstick nearby, do you?"

"A yardstick? Out in the garage, I think. Why?"

"Would you do me a favor, Vince, and measure it so we can get something official? I like to have accurate information before I make any decisions."

"Oh, sure. Hold on. I'll go get it."

"Thanks."

I put the phone down on the kitchen counter, rinsed and filled the kettle, put it on the stove and turned on the burner. After making some door sounds with the cupboards I picked up the phone. "OK, Simon."

"How much are we looking at?"

I looked through the sliding door at the buried deck, at the covered shrubs, at tree limbs bent under the weight of the snow. "Hold on," I said. "It's really cold. I'm just in my pajamas." In a patch of fog growing on the glass I drew a Superman S symbol. "Jeez Simon, I'm showing eighteen inches so far."

"Wow!"

"Uh. But there's some drifting on my deck, so it could be a little less?"

"That's fine, that's fine. Get back inside, Vince. I don't want you to freeze. I could never run the store without you."

"Whew, my hands are all tingly now." The water was starting to boil; I took it off the burner before it had a chance to whistle. "So what do you think, Simon? Eighteen inches. I could probably make it in..."

"Hmm." From the other end came pensive breathing, as though Simon was savoring having to make this executive decision. "Stay home," he said finally. "People can live without their comics for a day—never thought I'd say that! Don't you think?"

"I totally agree." I held the phone with my shoulder and dumped some coffee into the French press. "Has Golden Age ever closed before?"

"I'm sure we have. Well. Who's on the schedule with you today? Zane?"

"Marissa."

"I'll give her a call, let her know. Go make a snowman!" He hung up.

"Oh yeah," I said to myself. I knew today was going to be cool.

My coffee wasn't quite hot enough but I carried it down the hall. I stepped up onto my bed, walked across the mattress in my boxer shorts and thick blue socks and put the coffee on the nightstand. I stood there a minute, my buzzed hair grazing the ceiling, pulling absentmindedly at the waistband of my boxers, and then I said "Ha!" and collapsed into the warm, disheveled sheets.

The thing about snow days is that they're blissful in theory but always kind of intimidating when they actually happen. The day loomed as blank and white as my backyard. I pulled the blankets up to my chin and rubbed the sateen hem against my lips. I figured I'd just sleep through a few more of the daylight hours ahead—no reason to call Zane just yet. There was plenty of time on a day like today. I pulled my legs up into a ball to stay warm on my usual side of the double bed, rubbed my face into the pillow.

When I was a kid, like elementary school age, I used to tape notes to the headboard of my bed on the nights before forecasted storms. In block letters I'd write SNOW DAY or NO SCHOOL TOMORROW—little affirmations, little prayers to the weather gods and the superintendent. Now that I was twenty-four there was still something romantic about snow. The excitement of snow-days never really went away—in college, in the hands of hundreds of teenagers faced with unexpected idleness, they'd even grown more magical. When I remembered this I had the sudden desire to be out in it, to be buried in it, to feel it all around me. Maybe even, as Simon recommended, to build a snowman.

A small wall of snow collapsed into my living room when I pulled open the door. I went out and breathed in the cold air. Drifts rolled like white sand dunes across my front yard and climbed high against the sand-colored siding of my little Cape Cod house. I quickly kicked clear the steps just enough to sit down. The rest of it—the walk, the driveway—all that could wait.

I took a sip of coffee, touched the warm mug to my chin, my cheeks. In the sky, lines of blue looked sketched among gray clouds like an unfinished Van Gogh, and from somewhere not too far away I could hear the beep-beep of a plow backing up. A single car crept up my street, its wipers knocking back and forth fast-fast like hummingbird wings. I pushed the mug into the snow by my knee and doodled a spiral around it with one gloved finger. It was just after nine o'clock in the morning, and the neighborhood was quiet. It was easy to imagine this as an icy, isolated Fortress of Solitude.

From outside the house, the Billie Holiday record I'd put on sounded sweetly distant, like a memory of a song stuck in my head. Zane liked to play music quiet like this. He said it made him focus on the song more than if the volume hit him hard.

I would shovel, I decided, just enough for him to get his car in my driveway, and then I'd call him. I pulled my peacoat's floppy collar up around my neck and my hat down to my eyebrows. If he wanted to come over we could listen to records and look through the yellow, dog-eared comics in that cardboard box in my spare bedroom, the ones Simon had loaded into the Dumpster because they weren't worth anything. The ones Zane and I, months ago when things were easier, snuck out as treasure. I'd make us hot chocolate.

Across the street my neighbor opened her front door and took a surprised look at her buried front steps. She had white hair and wore a navy blue housecoat. She bent down slowly and dipped a wrinkled hand into the snow.

I put my hands against my mouth and shouted, "I'll come over and shovel you later, Mrs. Bradford!"

She waved and held out her arms, as if to catch a schoolyard ball.

I took another sip of coffee, watched my breath mix with the steam. If I made hot chocolate for Zane, I wondered, would that make it seem too much like a date? Would floating marshmallows, white and shiny in halos of melting, suggest an eroticism I'd be better off avoiding? Maybe. Maybe I'd swap the hot chocolate for beer, or apple juice, or Coke. Or something. Or maybe hot chocolate *without* marshmallows. If he even wanted to come over at all. Shit—if I even called him.

He probably shouldn't drive in this snow, anyway. And shoveling would be hard.

Mrs. Bradford held her hand out in the air and then put it to her lips, pulled back inside her house and closed the door.

Suddenly my knee was warm and I noticed my mug had lurched in its melting cupholder and sloshed coffee on my leg and into the spirals of snow. It hissed and a circle of brown slush sprang outward from the mug. I lifted it out of the snow, rescuing an inch of coffee, and leaned back against the step.

That's when I saw the figure walking up the narrow street. The puffy red vest he wore over a hooded sweatshirt stood out like an explosion against all the white, and he carried a backpack, the kind with the frame and the waist strap; there was a layer of snow on top. The snow was starting to pile up on my own outstretched legs, and the coffee spot was getting cold. I thought of going back inside to Billie, to the fire I built before coming out, but I decided to wait to see where this snow-covered stranger was headed. I took another sip of coffee.

He made his way slowly up the street, each step a search for a foothold in the slushy ruts left by plows. He was looking at each white-covered house as he passed it. When he came to the front of mine he stopped and stomped his boots and lifted the edge of his hood away from his eyes. Was he looking at me? Was he trying to make out the snow-dusted brass *63* on my door? I stood up, brushed off my legs and shoulders. The man on the street, though I could only see the small circle of face his scarf and pulled-tight hood revealed, was looking for someone.

Was it me? I was not expecting a visitor.

"Vince!" the stranger called. I started at the sound of my name, unexpected and booming through the muffled neighborhood. He laughed a laugh that sounded full of relief and waved. My pulse quickened. I wanted to think this was Zane but I knew it wasn't.

"Who is it?" I called, and began to wade out into my yard with clumsy, teetering steps. Snow went down my boots and bit my ankles through my socks. The stranger looked back and forth along the piles of snow along the street that formed a barrier between him and my yard. He threw up his hands in mock desperation and waved again.

Part of me knew who it was by then—a part that could tell just by the way he moved his hands, by the tone of his scarf-dampened voice. In fact, what I doubted now more than the person's identity was whether I was really awake at all, and not still in bed dreaming all this up. But when I got closer I was able to see his eyes through the opening between his hood and his scarf. They were green and bright. They belonged to the person in the photos on my living room wall.

The last inch of coffee slipped from the mug as it left my fingers and disappeared in a poof of white.

"Griffin?" It came out of me as a whisper. There was an inclination to run away, to dive beneath the snow and burrow away. I stepped hesitantly at first, not bothering to look for the mug, and then walked faster, stumbling, like I was running along the beach, overcome now, amazed, amazed. "Is that you?"

"It's me! I must look like a snowman."

"What're you— You do! Frosty!"

"I know! Haha!"

I was shivering, not just because my boots were full of snow. "What are you doing here?" I said, wading closer. "How the hell *are* you?"

He hugged himself. "I'm cold!" He pulled aside his scarf and put his gloved finger to his unshaven chin, as though trying to determine the best way to reach me. Then he started climbing up one side of the snow bank that divided us. I climbed up the other. We met at the top, overlooking the street and my yard, steadying ourselves in the loose snow with the same motion used to stomp grapes.

I opened my mouth to speak again but only white breath came out. My heart was pounding, my mind spinning. I started to lean in to give him a hug and we did that hesitant, shaky dance while a hug worked itself out. When he finally had his arms around me, though, he hugged me really hard, hard enough to make me slip.

"Whoa-ho, careful," he said, grabbing my sleeve. "Look at all this, huh?"

Was this really him? Could it be? What the *fuck*? I felt like rubbing my eyes like a surprised cartoon character. *Weeker-weeker-week*.

"This sure is a surprise," I said. "How the heck did you get here? I'm guessing you didn't walk the whole way."

"Bus," he said. His lips were chapped, his nose windburn-red. "I took the bus."

"Wait a second— From where? I guess it's been so long..."

"From Boston. I was living with Beth. Beth O'Shea. Do you remember—?"

"Of course I remember Beth. So you're together then?"

"Well— No. Not really, no. Not anymore."

"Oh. That sucks. I'm sorry."

"Eh, you know." He lifted his arms and let them fall against the padded waist strap at his hips. Snow, disturbed, tumbled off his hood and shoulders and backpack in tiny avalanches. "Not everything works out. Story of my fucking life, right? I know it's been a while, Vince, but some things never change."

"I guess. ...So you came here?"

He shrugged his shoulders as best he could beneath the straps and nodded.

"But what made you? It's been so long."

"Figured you'd take me in," he said. His scarf, which had risen back to the position it froze in, bunched against his cheeks, conveying a nervous smile beneath.

A car went by below us. Its exhaust puffed white behind it. Little snowballs danced and crumbled with the vibration of the tires. My eyes traveled up the snow pile. Snow caked Griff's pant legs. This was too detailed. This was no dream.

"I wasn't wrong, was I?" he added, the corners of his eyes revealing a subtle wince.

"Well no— I mean, of course you're welcome. I'm just— This is a surprise."

"Bad one? Good one?"

"Good one, sure."

"So that's your house?" he said, gesturing to it.

"Yup."

"Looks warm."

"Jesus, yeah. Come in. Come in, I'm sorry. You must be freezing." I began to climb down off our mountain.

"Thanks. I am." He sat down and shimmied on his butt down to the yard. "The snow was already coming down pretty hard when I got into town last night so I slept in the bus place. Well, maybe not slept. Dozed. I got the first cab I saw—it got stuck a mile or so back." He pointed down the street.

"A mile's not bad," I said.

"Mm."

We waded back across the front yard along the path I had made.

"How deep do you think this is?" I said.

"The snow? I don't know. Fourteen inches? Fifteen?"

"My boss wanted me to go out and measure and I was like, *Screw that, Simon*, so I took a guess and I said eighteen."

"The drifts are probably eighteen."

"Yeah, that's what I told him."

I stomped on the steps and smacked snow off my jeans with my gloves. Billie Holiday's voice grew louder when I pushed open the door. The warm spicy smell of burning firewood greeted us.

"Oh, heat at last, thank god." He yanked off his gloves and held his hands in the air like a hobo at a trashcan fire.

"You can kick off your stuff here," I said, stepping out of my boots.

"Sounds good." He wiggled out of his backpack and leaned it against the wall. He shook off his vest and sweatshirt before stepping inside and closing the door. "Nice place," he said. He bent forward and rubbed the small of his back. "*Ooof.*"

In the picture glass that hung beside him I caught a reflection of me sporting a dumbfounded expression. No way was Griff really here in my house. I turned around. "Let me give you the grand tour," I said. "I can pretty much do it right here, from the welcome mat. Ha."

"Nah, it looks like a great house," he said reassuringly as he untied his boots. I hadn't meant to seem embarrassed; I liked my house. I appreciated its weird color schemes (the living room's walls were burnt sienna, the kitchen's teal blue), its faux-wood–paneled cabinets and its drafty windows. Rather than reflecting a mash of hand-me-downs and yard-sale items, each one making its mark, the house looked carefully designed. It flirted in places with dumpy or tacky but always pulled back into quaint. At least I thought so.

Still, if I'd known he was coming I would've taken days, maybe weeks, getting everything just-so.

"Well this is obviously the living room here," I told him, gesturing like a game show model. "I believe in the olden days it was called a sitting room but I'm not quite that old-fashioned."

"Corduroy, Vince? Really?" He smiled, pointing at my two corduroy armchairs, one brown, one dark blue, both faded in the seats. A long leather ottoman stood in front of them. In a cabinet in the corner, beside the glowing fireplace, was the record player. There was the small television. There was the picture window— dual-named, because on either side of it hung framed photos, some black and white, some color.

He pulled off his boots, hopping on one foot then the other, and followed me through the arched doorway into the kitchen. A half-wall capped in a bar-like countertop and tiled on both sides with glossy sea-green squares separated it from the living room.

"This is where I do my modest cooking," I said. "Slightly more advanced than the dorm-room hot-pot ramen, but only slightly." I laughed, but he didn't seem to be hearing me; he was looking at the picture on the wall above the table.

"You still have the blue dog," he said, smiling. "Hey boy, long time no see." Yes, he was speaking to my art. It struck me as so cute I almost started crying. And I imagined the perpetually expectant look in the blue dog's oil-on-canvas-on-posterboard eyes softened just a little at the sound of Griff's voice.

I cleared my throat. "Come on," I told him. I led him out of the kitchen and down the hall to the rest of my little house, wishing for the first time that it was bigger. When the tour ended we'd have to talk about something other than furnishings and blue dogs and snow, and I had no idea yet what that would be. It was easier to continue stating the obvious. "Bathroom," I announced, pushing open the door and discreetly kicking a pair of underwear into the corner against the hamper.

"Bathroom," he repeated, nodding. "All the amenities."

"And this is basically a junk room," I said about the second bedroom, which contained my desk, an overloaded bookcase and that box of Simon's old comics (I realized, for the first time, they smelled). "And my bedroom." I didn't take him in, but rather just walked past it, and then I tapped the two remaining hallway doors. "Closet. Cellar. Cellar's kind of gross, so we'll leave that alone."

And then it was done. We returned to the kitchen, kind of facing each other a few feet apart—on a map of us this space would be labeled Awkwardland. I turned and began wiping off the counter, just something to do, while he looked around taking in details. I wished again that I'd had a chance to clean up more. "So that's, uh, pretty much—"

"I like it," he said with a smile. "This place is exactly you."

"You think so?"

"Yeah."

"Thanks."

"The fireplace smells good," he said.

"That's my favorite part."

"Can I stoke it?" he said. "Is that a word? Stoke?"

"I think so." I looked over the half-wall. The glowing coals in the charred cradle were low and hungry. "Go for it. Stoke away."

He went to the living room and moved a few pieces of split wood from the bin onto the embers. They snapped at the weight and he leaned away and touched his hair.

"You own this place?" he said. "Or rent?" He curled up in the brown chair, tucking his feet underneath him. He looked at home. He used to sit that way on his bed when he was doing homework, tapping his pen against the spine of a textbook, humming, swearing, asking me to come look at something real quick. Something about roommates, good roommates at least, is that once you live with someone, you always feel like whatever place they're in now is a little bit yours. Same smell, same stuff— same trinkets and furniture—that once intermixed with your own. He reached over to the stereo and turned my music down, as he'd done so many times before. The familiarity of the action quieted my buzzing nerves.

"My grandparents bought this place a few years ago when my grandpa was sick," I said. "They were planning some renovations and then they'd move in after he got better—they loved the Cape. Something to look forward to, I guess." I went into the living room and sat down in the other chair.

"Light at the end of the tunnel?" he said.

"Yeah, well he found the other light first. They never moved in. My grandmother won't sell it. So yours-truly took over as the official custodian person guy."

"Sweet." He laughed. "So you're squatting."

"I'm not squatting. Come on. I'm paying the mortgage. It's fair."

"Good deal," he said. "Well not the grandfather part, but you know." Then I saw the photos on the wall catch his eye. "Hey— is that me?" He got up and went over to them.

"There are a couple of you, yeah." When I saw him coming up the street I should've run inside and taken them all down. They made me feel like some kind of stalker.

He stood with his arms crossed, eyes moving back and forth across the photos. "This one's fucking funny," he said, tapping the frame. "Our antics. I like that you have these. Hey, that reminds me—I brought you a present." He went to his backpack, unzipped a nylon pocket, rummaged around, took out some t-shirts, a few sci-fi paperbacks. "I don't mean to keep you in suspense—there's no drum roll necessary. You paid about a hundred and thirty grand for this so I wanted to make sure you got it." He managed to yank out what he was looking for and held it out to me.

It was my Shuster College yearbook. I took it from him and his fingerprints evaporated from the glossy cover. I traced my finger along the raised gold letters of my name. Vincent J. Dandro. "How'd you get this?"

"You didn't pick it up at gradua— Ow, fuck that's *cold*!" He shook a socked foot out of the puddle by the door. "You didn't pick it up at graduation, I guess. Beth was on the yearbook staff. She has a whole box of unclaimed books. I don't know if it's really legit, but she has them. I guess she's supposed to mail them out if someone requests theirs, but it doesn't seem like many people ever do. I was looking through last fall and found yours. Got me thinking about you."

"I beat it out of there pretty quick that day," I said, meaning graduation. I opened the yearbook—its spine creaked and it smelled new, like paper, but like something else too. Was it Griff's house? Their house? I sat down on the ottoman.

"I looked for you after the ceremony," he said softly, "but yeah, you were gone. Anyway, there was a supplement thing they put out with grad photos and stuff, but I don't know what happened to that. I think you had to order it or something."

"It's OK," I said. "Thank you."

"You're a memory person. It's good to have." He gathered up his scattered belongings, separating from them a change of clothes and a baggie containing a toothbrush and a stick of Degree deodorant. "Would it be cool if I grab a quick shower while you're looking through that? I feel kind of rank."

"Sure, of course. I think you remember the bathroom from the tour?"

"Haha."

"Water takes a while to heat up, but it gets really hot so be careful. Towels are under the sink."

"Thanks. I'll try not to melt my flesh off."

"Hey, are you hungry?"

"Starved."

"I could make pancakes?"

"That would be awesome, thank you." He went into the bathroom and closed the door. I listened for the sound of the lock, wondering if he would turn it, and then it came. *Tink.*

I flipped through several glossy pages of the yearbook, but when I heard the shower turn on I closed it and set it on the arm of the chair. It felt cold in my hands, and not just because it had been outside.

I pulled a dusty griddle out of the kitchen cupboard and put it on the counter and cleaned it off. An icicle, thick and clear enough to make the yard behind it wobbly, hung behind the frosty window over the sink. I could see an orange snowblower against the white, spewing a snowy fountain into the air above my neighbor's yard.

I cracked eggs into a green plastic bowl, sniffed what was left of the milk, was glad there was almost enough, added a little water to compensate, poured, began to whisk it into pancake mix. I focused intently on the batter, making sure to pop every pocket of powder.

There was a yelp in the bathroom.

"Told you it gets hot!"

When I heard the shower turn off I ladled raw pancakes onto the griddle. Watching them bubble, listening to Griff putter in the bathroom—the click of his toothbrush against the sink, the *fwap* of pants being unfolded—I felt nervous, almost queasy. Before today I hadn't spoken to the guy since graduation two years ago, and even that brief conversation was just a blip in the span of our silence. You really had to go back four years to get to the last time were close. I noticed my hand was shaking. I started whisking what remained of the batter.

The bathroom door opened and Griff emerged in a cloud of steam, the grand entrance of every B-movie alien I'd ever seen. Maybe this wasn't Griff at all but some interstellar prankster setting me up. Forget about abductions, anal probes and secret alien cookbooks—the real fun was in poking at the Earthlings' old heartaches.

"Feel better?"

"Much," he said. "I hadn't been warm in like—thirty-six hours!"

He stopped at his backpack, carefully stepping around the cold puddle this time, to pack away his dirty clothes. Then he took a seat at the kitchen table.

"How're those pancakes coming?" he said, flicking at a bubble in the bottle of syrup I put on the table.

Griffin Dean at my kitchen table. He looked the same, mostly. His blond hair hung past his jaw in damp waves. He'd worn it long in college to hide the acne he'd been constantly at war with. His skin was clear now but scars speckled his temples and jaw. His green eyes were framed by eyebrows several shades darker than his hair. He was tall and lanky and apparently still wore his shirts too big. On his right shoulder-blade, I knew, was a tattoo of a knobby and twisted joshua tree. His white-socked toes curled around the bottom rung of the chair.

"They're getting there," I told him. "They may be a little bland—I didn't have enough milk."

"That's OK, that's what syrup is for."

"I have this thing about going to the supermarket. I hate it. So I like never have any food around here."

"I hear ya." He rocked the syrup bottle back and forth with his thumb. "At Beth's we'd have to carry all the groceries from the market to the apartment. That was a bitch, let me tell you. The handles on those plastic bags turn into razor-wire in about ten seconds."

"What part of Boston do you live in?"

"What part *did* I live in?"

"Sure. Yeah."

"Down by Fenway. One of those brownstone-type places. Cool location, but yeah, buying groceries was the pits."

"Perks of city life, huh?"

"It just forces you to be creative. We got stuff that could do double, triple meal-duty. A lot of cereal. Kix, Cheerios—they're good for breakfast, lunch, snack. And they're light."

"I like cereal. Oh, grab a plate." I gestured with my chin to the cupboard and began to pry the pancakes off the griddle. They were a little burned and I felt embarrassed.

He got up, reached for the cupboard door, showing dark dots on his sleeve where he hadn't dried thoroughly. He should've been gorgeous, really. On paper he was. He had the blond hair, the bright eyes, the strong jaw with a shadow of golden beard—all the elements, all the materials—but he looked somehow more boy-next-door than runway model, and that was fine. It made him seem more within reach, more attainable, even though as a straightboy he was no more attainable for me than a runway model. He pulled out two plates, put one on the counter and held out the other. I slapped a half-dozen pancakes onto it.

"I probably don't need *all* those," he said.

"Oh, I thought you were hungry?"

"I am," he said, blushing just a little, or maybe those were his freshly-showered cheeks. "But some things never change."

"Still have the legendary weak stomach, huh?"

He smiled, as though he was happy I remembered, and I pulled two of his pancakes onto my own plate. "That OK?" I said, and he nodded.

"Could I have some coffee?" he said, reaching for the French press with his free hand. "Is this coffee?"

"Yeah, but it's probably stone cold." I touched the back of my hand to the glass. "Might be OK, actually."

That it was still warm, the pot I'd made before going to sit on the stoop, made me realize how little time had passed since the coolest thing about today was that I didn't have to go to work. It was just over forty-five minutes but felt more like a year. Or—no—it felt like some kind of space-time portal had opened up and I'd fallen years-deep into an alternate past.

He poured himself some coffee—he always drank it black, luckily—and brought his breakfast to the table. I put the last pancakes on the other plate and sat down with him. He divided his pancakes into two piles of two and cut them neatly into sections, like a pizza. He ate from both stacks at a time, dipping each forkful into a creeping pool of syrup he maintained at the side.

"These're good, thanks."

"No problem." I squirted zigzags of syrup across my plate—too much, but it was something for my hands to do. "Let me know if you want any more."

He chewed and nodded.

"So how is Beth?" I said. "I guess I haven't seen her in like four years." He looked a little uncomfortable as he tipped his mug to his face, and I realized she was bound to be a sore subject. "Oh, I'm sorry, you probably don't want to—"

"Nah, it's OK. She's good. Hasn't changed much."

"It's hard for me to picture her outside the dorm."

"Yeah."

"So wasn't it—I don't know—kind of mean? That she made you leave in the middle of a blizzard?"

He swallowed. "Like I said, same old." He grinned for a second. "No, it was a pretty mutual thing." He stabbed another pancake wedge, looked around for another one that matched its size, dunked, and brought the fork to his lips. "We just took it as far as we could take it, and then... Well, Beth has never been into wasting time. You know, go go go." He chewed.

"Well that's good it wasn't messy. It's always easier when things aren't messy."

"No, not messy," he said and considered for a second, "but like final, you know?"

For a while we ate in silence. A lump of butter slid across one of my pancakes and plopped into a puddle of syrup. I dragged a piece of pancake through it.

"So you gathered up your stuff and decided to pay me a visit, huh?" I was still trying to work up to the question of why. It seemed a long way off still, though.

He was looking up at the blue dog with a content smile and turned to me. "I still have some shit at her place," he said. "I would've been fine with staying a little longer. But she was visiting her parents and I thought I should sort of make my official exit before she got back."

"Where's she from again?"

"Rochester," he said, but that didn't ring a bell. "New York. Anyway, don't blame me for not calling you first. I would've if you had a phone!"

"What do you mean? Of course I have a phone."

"Haha. Maybe they just didn't have your number?"

"Who? Where'd you even come across my address, anyway?"

"Shuster alumni directory. It's all there online."

"It is? Jeez. I don't even own a computer."

"Really? Why not?"

"Just don't see the need, I guess."

"Well it's all in the directory, all your vital statistics."

"So *that's* how you found me," I said.

I meant it to be funny but there was a sting in his eyes, as though a soap bubble burst on his cornea. He got up from the table, rinsed his empty plate. He stood smoothing with his foot a square of yellow linoleum that had curled up away from the baseboard under the sink.

I felt bad.

"When you finish eating," he said without turning around, "I'll help you shovel."

Pulling on my boots again, I noticed the photo Griff was looking at earlier. It was a snapshot of him lunging off his bed in our dorm room, taken mid-jump by me from my bed, where I was sitting. Jumping back and forth between our beds, a game kids play in motel rooms, had been Griff's stress relief when writing research papers. In the picture his body was a blur but his face was clear, frozen in an airborne gasp, his hair fanned out behind him. A split-second after I snapped it he landed on my bed with a force that slid the mattress halfway off its black metal frame— and me along with it. Laughing and red, he'd hauled me to my feet.

It was something I thought about a lot. College memories played through my mind like television reruns on a high-digit cable channel dedicated to making my present feel inadequate. Watching Griff stomp out into the snow in his sweatshirt and scarf, I thought maybe that's why having him here didn't feel quite as strange as it probably should've. I'd spent so much time remembering, that even though we hadn't talked in years his name had never left the tip of my tongue.

I buttoned my coat and followed him outside. The yard tools were in the garage, which also housed my Jeep. The garage door opened manually, and to get to the handle we had to dig down into the snow. It took our combined strength to get it to screech up along its frozen tracks.

"If I hadn't come you would've been stuck," Griff said.

"Nah, I probably wouldn't even have shoveled," I said. In fact, I wasn't sure I'd ever shoveled this driveway. After the neighbor lady's was done I usually made do with ruts in my own.

I could only find one shovel, stuck to the wall with springy metal grips, alongside a rarely-used rake and a never-used hoe.

"Give it here," he said, taking it. "I'll do it until I get tired."

While he shoveled I kicked a crater in the snow by the edge of the driveway and sat down. Crazy how being surrounded by millions of flakes of ice can feel so cozy. A boy and a girl dressed in snowsuits walked down the street pulling red plastic sleds. There were no hills around and I wondered where they were going.

Griff tossed the snow back over his shoulder with the enthusiasm of someone digging for treasure. When he'd cleared half the driveway he stabbed the shovel into a pile and rested his chin on the green plastic handle. I got up to take my turn.

He waved me away. "I have a little left in me," he said.

"... Suit yourself." I settled back into the snow.

"So since we've covered my romantic disaster," he said after heaving a load of snow against the fence that separated my yard from my neighbor's, "what have you been up to? Seeing anyone?"

"I was for a while," I said. "In the fall."

"Guy or girl?"

The question—the matter-of-factness of it—made me smile. Unlike some people, Griff had never treated my bi-ness as something I might outgrow.

"Girl. Melanie. She works at the art gallery down the street from my comic shop. Or worked. I assume she still does."

"You working there? At the comic shop, I mean?"

"Yeah. Sort of a manager. We don't really have titles. My boss Simon owns the place."

"Can't say I'm surprised. You always liked your funny books," he said with a laugh. "Anyway, go on— Melanie?"

"Yeah."

"Hot?"

"Very." She'd had the most beautiful chocolate-colored hair. It was long, went down to the middle of her back. When we kissed we could hide in it, like people behind a waterfall. "There's not a lot to tell," I said. "We dated for like four months. Fun, cute. I thought it was going pretty well. Then her ex came back from Iraq and was worth a second look, apparently, now that he was some kind of war hero. Suddenly me and my superheroes were second rate."

"What happened?"

"She gave me the heave-ho in a McDonald's drive-thru."

"Ouch."

"Yeah. Burgers went cold that night. I was pretty pissed off."

"About the burgers or the dumping?"

"Well, both." I gathered a clump of snow in my hands and pressed it together, but it was too light for snowballs and sifted through my fingers. "But what can you do, right?"

Griff nodded and tossed a load of snow over his shoulder. "Yeah, what can you do." He'd cleared most of the driveway and was breathing out big white clouds.

"Aren't you tired?" I said, getting up and really hoping he'd hand over the shovel before he passed out. "You said you barely slept last night."

"Now that you mention it, yeah." He started to take another scoop but slowed and stopped. "OK. Here." He harpooned the shovel into the remaining square of snow.

He walked up the driveway and took over my vacated snow seat. "So what did Melanie think of the bi thing?"

"Oh, I don't know. She seemed OK with it," I said, heaving a shovelful of snow. "I think she thought it was interesting."

"Cool."

"It's funny how it works. Gay guys love it when they just want to hook up because they think I'm actually straight and hooking up with straight guys is hot."

"Seriously?"

"Apparently, yeah. But they hate it for a relationship. And I'm not really a one-night-stand kind of guy, I guess. Then girls usually hate it flat-out because they think I'm actually gay and just waiting to break out of the closet. It's kind of rough."

"I get that. There's so many variables and stuff that can make people wrong for each other, though," he said. He waved his arms through the snow on either side of the snow-chair, giving it angel wings. "You probably have more crap to deal with than average, I'll give you that. But it's not like it's a cakewalk for me either, you know?"

"I guess."

I finished clearing the driveway down to the sand and the crushed purple shells, hacked through the snow bank at the end, opening my house to the street and to Harwich beyond. Finally I cut a path along the walk up to the front porch. Griff had been quiet for a while and I noticed after putting the shovel away that he had fallen asleep.

"Griff, wake up," I said, shaking him by the shoulder. "You can die doing that."

"I need to crash," he mumbled.

"Come inside," I said, pulling the garage door closed, "before you get hypothermia."

There was no bed in the spare bedroom, and in the living room just the two corduroy chairs.

I offered him my own bed, glancing down at the chipped teal paint on the baseboard heater as I said it, my arms crossed masculinely over my chest. With Griff I'd always been afraid of implications.

He mumbled something that sounded like *thanks* and scuffed down the hall to my room. I heard the headboard smack the wall. I felt like smiling, and may have, but at the same time my heart began to pound with the full weight of whatever was going on here. Through the picture window I watched a flashing plow grind its way down the street, leaving in its wake a new snow bank at the end of my driveway. We were snowed-in all over again.

The yearbook was still lying on the chair. I sat down and opened it across my lap, flipped through the pages like a squeamish med student through a medical textbook, afraid that on the next page, or the next, would be blood and guts. My memories were carefully filtered and I was wary of seeing a photo that rekindled one I was happy to have forgotten.

I didn't expect to be in much of the yearbook, though, and I wasn't. Amidst the standard thumbnail photos I found the one starring Vincent J. Dandro: I was leaning against my Jeep, new when the photo was taken and gleaming cobalt blue in the sun. In the space beneath the photo that most graduates filled with inside jokes and cryptic memories, I was surprised to find that I'd written only "I never drink when I fly," a line I recognized immediately as coming from the movie *Superman*, but which I had absolutely zero memory of writing. I cringed. The quote looked awkward, uncomfortable, even sad, especially in comparison to other people's. It couldn't have really meant anything to me; it was probably just the first thing that came to mind when I was filling out the form. It was profound only in that it showed I had nothing more meaningful to say.

To the right of my photo was Virginia Daniels, a good-looking auburn-haired number with perfect eyebrows and pouty lips, and to the right of her, there he was: A. Griffin Dean.

His smile looked a little forced but it was a good, professional picture. His hair was shorter than I ever saw it back then. A tie hung loosely around the collar of his paisley shirt, over which he wore a solid brown vest. Beneath his photo was an unpunctuated list of things I didn't understand, and that stabbed me with sadness. They must've been from the two years I hadn't been part of. Ah, but here was one I did recognize. It said simply, *Pantie-O's*—a reference to the breakfast cereal with undergarment-shaped marshmallows we'd crafted from an empty Cocoa Krispies box.

I wondered, not for the first time and as always with a mixture of loneliness and guilt, how much he'd thought of me during our second half of college. Had he put that in there just for me, or were Pantie-O's a joke he let other people in on? Was it no longer just ours?

I turned the page.

The club photos were next—I hadn't been in any of the clubs—and then came the sports teams, the intramural baseball team being the second and last photo I expected to be in. I was OK. I played outfield—never liked hitting. I liked being far enough away to almost just be a spectator like the rest of the crowd, but with the special potential, unique among them, to at any moment appear out of nowhere and make a game-winning catch. It barely mattered that I never did.

After the teams were the general campus photos: the dining hall (I could remember the plates clinking, the symphony of conversation, the routine comfort of soft-serve ice cream eaten at circular tables with friends), the library where I'd worked a couple semesters, the white-washed marble arches of my dorm's ancient lobby. These were places I didn't have my own photos of. I hadn't seen them since graduation. It was almost a surprise to find they existed outside my own brain.

Stapled to the last page of the book was a manila envelope. I ripped it free and pried back the brass fastener. The graduation supplement was inside after all. It was nothing fancy, just a ten-page collage of photos from graduation. Our class speaker—the CEO of a dot-com that had since gone under—and our valedictorian; lots of people I didn't know in blue and green robes. But then out jumped someone I recognized: Griffin—and there beside him, me. The photographer was more interested in a mortar board a girl had decorated with elbow pasta, though, so we weren't in focus. We were off to the side. We were blurry.

In my memory time had managed to make the end of our friendship seem practically romantic, a tragedy out of Shakespeare or Dickens, a tale of heartbreak and stiff upper lips. But this photo brought that shit tumbling like a house of cards. There was nothing romantic about this photo at all. It had no more relationship to romance than a dying soldier has to war movies. We were standing side by side and there was enough glaring awkwardness in our eyes to taint even the happiness in those of the main subject.

I remembered seeing him, standing alone in the crowded lobby of the ritzy theatre we graduated in. I remembered the shock of seeing his face two years after we roomed together, at once so familiar and so different. I'd turned away, hoping he wouldn't see me—I probably thought about ducking behind something. It wasn't easy but somehow I made myself walk over to him. He had on red Converse All-Stars with his navy blue pin-stripe suit. His graduation gown was tossed over his shoulder like a locker room towel.

"Look at you all dressed up," I said as I approached, doing my very best to sound like I'd seen him the day before and every other day before that, too. But of course the act was useless.

"Hey," he said softly and almost with suspicion, as though he wasn't sure I was really there. His dark eyebrows furrowed but he stepped forward to hug me. It was a quick clap-on-the-back hug, though, a hug of strangers. "Hey Vince. How you been?"

"Good. You know. Keeping busy. Looking for a job and stuff. Big day, huh?" I pulled my hands up into the wide sleeves of my gown.

"I could take it or leave it," he said. "I feel like I owe it to my mom to walk across the stage." His mouth opened to say something more, but then he rubbed his nose and looked away.

"Hard to believe we're this old, huh?" I said, looking not at him but following his gaze to the crowd of our fellow students.

"Hard to believe. Yeah."

We made small-talk about our job searches, about finally being adults, stuff like that, but there was no mention of the past.

An onlooker probably would've guessed we were just two random students who'd had a class or two together.

When the doors of a large ballroom opened and an announcement was made for us to line up outside, we walked quickly to the entrance, thankful for motion. I expected, because of the spelling of our last names, to be lined up close together. But when the woman at the door asked not for our names but for our majors, it felt like an escape.

"Industrial design," Griff told her, and the woman's chubby finger directed him to the left and down the hall.

"Business," I said, and I was pointed straight ahead. I turned to Griff. "Well I guess—"

"Remember to smile—"

And we were split up there, in the entry to that ballroom, robed graduates swarming around us like a school of jellyfish. Cut-off meaningless sentences were our goodbyes. Before today, the last time I saw Griff was from my seat in the audience as he walked across the stage to get his diploma. I'd cheered for him then.

Now, two years later, I closed the fucking yearbook and looked at the picture window, past the pictures of Griff, out at the snow.

There was a thump at the front door. When I opened it I found a newspaper on the stoop. A car threw one at the old lady's house too and continued down the street. Her door opened and she plucked the paper off of her freshly-shoveled steps, waved at me.

The snow on the ground was nighttime blue now. I could see in the car's headlights and in the glow of the old lady's driveway floodlight that the snow was still coming down, but in fine flakes almost like mist. I picked up the paper, slid it out of the translucent bag. The headline proclaimed *Blizzard!* in giant text.

"What time is it?" Griff said behind me, startling me. I shut the door. His t-shirt was wrinkled and one of his pant-legs was rolled up.

I looked into the kitchen at the microwave. "Well the paper just arrived and you're just getting out of bed, so it would appear to be 8:30 a.m. But in this upside-down world it's actually 8:30 *p.m.*"

"Strange times," he said, wiping his eyes. He still looked tired.

I tossed the newspaper onto the ottoman. "Paper claims it snowed."

"Can't believe anything you read nowadays." He grinned, hopping on one foot to fix his sock.

"There's pizza on the stove," I said.

"Cool, thank you." He went into the kitchen, sliding his socks on the linoleum. "Oh, homemade, nice!" He took a bite, testing, approving. "Have any milk?"

"No. There's juice. Sam Adams in the drawer." I put my hands in my pockets and stood in front of the picture window for a moment before drawing the dark floral curtains across it.

"Sorry I slept so long," he said. "That was probably kind of rude."

"No, it's fine. I don't mind."

"What'd you do all day?" he said. He had the grapefruit juice container in his hand. "Ah—*Shoveling the lady nextdoor*," he read from the note I'd stuck on the fridge. "That sounds hot. Or— But not as good as *plowing*."

I smiled.

After finishing his pizza he sat down sideways in the brown corduroy chair, legs draped over the arm, feet close to the fire. He watched me flip through records for a moment and then grabbed the remote and turned on the television. The screen looked like snow, a portal into twenty hours ago.

"Is it out or do you just not get cable?"

"Cable shmable," I said. "Use the rabbit ears."

"Right." He rolled his eyes and turned off the TV.

I held up two records I'd chosen from the stacker in the cabinet. "The Cure or T-Rex?"

He pointed to the T-Rex. As I was sliding the record out of its sleeve he asked, "Do you have snow tires on your Jeep?"

"Yeah." I lifted the clear plastic cover. The Billie Holiday was still on the turntable. "Why?"

"Would you want to go for a drive or something?"

"Now?"

"Maybe just a quick spin to get some air? You haven't been out all day."

"I've been out most of the day."

"I mean *out* out."

I thought for a moment, slid the record back into the sleeve. Being out was something to do, offered less chance for awkwardness.

"OK," I said. "Put on your boots."

The roads were still in pretty rough shape and there weren't many cars out other than us. My wipers swooshed back and forth, batting the stubborn fine flakes that continued to fall. They didn't seem to be accumulating much anymore, just added a sugary dusting to the twenty inches already there.

On Oak Street wide piles lining the shoulders reduced it to one lane. Ahead of us a plow turned onto the street. It rumbled toward us. Its revolving orange lights were bright and it shrieked warnings at us to clear the road.

"You need to make room," Griff said helpfully.

"Where's he think he's going?" I looked in the rearview; the street behind us was clear but there weren't any easy turnarounds. "One of us needs to back up."

"Nah, there's room," Griff said. "It's fine. Just pull over a bit."

I turned the wheel and drove the Jeep onto the shoulder, more hastily than I should've. The passenger side scraped against the snow bank and the Jeep thumped to a spongy halt. Snowballs skittered across the hood. The plow was in front of us now. I could feel the vibrations.

"Hold your breath, here it comes," Griff said. I wondered if he was also one of those people who ducks when driving under a bridge.

The plow passed us slowly. I could see each individual snowflake clinging to the truck's yellow paint—could see their fractal patterns receding to icy infinity.

"Sweatless," Griff said.

"Sure, you're on the passenger side. I almost shit my pants."

I put the Jeep into drive and stepped on the gas, giving it a little extra to get out of the snow. The rear tires spun and the Jeep didn't move. I put it in reverse and tried again, then tried forward again. Rocked back and forth, no luck. I grumbled and squeezed the wheel.

"I'll check it out," Griff said, but his door only opened a few inches before crunching against the snow bank.

"It's OK." I got out and walked around to the front, steadying myself with a hand on a snow pile. The headlights spotlighted me and inside the car I could see a wavy image of Griff obscured by the wipers. The Jeep was half buried in the bank; its passenger-side tires had all but disappeared. I got back in.

"I should've just backed up," I said, thumping my forehead against the wheel.

"I could push," he offered.

"It needs to like come out sideways, not forward."

"We could use that huge winch you've got on the back. Tie it to a tree or something."

"What, and then reel it in like a fish?"

"OK, bad idea. What do you have that thing for anyway?"

"Oh, I went through a WWSD phase last winter. *What Would Superman Do.* Like a Good Samaritan thing. My specialty was towing people out of ditches and snow banks and stuff."

"Did you ever?"

"A couple."

"And now you're stuck yourself. How ironic." He breathed into his gloves and pulled them on—I'd turned off the car to keep the exhaust from backing up and killing us, and it was cold inside already. "Got a shovel?"

"Nope."

"We could knock on one of these houses and borrow one."

"…"

When I didn't respond he added, "OK, then we push."

Blazingly lit by the headlights of my Jeep, with snowflakes twinkling down around him, he looked like a dream, a figment of my imagination. This was too real to be a dream, but too surreal to actually be happening. Griff, who I hadn't talked to in two years or really in four, was standing up to his thighs in a snowy backstreet in Harwich, trying to push me out of a snow bank. He must've been an apparition, the Ghost of Christmas Past.

At his command I floored the Jeep in reverse. It came unstuck easily, much easier than either of us expected, and as the front bumper whisked out from under his hands he fell forward into the snow. He reappeared in my headlights a moment later with snow on his chin, laughing.

I got out and stood around while he smacked snow off his clothes, then we got back in the Jeep.

"That was something," I said.

"That *was* something."

"Maybe we should cut our losses and head back?"

"We can't just go home after that! It won't have been worth the trouble. Drive me somewhere. Show me your life or something."

"My life?"

"Give me a tour. Just watch out for plows."

The comic shop was on the first floor of a two-story building. Its upstairs neighbor was a family dentist. Bloody-mouthed boys let loose on the action figures by their moms as a reward for good behavior were big customers at Golden Age Comics. (Simon, the owner, was a collector/historian and had named his store after the oldest and most valuable books.) Beside Golden Age on the first floor was a Copy Cop, and above that the offices of a small law firm. Light from a floodlight shined down from the eaves of the building but all the windows in all the businesses were dark. The sidewalk looked like it'd been shoveled about halfway into the storm. We trampled through the snow and up the three buried concrete steps.

"I'm excited," Griff said.

28

I was too. It was like we were archaeologists, discovering this place.

I wiped the gauze of snow from the sign hanging beside the glass door. The *O* in Golden Age, yellow, was shaped like a word balloon, its point jutting off the sign and away from the other black letters in a 3D effect. The tip of the point had once pricked the finger of a nine-year-old customer, *Sleeping Beauty*–style. Now it was blunted with duct tape.

I unlocked the two locks, pushed open the door. The bell above the door jingled.

"Hold on a sec," I said.

I flipped on the fluorescent lights—*tink tink tink*. On the wall beside the counter where the register sat was a glowing keypad. I mumbled the numbers as I punched the keys. The alarm chirped and released its grip on the store.

"I like this," Griff said, smiling. His hands clasped behind his back, he browsed around with the quiet intrigue of a person touring an ancient tomb.

It was a cozy store with bright yellow walls that on sunny days seemed to glow, and that made the superhero costumes in the comics and posters against them even more vibrant. It wasn't like all the other comics shops I'd ever been in, most of which were dark and claustrophobic, almost ashamed. This store said *Wheee!*

It was L-shaped and not more than twice the size of my living room. Shelves stretched from floor to ceiling. The check-out counter of wood and blue Formica was opposite the entrance. New arrivals lined the side wall on the left. Hardcovers and trade paperbacks were in an island of shelves in the middle. Rows of long white boxes full of back-issues were stacked at the back of the store. In front of the register hung a free-standing rack of action figures; behind it was a glass case showcasing limited edition figurines and knickknacks and several of the more valuable comics. Beside the door hung posters hyping DC's and Marvel's upcoming summer crossovers.

It was like my second home.

"So you manage it?" Griff said.

"Sometimes I feel like I live here," I said. "Simon comes in on Wednesdays for new arrival day, which gets busy, and on other days he'll pop in and out. Aside from that it's pretty much mine."

"Is it just you and him?"

"No, there's two college kids who work a couple afternoons." I told him about Marissa and Zane and how they both went to Cape Cod Community. When Simon taught a comic history course there two years ago he came away with sidekicks. "Marissa's pretty angsty," I said, "but when it comes to comics she knows her shit. And Zane is... well, Zane's Zane."

"Your comic book *familia*," Griff said.

"I guess we are, a little bit."

He smiled and strolled past the Indie section. I liked seeing him here; it was a nice collision of worlds. "How's the comic book business these days?" he said.

"Hanging in there. Little ups and downs, but steady for now. There will always be geeks."

"That's true," he said. "Hey," he added, pointing to an *Adam Strange* comic, "I know him. This guy used to be in the *Mysteries in Space* comics my dad had a bunch of. You know him? He catches some kind of transporter beam and gets whisked to another planet where he has a beautiful wife and goes on amazing adventures. It was very spacey."

"I like his ray gun," I said. "It looks like it came from the 1940 World's Fair or something." I made a gun with my fingers and fired at him. "So are you about ready?"

"Oh, I thought we were going to hang out for a while?" His eyes were earnest. If I imagined a chunk of gauze dangling from his lips like a bloody stogie, he wouldn't be much different from the kids who came in with their moms.

"Oh. Yeah. Hang out? I guess I figured there isn't much to see."

"Here," he said, handing me the *Adam Strange* comic and then taking another one for himself. "Let's read comics."

We sat down on the floor, our backs against the Marvel trades, and it felt like a thousand different things might happen.

But the only one that did was that we sat and read the comics. He didn't touch me or even look at me in a way that made me think he wanted to. We just sat side by side and I turned the sweet-smelling pages when he turned his, but I didn't actually read a single word.

We locked up the store and started back to the parking lot. In the distance we heard the ominous screech of another plow, like a huge beast making its presence known on the snowy savanna.

"You've been walking all over Massachusetts in the snow today, haven't you," I said. I blew out a puff of white breath. Yes, the visible breath coming from the mouth and nose did look cool, and that was why there would always be smokers.

"This morning feels like yesterday to me, though," he said, "so not really."

"Oh, that's right. I forgot you're a whole consciousness period ahead of me."

"Which is probably why I'm so wide awake," he said. And then, pointing across the street, he added, "That Dunkin' Donuts looks open. Buy you a hot chocolate?"

I'd been in here almost every day for the past year—summer days, winter days, in rain and snow and sunshine, with Zane, with Marissa, with Melanie and with Simon—but it had never felt like this before. I never expected to look across the table and find Griff sitting there, licking chocolate from his lips.

As I sipped mine I remembered that tonight was the night I was going to make Zane a hot chocolate and tell him how I felt. If all had gone according to plan, he and I would've probably been in bed together right now. But if it hadn't, maybe I'd have been alone instead. The whole idea felt so distant now, so odd in light of these new circumstances.

"So what's going on in Griff Dean's life?" I said. "Other than the Beth stuff. Where are you working? What do you do?"

He looked surprised. Before answering he blew on his hot chocolate and then took a long, slow sip. "Nothing," he said. "I'm rich."

"Of course you are. Did you buy stocks with all the money you made sitting desk in college?"

He laughed, a nostalgic chuckle, and looked up, rubbing his chin with one hand. "I was always sitting desk, wasn't I? No, my grandmother died last year."

"Oh." I lowered my eyes to the steam rising from his drink. "I didn't know that. I'm sorry, dude."

"We weren't close. It wasn't that big a deal."

"Oh..."

"She and my mom argued like rabid badgers, so..."

I waited for more; it was beginning to dawn on me that maybe he hadn't been joking.

"She left my mom a hundred bucks." He paused and then a soft smile appeared around his eyes and crept down his cheeks to his chapped lips and he said, "And she left me eight hundred and fifty big ones."

"No way. Thousands?"

"Yeah."

I recoiled as if shocked by a lightning bolt, my spine knocking back against the plastic chair, and then started laughing so hard I had to press my hands over my mouth to keep from making a scene. The amount of money was absurd, of course—as ridiculous as a number like fifty gazillion to a recent grad running a comic shop—but that wasn't even what struck me the most.

"She left you inheritance for *spite*?!"

"The old bird left me inheritance for spite," he said, "yeah," shaking his head but looking like he was trying for all the world not to get up and jump around the Dunkins.

"Spite money. Wow."

"Can you believe it?"

I couldn't. For what must've been close to five minutes we laughed about his late grandmother's final shaft. Finally, when we'd mostly calmed down, I asked if he offered any to his mom.

"I did but she wouldn't take a penny," he said, wiping tears off his cheeks. "She even donated her hundred bucks to the Democrats because Grandma was a fierce Republican."

"Your family belongs on a soap opera."

"Tell me about it."

My throat felt itchy from laughing so hard. "So what's it like having a million bucks fall into your lap?"

"It's not a million."

"Just about."

"Don't make it crazier than it is. It's crazy," he said. "Crazy cool but crazy scary, too. Brings out the angel and devil on your shoulders pretty fucking quick, let me tell you."

"Do you ever feel like flying to Vegas and just blowing it all on hookers and booze?"

He shook his head. "The opposite. I almost feel like it's some kind of exotic and poisonous fish and if I don't consume it in just the right way it'll kill me. I want to save it for something, make it last. It's so much potential, you know? That's what's scary." He smiled. "I quit my job."

"What'd you do?"

"I made blueprints at an architecture firm. It sucked."

"Why'd it suck? You used to like drawing buildings."

"I did, but that's not what this was. I just took other people's drawings and made big blue copies. With this special paper and this giant machine." He spread his arms wide to measure. "I went home reeking of ammonia every day. But I knew the shit was hitting the fan with Beth and I'd be bouncing soon. So a couple days after New Year's I left for lunch and just never went back."

"Wow. And what now? Just living off your inheritance?"

"Not even. The interest." He paused and seemed to be watching me for a reaction, to see if I approved. I wondered how much crap he'd taken from Beth about this, quitting his job and stuff.

"That's awesome," I said, and he smiled.

"I've got it all in this high-yield savings account thing," he went on. "I'm making more in interest than I did at the firm. Life is fucking bliss."

When we were putting on our jackets he realized he didn't have his phone. He looked around under the table and said, "I hope it's in the car."

But it wasn't, so we drove back across to Golden Age to check there. Waiting to make the turn into the parking lot, I let a minivan pass. The driver's teeth were clenched and his hands squeezed the wheel at a perfect ten-and-two. He looked like someone I'd once towed out of a ditch.

A plow had gone up Main Street while we were in Dunkin' Donuts. I sped up to make it over the crest of snow at the edge of the lot. The lot had been plowed a few hours ago; now, in addition to my first set of tire tracks, there was a second set in the half-inch snow. I didn't recognize the car that had made them. It was parked at the back of the lot, a pick-up. Blue, maybe black—I couldn't tell in the dark. I pulled into a spot in front. We got out.

"Looks like company," said Griff, pointing to footprints that ran up the walk amongst the ones we'd left.

"Tooth emergency, maybe?" I said. But when I looked up, the second-floor windows were dark. "Probably Simon," I added when it became clear the new tracks led to Golden Age. Doubtful, but it was my only explanation.

The lights in the store were off and through the glass door, between the sign that said CLOSED and the edge of a *Green Lantern* poster, I saw movement at the register. My pulse quickened and my tongue tasted suddenly sickly. I had my keys clenched in my fingers, ready to use as a weapon.

"Under the register counter there's a phone," I told Griff. "If I get taken down, go for it."

"OK, dude," he said, patting my shoulder.

"I'm serious."

"Oh... You know, maybe we should just find a payphone and call the—"

"Fuck that—it's my store." I unlocked the door, careful not to rattle the keys too much, and swung it open.

The bell jingled. There was a bump, a gasp at the register. Two men. Light from the floodlight behind me illuminated a bare ass. Jeans were yanked up over it. The second man jumped off the counter clutching at his own jeans. Beside me, Griff stifled a nervous laugh. Someone else yelled *fuck*. I recognized the voice.

I flipped the row of switches by the door. The fluorescents blinked on. The man, the one who'd been standing, or maybe he'd been on his knees, spun around and threw his hands in the air. The other—

"Zane!"

"What the hell are you doing!" There was a *zoot* sound as he zipped his fly, and now he was fumbling with his belt buckle.

"What the fuck, Zane!" I pulled the keys out of the lock. I was shivering—no, shaking. My face grew warm. "You," I pointed at the other guy—a kid really, jockish, crew cut; his hands were still up, his eyes wide—"you wait outside. Griff, give me a minute please?"

The kid looked at me and then at Griff. "You won't tell anyone, will you?" His voice was deep but quivered.

"Not if you cooperate," Griff said, a little bit theatrically, and shut the door behind them as they went out.

I put my hands over my face and sighed. "I refuse to be the one embarrassed about this," I said.

Zane clenched his teeth. He wore a white hooded sweatshirt that accentuated his flushed cheeks. Was he red from what had been going on, I wondered, or just from getting caught at it? His left ear was pierced with three small silver hoops; his right ear had two. His eyes were pinched softly at the corners—as easily the result of a cute cozy sleepiness as the DNA influence of his Japanese grandmother.

"This isn't your personal motel," I said.

"No, I'm sorry, I didn't realize you already had a reservation." His voice was low, hard. Anger was hiding his embarrassment.

"Reservation?"

"Him." He lifted his chin toward the door. "Hot stuff, Vince."

"Oh for fuck's sake."

I stomped to the back closet, pulse throbbing, just to get away from him, wondering what I should do next, wondering whether I should take his keys away. I wanted to take his keys. How dare he embarrass me like this in front of Griff? And be so disrespectful of this store? I paced around the little closet. If he was still there when I went back out, yes, I'd take away his keys. But only if he was still there. I started to go out but I wasn't ready to deal with it yet, so I stalled. *Who was that guy?* I wondered. *Are they dating or was he just a trick? I was going to make him hot chocolate!* I watched snow puddles form around my boots. Finally I switched off the light.

He'd waited. He was still there.

"I'm sorry, Vince, I know, I know." He was standing with his hands stuffed in his jacket pockets. "It's just that he was nervous and we didn't have anywhere else to go. You know I can't bring him to my house. My parents—"

"Your homophobic parents are not my problem. Have a little fucking respect." I sighed and then actually said, "Give me your keys."

He cringed. "...What? Why?"

"Just do it."

"Don't you have to talk to Simon first?"

"And what would I say, huh? By the way, Simon, Zane was getting sucked off on top of your cash register last night. I'm sure that'd go over well."

"Give me a fucking break, Vince," he said, jerking his head. His earrings clinked together. "It's bad enough that because of you I have blue-balls now."

"Sorry." I held out my hand.

"Fine."

He dug in his pocket and pulled out a red carabiner looped with key rings. He picked through the rings and slipped one off. He bypassed my open hand and slammed the keys down on the counter. He walked to the door.

"Hold on," I told him. I felt a stab of guilt when he turned expectantly—I'd only meant to turn on the security system. I punched the numbers. When I said OK he opened the door. I grabbed the keys off the counter and on my way out spotted Griff's phone on the floor where we'd been reading the comics. I detoured to get it and followed Zane out.

"Where'd they go?" I locked up with Zane's keys.

"I bet Jeremy took off," he said without much regret, looking toward the parking lot. In the floodlight his spiked black hair looked almost blue. "Your boy's in your car."

"He's not my boy."

"Well whoeverthefuck."

Our tracks were a beaten path now from all the late-night back and forth. My Jeep was alone in the lot. I opened the door.

"That kid hit the road," Griff reported from the passenger seat. "He was pretty freaked out."

"He was just a queerling anyway," Zane said, and looked at me. "And his head sucked."

"Pun not intended, I assume," Griff said. Zane grinned. Griff leaned over the driver's side and offered Zane his hand. "Griffin," he said. Zane took it; they shook.

"Zane."

"Ah, the famous Zane of Golden Age Comics?"

"Formerly of Golden Age," Zane said. I felt his eyes on me again, heavy and dark.

"Get in," I said, pulling the front seat forward. "I'll drive you home."

I could tell Griff was glaring at me even though his hat covered his eyebrows. "You really fired him?" he said.

I pulled the door shut and buckled my seatbelt. In the beams of my headlights I watched Zane stomp his sneakers on his parents' front steps and go inside their blue-sided colonial.

"I took his keys." I backed out of the driveway and pulled onto the street. "Whether I fired him depends on whether he shows up for his next shift, I guess."

"Sounds a bit harsh."

"Griff, he was in the store when he wasn't supposed to be. Oh and lest I forget, he was having a fucking suckfest."

"C'mon, it's a comic shop. It's all about fantasy."

"It's a business."

"It's a business to your *boss*, Vince. To you, it is a comic shop. Hell, it was almost *appropriate*. Do you know how many times I've spanked it to *Wonder Woman* comics?"

"Doesn't matter." But Griff had always had a knack for silencing me with his bizarre logic, the kind that took the wind out of my dramatic sails, and now there was nothing I could say back to him, nothing besides—

"You've spanked to *Wonder Woman*?"

He chuckled, remembering fondly the sweet secret fumblings of an intense affair. "When you were in class, I'd peruse your *Justice League* books."

"You spanked to *my* comic books?"

"Once or twice."

"I can't believe it."

"Why not? She's hot!"

"She's *Wonder Woman*, for god's sake. I can't think about her that way. She's like the mother-figure of the entire DC Universe."

"So then she's a MILF," he said, darting his tongue in and out. "I'd let her tie me up with that magic lasso of hers."

"You're unbelievable, you know that?"

He leaned back against the headrest, smiling smugly at the huff he'd gotten me into. "What time is it anyway?" he said, flicking the broken clock on the dashboard with his thumb. A green eight lit up briefly.

I pushed up my sleeve and looked at my watch. "Almost midnight."

"Late," he said, resting his head against the window. And then he added, making me smile, "Bring me home, Vinny."

Using all my weight I pulled the squeaky garage door down on its tracks. Above us the motion-detecting floodlight blinked off and then turned back on when Griff waved his arms.

"I should be tireder," he said. "It was that nap."

"I never nap."

"So you've basically put me up for two days so far," he said.

The last flakes of the storm had stopped falling and now the sky was opening up, showing its first stars in days. They reminded me that there was a wide world out there, one that would take Griff back.

"No problem," I said, kicking my boots against the front steps. "So do you know how long you plan on, like, staying?" As soon as I asked I regretted it—I wasn't sure I wanted to lose the mystery. "Or, if you don't know, that's cool."

He pulled off his gloves and stuffed them in his pocket. His hair went up crazy when he pulled off his hat. "Is a few days OK? Definitely no longer than a week, max."

"Sure, that's fine. It's not like there's a lot going on here."

It was exactly the amount of time I'd expected, even the same as I'd hoped at first, but hearing it out loud really cut down on my ability to imagine something more.

"Just until I can figure out the next stop on the Griff Express and stuff," he said.

"Any ideas?" I went to the thermostat and turned the heat up a few degrees. "You want some coffee or something? Tea?"

"Tea would be nice. Green?"

"Sure."

"Yeah. Thanks."

I went to the kitchen to put the kettle on and he flopped into one of the corduroy armchairs. My kitchen was separated from the living room by a half-wall; above it I could only see the top of his head.

"I've been in touch with my cousin Dave," he said. "He's the one in Phoenix. Close to Phoenix."

"I thought Dave lived in Florida?"

"Oh—he moved to Arizona like three years ago."

"Three years ago. Oh."

"Yeah."

"Does he like it? I wouldn't mind visiting Arizona someday."

"Yeah, me neither," he said. "So you know, I figure... He's putting in a pool. Or a hot-tub. Something—some kind of construction. Said I could crash at his place for a while if I give him a hand."

"You're going to fly across the continent to help put in a hot-tub? Doesn't he have friends?"

He shrugged. "You don't mind me staying until I can get things together, do you? I wouldn't want to impose."

"Nah. Once a roommate always a roommate, right? Stay as long as you like."

Around us the house grew warmer as we sipped our tea.

"I like your house," he said, gazing into the fireplace.

"Thanks."

"How's the whole *being graduated* thing working out for you?"

"I don't know. Hard to say."

"I actually looked into going back," he said, "if you can believe that."

"To Shuster?"

"Yeah."

I laughed because I'd had that same idea many times. "To study what? Or does that even matter?"

He smiled. "Didn't matter. I just wanted to— I don't know. When I found out that grad students don't live in the dorm..."

"It wouldn't be the same," I said.

"No." He looked over again at the photos on the wall. "It's just so weird, you know?"

"Life after college?"

"Yeah."

"No shit, Griff. It's really weird."

"Nobody ever told us what it was going to *feel* like," he said. "Nobody fucking *warned* us."

"Warned?"

"About how much it was going to hurt. There was no preparation for that at all. All we got was the stuff about finding a career, blah blah blah. As if that's all there is to it. The actual day-to-day feeling is a complete surprise no one even tries to prepare you for."

"How do you mean?"

"Little huge things like measuring time."

"No kidding. Yeah. Everything since graduation feels like one long month."

"For as long as we can remember," he said, "I mean literally our *whole conscious lives*, time has been neatly divided into semesters and years. Each year completely distinguishable and unique. First grade, third grade. We didn't measure by age, we measured by grade. Like I know I broke my arm in sixth grade but I'd have to do the math to figure out what year that was, or how old I was. That was our world view."

"And now it's gone."

"Now there's just this huge, unlabeled expanse. It's so empty and—I will admit this to you—it's terrifying. You know?"

"It's the void," I said. "The post-college void."

"That's exactly what it is. Sometimes I feel like I'm just floundering in it, Vin." He leaned back in the chair and closed his eyes. "Sometimes I wonder if the average person thinks about this stuff the way I do. Major life things like this. If they have words like *post-college void* or even know what one is."

"No, I don't think most people do," I said. "I do."

"I know you do." He blew a wave of hair away from his mouth. "Is it good or bad, to be this way? So introspective."

"I don't know. Bad probably, but I wouldn't want to be any other way."

"My Vince," he said, and the tone of his voice made me want to go to him. He thumped his head back against the chair and pushed the wave of hair behind his ear. "I feel like green with tiny flecks of brown."

He had synesthesia, a mixing of senses. Some people with it taste shapes or hear music in letters or numbers. Griff experienced emotions as colors. I thought of it as a super power. In college I'd drawn and taped to our door a serial comic strip about Mood Ring, Griff's secret superhero identity. The character wore a tie-dyed jumpsuit with a glistening stone on his chest. There wasn't a lot we could do with Mood Ring because, admittedly, shooting emotions out of a ring was kind of lame.

"Is green with flecks of brown good?" I asked.

"It's a quiet feeling," he said. "Cozy. It means bed time."

It was almost 2:00 a.m. now and I was falling asleep myself, but my feet were warm beneath me and I was reluctant to put them on the chilly floor, and equally as reluctant to tackle the upcoming hurdle of awkwardness: I had no couch. "OK," I said finally, dragging myself off the warm corduroy. "I need to sleep too. I barely slept at all last night because of the storm."

"I was just going to ask for a couple blankets or something," he said, "but do you think it'd be OK if I stole half your bed? I mean just for tonight?"

"I guess that would—"

"I mean, tomorrow we can find a Wal-Mart and I'll grab a camping mattress or something."

"Oh. Yeah. Sure, no biggie." I said it with as much confidence and nonchalance as I could muster, but in my head it still sounded rife with insinuation. I thought I might vomit from nerves. "Why not just furnish my spare bedroom for me? I know you can afford it."

He laughed. "I've never bunked with a dude before but I'm too tired to pretend I'd be more comfortable sleeping sitting up."

"It's cool." Oh my god. "Yeah, tomorrow we'll go buy an air mattress," I said, my mouth just running now. God forbid I give the impression that I think he would enjoy sleeping with me...

"Just so you know, though," he said, "I sleep in the nude."

I froze.

"Kidding!" he said with a smirk.

I went in the bathroom and brushed my teeth, and with every stroke of the brush my outlook seemed to change, bristling sudsily back and forth between *this is a dream come true* and *this is a fucking nightmare.*

In the bedroom the blankets were still askew from his afternoon nap. I started to straighten them but thought it would be better to already be in bed when he came in, so that symbolically *he* would be getting into bed with *me*, something that would make me feel less like I was trying to seduce him or something. But I'd have to hurry. I wondered what I should wear, considered sweatpants, a t-shirt. Finally I decided it was best to just wear my boxers. We'd lived together once upon a

42

time, after all—he knew that's what I wore to bed sure as I knew he didn't sleep naked.

My pillow smelled like him and that made this all seem suddenly very real. What if I got a boner? What if I couldn't stop myself, and kissed him?

He appeared at the door, silhouetted against the amber light from the hall.

"Is there a place I can hang my shit?" he asked, leaning in with his hands against the jambs.

"Closet in the other bedroom."

"Thanks."

He pulled the door almost all the way shut behind him. For a while I listened to him unzipping pockets in his backpack, jingling wire coat hangers, rinsing dishes, moving around the house with the familiarity of someone who belonged there. The sound of someone else in my house was new again and as comforting as a lullaby.

Something woke me a short time later. I squinted at the glowing green clock on the bedside table—3:12—and was startled by the man lying next to me. After a second I remembered it was Griff. Griff and not some random stranger. Griff and not Melanie. Griff—and not Zane.

I lay still, afraid of waking him, afraid of what fumbled conversation we might force into the six inches of space separating us. He was facing away from me, hugging his pillow against his chest. Between us he had placed another pillow, apparently to serve as a boundary line running down the middle of the bed and to prevent any direct contact, accidental or otherwise, during the night. His head lay on the mattress. The joshua tree tattoo on his shoulder was visible above the hem of the sheet. I stared at it, at his neck and the back of his head. Two coils of hair twisted together and formed an upside-down heart. I separated them gently with my finger.

There'd been days upon days when all I wanted out of my life was to share a bed with Griff. Sometimes I thought about sleeping *with* him, about making love, about what that would feel

like, but more often, when I was loneliest, I thought about sleeping *beside* him, exactly as was happening now: him drooling beside me, me trying to make sense of the things he sleep-mumbled into his pillow and being enveloped in the nighttime smell of his skin. Now here he was. Out of the blue. Out of the *white*. And I didn't know what to make of it. Tears filled my eyes but I wasn't crying, not exactly.

He'd come to my room in the dark, quietly undressed, placed the pillow between us, and got into bed beside me, all without waking me up.

He tossed and made a snorting noise and his foot—bare—grazed my shin. It was too much. My disbelief at his presence suddenly fell aside when I wondered if he'd not really been kidding about sleeping naked now. Was he naked? Griffin naked. *Griffin naked.* Even as my eyes were wet my underwear got tight.

I had to know, and felt gross for having to know. I lifted the blankets but it was too dark to see under there. I reached under the covers and moved my hand slowly across the mattress and allowed my fingers to graze his hip. They touched cotton.

I felt silly for expecting anything else. Vince, I told myself, he's not trying to seduce you, he's only looking for a place to sleep. All he wants is sleep. A simple thing and you have not, after all these fucking years, gotten through your head that he wants nothing more than a comfortable place to sleep. I hated myself for touching his underwear, for violating him that way.

I felt sick, and I had to get up.

Slowly I rolled over and dropped out of the bed. I grabbed a sweatshirt off my dresser and slipped out of my room, carefully closing the door behind me.

The fire was low so I dropped on a few pieces of wood and pushed everything around with the poker. The corduroy chair felt warm and I pulled a polar-fleece throw around me and sat Indian-style with the blanket tucked under my bare legs.

I watched the fire thinking I should go into the bathroom and jerk off, to help me not care so much that Griff was in my bed, but that wouldn't be right—I wouldn't feel any better doing that right after touching his underwear.

So I just sat and watched the fire—fire and ocean are two things I can watch for millions of years without getting bored. I don't know how long I sat that way before I heard the bed creak and then I heard him call out, very clearly, "Beth?" A moment later: "Vince?"

A few minutes after that he came down the hall. He was in his underwear, his arms wrapped around his thin chest, hugging himself.

"Oh," he said when he saw me.

"I'm out here."

"Sorry, did I keep you up? Was I hogging the bed?"

"No, it was fine. I just couldn't sleep."

"Oh. Want some company?"

"OK."

He started to walk into the living room but then he turned and went into the spare room. I heard some zippers and he emerged a minute later in sweatpants and a hoodie. He sat down in the other chair.

Reaching out for the poker he said, "Can I see the thingy?" I grabbed it and handed it to him. He leaned over and stuck it into the embers, not doing much of anything except making sparks that drifted up into the chimney. "I'm all thrown off," he said, "time-wise."

"Yeah."

Settling back in the chair, the yearbook on the ottoman caught his eye and he picked it up, began to page through it.

"Hey," he said, "what was that thing you wrote about drinking and flying or whatever? What did that mean?"

"It's a line from *Superman*. I really don't know why I put it in there."

"All mine are stupid too," he said. "People are so cryptic with these things, I bet most people look back and have no idea what they mean. I don't understand half the things I wrote. Like what the heck are Pantie-O's?"

It hurt that I had to remind him; it hurt that he didn't remember whether he'd written it just for me.

As he turned the pages the supplement fell out, slipped down between the cushion and the arm. He plucked it out.

"So it *was* in here," he said.

"Yeah. There's a picture of us on graduation day."

"I remember that picture," he said, nodding. His voice was croaky, a nighttime voice. "We're all blurry."

"Blurry, yeah." I looked into the fire. "It's like the camera somehow saw what we really were, you know? Like a mirror does to vampires. I remember the look on your face when I came up to you at graduation. You looked like I was back from the dead. You wanted to know what happened."

"Yeah, I did," he said. "I *was* confused. But all that stuff was a long time ago."

"Not to me." I gestured at the wall, at the photos. I could feel my throat tighten up and I laid my head back against the cushion.

He nodded. He zipped his hoodie higher, slowly, obviously taking care not to snag any chest hairs, and resumed hugging himself. I almost offered to go get him a blanket, but didn't.

"So I guess at some point we should probably talk about why you stopped acknowledging my existence," he said. "I kind of feel like it's the elephant in the room. Maybe it's the elephant in the decade."

I didn't say anything.

"We don't have to," he added. "I came here to hang out with you, not interrogate you."

"I don't know, Griff, it happened because I was embarrassed. I was *embarrassed*." The word came out one biley green syllable at a time, each one burning my throat on its way up. "I was never really able to get past that fucking email. It was easier just to stop talking to you."

"What email? Wait—you mean the *Truman* email?" He sat up straight. "You're kidding. Is that what this has always been about? Why didn't you tell me?"

"Um. Embarrassed?"

He closed his eyes for a moment. "So asking me out on a date when we were teenagers is an unforgivable sin in your book? Is that in Leviticus or something?" He looked at me and I rolled my eyes and felt just like the teenager I'd been. "No," he said, reading my face, "just embarrassing. Huh."

"I was afraid that you were always wondering about my motives."

"Motives for what?"

"I don't know. For being close to you. For being your friend." I feared that every glance he would think I was mentally undressing him, every handshake an excuse to touch him. That when he came out of the bathroom wearing only a towel, I— Or when we sat side-by-side at the movies—

"Then apparently you didn't know me as well as I thought you did, Vince." He was angry, but in his eyes there was also relief. At least now he knew it hadn't been his fault. "I told you it was cool and I wasn't lying."

"I know you weren't. It's my problem, not yours."

"Well Vince, man, you need to fucking get over yourself." He bounced his fist like a gavel on the plump arm of the chair. He got up and kneeled down on the brick hearth, worked busily at the embers with the poker. I watched his shoulders rise and fall with a deep sigh. Finally he put the poker down and slid across the floor, leaned against his chair. "OK," he said, looking up at me, "if the email was the problem, let's just go through it. Let's just get it all out in the open. Isn't that what I told you the night I figured out your little secret? Maybe if we'd gotten it out a long time ago we wouldn't have all these—" He looked from me to the fire. "Whatever. How did it start? You saw me in some class we had or something."

"Rebellion in Literature," I said.

"Ah, that's right. Rebellion in Literature." He gestured *come here* with a wag of his fingers, and my living room became a time machine.

***

Spring semester of my freshman year—that's when, as they say, the magic happened. It really did seem like magic that first day of class. Magic, lightning, fate—whatever you want to call it, it was it. It was magic when he came through the door, backpack slung over his shoulder—magic when he strode across the scratched tile with a cocky swagger I'd later understand was a clever disguise for his shyness. The chairs were arranged in a circle, filling slowly as students trickled in. He took a seat on the other side of the circle from me, almost so we were facing each other across the empty middle. When he looked up I looked down at my hands, felt my face redden.

I learned his name when the professor, a young woman named Nicole, not yet jaded by experience and who still believed she could change her students' lives (and, via them, the world), took attendance the first time.

"Ariel Dean," she read from her roster, then looked up to scan the circle.

Griff raised his hand. That act of drawing attention to himself permitted me to look at him full-on for the first time since he sat down.

"I go by Griffin," he told her. "My middle name. Or Griff, less formally. Uh."

"Griffin Dean it is, then." The professor noted it on her attendance roster and I began doodling a capital *G* on a sheet of loose-leaf paper.

After attendance Nicole made us go around the circle telling what our favorite book was, making an effort to remember our names but actually only remembering Griffin's. His favorite, he said, was *The Positronic Man*, by Isaac Asimov, which he added was turned into a bad movie starring Robin Williams. I agreed aloud that it was bad.

"I'm glad it's not just me!" he said, and he pointed at me and smiled. I perceived the flip of his finger as a mind-blowing and unqualified show of affection and blushed, thinking it was obvious to everyone else in the class that our souls were entwining before their very eyes.

When I got back to my dorm room after that first class I looked him up in the student directory and was heartbroken to find no Deans at all, Griffin or otherwise. In the days before Facebook the thin booklet was all I had, and apparently I had nothing. During the next class, though, I received a consolation prize: a list of the whole class's contact info, which the well-intentioned young professor provided so we could get in touch with each other outside of class. Griffin had written his name and his email address in tiny, cramped letters. I ran my finger over his letters even though they were only photocopies.

For more than a month I lived and breathed for Mondays and Wednesdays—for class days, Griffin days—and every other hour of the week served only to anticipate, to prepare. I arranged my laundry schedule so my best jeans would always be ready for Rebellion in Lit. I got up earlier on those days so my hair could be carefully messed according to current style. All in case that day was the day we were to speak.

But no matter how I tried to align the planets or bribe fate, each class was a bigger disappointment than the one before. There was no conversation with Griffin, no chance encounters before or after class, or in the dining hall, or on the sidewalk. Class after class my hopes were pummeled and even though I was naturally optimistic it began to wear me out, made me feel numb and indifferent and bitter. And sad.

At the end of February, our earnest young professor scheduled one-on-one meetings with her to discuss the progress of the course. When I arrived at her office for my meeting Griffin Dean was sitting in a chair outside her door. I took a deep breath. Six weeks into the semester, we would *talk*. My heart started to slam in my chest even as my muscles quieted into a rehearsed steady-cool slowness.

He had a U2 baseball cap on backward—above the strap were the appropriate words *Achtung Baby!*—and a paperback open on his lap. His right leg was crossed over his left, ankle to knee. His jeans were torn up and dirty at the heels where they dragged on the ground.

I sat down beside him. "Hey," I said, the simple word I'd wanted to say to him for weeks.

"Hey," Griffin said. His voice, for the first time since that first day, was for me. The sound as it entered my ears was as lovely as a field of sunflowers, something to treasure like a mint copy of *Action Comics* #1. He jiggled his sneaker and uncrossed his leg.

What was he reading?, I wondered. It was hard to look at the book without appearing to be examining his balls. Was it the book for class? I shifted in my chair and used the motion to disguise a glance. The book had a flying saucer on its cover.

"She running late?" I said.

"A little, yeah."

"Figures— I thought *I* was going to be late."

He smiled and returned to his book. I stared at the bulletin board on the wall opposite the chairs. A flyer announced auditions for the spring musical. *Think of something else to say*, I screamed in my head. This chance of a lifetime took weeks to arrive and likely would never come again.

"Good book?"

He stopped reading and marked his place with his thumb. "Yeah, but it's not really spacey enough."

Not spacey enough. I didn't know what that meant, so I just agreed.

"I'm reading this amazing book about dogs," I added. "I mean, it's called *Dogwalker*. About mutant puppies. Or—well some of them are. And this mole who hides under the couch and sings but turns out to be a tiny man."

"A tiny man, huh?"

"He hides and sings. And there's another one about a mattress. He has to find a mattress."

"The tiny man?"

"No, the narrator."

I heard the scrape of chairs moving inside the office and then the door opened. *Fuck. Not yet!* I hadn't had enough time with Griffin yet. *Take longer, damn you!* But a girl pulling on a Shuster Tennis jacket came out with the professor following her.

"Griffin, hi—I'm sorry—about the time," Nicole said. She had a red pen behind her ear. The cap was chewed.

"No problem," he said.

"Eliza was giving me *loads* of great feedback. I'll be with you in a minute, Vince. Thanks for waiting."

Eliza nodded at us and walked away toward the elevators. Griffin stuffed his book in his backpack, got up and went into the office. Just before he closed the door he turned around and winked at me.

*

"I think I just meant, you know, about Eliza giving the teacher *feedback*. They were both pretty foxy."

"I probably knew that and chose to ignore it."

"Man. I had no idea I was such a charmer. I can go around seducing people with just a mere bat of the eyelash, huh? I'll have to keep that in mind. So what happened next?"

"It drove me insane."

***

I had to know what the wink meant. Was it a secret signal from one closeted dude to another? It could be! I waited for more signals. In class I watched Griffin's hands and sneakers for discreet taps, for a queer Morse code. *Tap tap I think I love you tap tap tap ask me out tap tap.*

When I figured I wasn't picking up anything I decided to send out signals of my own. I made tiny attempts to copy his movements: I crossed my arms when he crossed his, sat on my leg when he sat on his. I hoped he would see this synchronicity and know I'd *noticed* him. It was never blatant, though. It wouldn't do just to attract his attention. He had to be watching for it. Closely.

But nothing happened. Not that class or the next or the next or the next. And I began to realize that my whole semester was unraveling waiting for something that wasn't ever going to come. Never unless I did more than scratch my nose when he scratched his. Never unless I just grew a pair and asked him out.

But not only did I not know whether he was interested—I didn't know whether he even *could* be interested.

How could I find out whether Griffin Dean liked guys?

*

"My turn," Griff said. He returned to the chair and curled up with his legs under him. "So you were a lovesick swain trying to figure out what to do. Finally you came up with both an idea and the nerve to put it in action, so you'd know whether to expect to get smacked if you asked me out. Although why you thought that was a possibility is beyond me. But anyway, anyway— You made a special screen name and sent me a nice and, I must say, well-written but extremely anonymous email asking me if I dated guys. Am I right so far?"

"Yes." I pulled the blanket down tighter on my shoulders. "Maybe we should skip this part?"

"Vince, if you can't see the humor in this you're taking life way too seriously. Right? Yeah, you know I'm right. So you sent the email. I got the letter, and yeah, I *was* weirded out. Not so much about it being from a guy, but I didn't know *which* guy. I would've been flattered if I'd known it was you. You've always had enviable biceps. But you could've just as easily been that dipshit with the hacky sack who was always blocking the front door. Remember him?"

"Ryan Sedgwick."

"Yeah, what a fucker. I hated that kid. So anyway, I didn't respond."

***

As the week went by I felt more and more guilty about sending the email. On top of everything, on top of my weird and overwhelming attraction to Griffin, I liked him. I *cared* about him. And the last thing I ever wanted to do was make him uncomfortable.

If he didn't like guys the way I did (and that was likely, right? like ninety-something-percent likely?), was he just totally confused about why some mysterious person going by the name of Truman thought he might? And if he did like guys but was closeted, was he afraid he'd been discovered? Was he scanning every face wondering if any of those people were Truman? Did he sit in the dining hall glancing around while his food got cold and his soda went flat? Did he lie awake at night? The whole thing made me feel lonely and villainous and sick to my stomach.

Nicole started the first class of March by announcing a group project and then began counting around our circle, dividing us into groups. I tried counting ahead, my eyes racing past the pen she was ticking against desks, desperately trying to figure out whether Griffin and I would be assigned to the same group—but Nicole's counting kept messing me up. Griffin got labeled a four. If I'd known about the group project I would've tried rigging the outcome. I thought, as it was, that my chances were not one-in-five, but somehow much closer to zero.

But at last fate had been bribed and the planets were aligned and when Nicole clicked her red pen on my desk and said *four* it felt like getting knighted.

Ninety-seven seconds later I found myself sitting directly opposite Griffin, our desks pushed together front-to-front. My happiness was bittersweet, though, because even in my happiness I felt guilty knowing what I'd done, and fearful too that he'd somehow uncovered my deceit, that he would at any moment reach across our desks and slug me. Ah, but he was here and it was worth it. There were two other people in our group—just scenery, just mannequins.

Maybe we would eat lunch together, I thought, nervously rolling myself up in the fantasy. His eyes were green and seemed to hint at things he wanted to say but couldn't, at least not here. I watched his hands as he jotted notes. He had nice fingernails and a very even skin-tone. Maybe we would hang out in each other's rooms, sixty-nine for hours while our roommates were away, become life partners, adopt foreign orphans.

While I was daydreaming of these things I could feel my mouth moving, could vaguely hear words coming out of it. I had some awareness of books being handed out, and of listening while Nicole gave instructions. But it was something Griffin said that blasted apart my reverie—the worst thing a guy who likes a guy can possibly hear:

"My girlfriend read this book last semester."

At first I thought maybe it was one of the mannequins in our group speaking, but—oh man, *oh no*—it was Griffin. The rest of what he said—the things the girlfriend had told him about the book, and how we could use that now in this project so we wouldn't have to actually read it ourselves—all blended into a monotone hum like that emergency alert tone they test on TV.

A girlfriend. He had one. At worst he was straight. But even if he was bi, he was taken. He was someone else's. Of course. Of course he was.

The tiny pessimistic devil who usually sat on my shoulder and who'd warned me not to even bother with Griffin in the first place suddenly conjured himself in my stomach and began crawling up my throat, making it tight. I wasn't sure whether to cry that fucker out or throw him up. I thought I might do both, and collapse in a puddle of tears and puke.

By the time class was over, though, I'd talked myself into being thankful that I'd made no real connection with Griffin before finding out he had a girlfriend. Somehow not having him in my life right now made it a little easier to know he'd never be in it at all.

One week later I laid my arms across the window sill and rested my chin in the crook of my elbow. Through my fifth-floor window and across Beacon Street, over the row of brownstones on the other side, were the tall glass buildings that made up Boston's ever more jagged skyline. Waning sunlight lit up the Hancock and Prudential buildings with blazing orange. As the sun descended behind the horizon the light crept down the sides of the buildings, burning them up, until finally it disappeared into dark embers at the bottoms. I tried to watch the sunset as often as possible.

"*God I hope I get it, I hope I get it,*" sang my roommate Brian. He was standing on his bed. His strawberry hair was pushed up severely in the front. "*Oh god I really, really need to get this job!* Wait, fuckadilly—how's this go?" He reached for a sheet of lyrics that lay on his pillow.

It was mid-March. Room selection for our sophomore year was in less than a month and I did not consider it an option to spend another year living with Brian Lauder (pronounced *louder*). My few other friends were either seniors or girls or both. As a freshman I wouldn't have a chance at getting a single. I was shit out of luck.

I needed a roommate.

*

"There's that total hunk you still have the crush on," Griff suggested as he poked the fire.

"You mean the one I just found out had a girlfriend?"

"Yeah, him. You could ask him.—No you couldn't.—Yes you could. You play Gollum/Sméagol for a while and finally decide that you're young and ridiculous—"

"And desperate."

"—and desperate—OK mostly desperate—and you do. You send me another email, this time from your real Shuster address, telling me that since we got along fine during groupwork and since you have no one else to ask, you wonder if I'm looking for a roommate for sophomore year."

***

I sent that second email on a Saturday morning (taking pains to use a different font from the Truman email) and all weekend waited in a state of near panic for Griffin to reply. I clicked refresh on the browser like a gambling addict at a slot machine, hoping, believing, that the next click would be the jackpot. But by Sunday night I was bitter and broke.

On Monday morning I sulked to class not wanting to see Griffin at all. I was angry not only because he'd given me no answer—again!—but because he was continually breaking my heart. The worst part was that he didn't even know it.

I chose a desk in the circle and sat down to read the homework assignment I'd been too busy refreshing my email to read the night before. When someone took the seat beside me I didn't look up, didn't so much as raise my eyes. The person was fidgeting with a click-pen, that much I could hear. *Clicka clicka clicka.*

"Hey, I got your email," the person said after a minute or two, mid-breath, as though he'd only just sat down. Or as though he'd been rehearsing.

I put my book down. "Oh, cool." Something was different about him. His eyes were brighter or his skin was darker. Yes, it was his skin—he had a tan. In March. It took my breath away.

"Sorry I didn't reply," he went on. "I was in Florida this weekend and I just got it this morning. A few minutes ago, actually."

"That's OK," I said nonchalantly, as though his response was of minimal interest. "How was Florida?"

"It was all right. My cousin lives there, so... Would you want to hit the dining hall after class?"

"Sure."

"Cool."

That was all. He put down his pen and folded his hands in his lap. I picked up my book and read the same sentence of *Letters From A Birmingham Jail* over and over. Goosebumps rose on my arms. It used to be that I savored every minute of this class because that was Griffin Time. But now that Griffin Time was about to extend beyond class, outside of class, and be *better*, I was desperate for the 105 minutes to be over.

When Nicole was done talking I packed my notebook into my backpack slowly, making every effort to be casual and suave. My post-class exit was no longer about trying to match Griffin's speed to the door so maybe I could hold it for him or have it held by him, with the chance of our fingers brushing. This was about waiting for him so we could leave together.

Together. Imagine!

"I'm starving," I said, trying to hide my giddiness.

"Me too," said Griffin. "What were the pages for the homework?"

"I think it—"

"Never mind, I'll get it from you later." He closed his book onto a sheet of paper and stuffed it in his backpack. "After you," he said, and held the door.

We walked up Beacon Street and through Boston Common. Spring had begun a few days ago, and while the trees were still winter-bare, the sun on the branches seemed to be selling the idea that it was time to start pushing out new buds.

"So you're having trouble finding a roommate too, huh?" he said, backpack slung by one strap over his shoulder. He was taller than me by a couple inches, even in his thin-soled Converse, but skinnier.

"Most of my friends are seniors," I said. "The guy I live with now is a musical theatre major. Let's just say I'd prefer someone a little quieter."

"Quiet would be a nice change," he said. He hooked a thumb under his backpack strap. "I'm in a triple right now. It's OK I guess but I'm kind of the third wheel. I'm pretty sure the other two guys are gay for each other, so, you know..."

"That's funny," I said, trying to decide whether he'd meant that the problem was the gay roommates or his third-wheel status. "Which dorm are you in?"

"Beacon-Storrow," he said.

"...You are? What floor?"

"Ten."

"I'm on Five. It's weird that I've never seen you around there." It seemed suddenly funny that while I was scanning through the student directory he was only five floors above me, sleeping, showering, practicing karate naked.

"I actually just transferred here this semester," he said.

Ah, that explained why he wasn't in the directory. "Where were you before?"

"Roger Williams. In Rhode Island."

"No good?"

"I don't know, it just wasn't right for me somehow and I was shit-unhappy about it. I couldn't get settled. I get kind of antsy sometimes." He wiggled his hands as though they'd fallen asleep.

Two Shuster girls were playing tennis in the Common courts. Like window shoppers we stopped and watched them without saying anything, our fingers hooked through the green chain-link fence that surrounded the courts.

"The one on the left is gorgeous," Griff said. "If I could draw people I'd draw her picture."

"Didn't you say you have a girlfriend?"

He looked at me with an embarrassed grin. "I didn't say I wanted to *sleep* with her," he said. "There are the girls you want to go to bed with, and then the girls you want to put a frame around and just gaze at, you know? Girls are art sometimes, I think. Don't you?" He looked at me again, swinging himself playfully on the fence, but his feet were still touching the ground. "Sorry, I sound like a total homo."

"No, yeah, I know what you mean. I like people-watching. Sometimes I crave beauty, too. Some people—some girls are just so beautiful."

"That's it exactly," he said. "I'm a beauty-craver. I need to see it sometimes so I know the world's going to be OK."

It hurt when he said that because someone who would say something so personal to a stranger, if he loved me, would've already told me that too.

When the girls noticed us watching we got back on the brick sidewalk that led to Tremont Street and to the dining hall.

"So do you like Shuster so far?" I said.

"It's better."

"Even with Professor Nicole and your gay roommates?"

He smiled. "Yeah, even."

We sat at a two-person table in the dining hall by the windows and had lunch; me a ham-and-cheese sub and he a grilled cheese with bacon. We talked about our Lit class (turned out we got a B on that group project) and his trip to Florida, and it was fun and easy. Even when the conversation drifted toward his girlfriend—whose name was Ashley, who he met at Roger Williams—it didn't make me nervous. He still seemed like the guy I'd made up in my mind. Maybe it was because somehow, against all odds, he was exactly what I expected. Maybe it was because she was so far away.

"So do you want to do it?" he said, wiggling a fry through a puddle of ketchup, officially broaching the topic. "Room next year?"

"You mean you've felt me out enough already?"

"I figure you won't stab me in my sleep or anything," he said. A blob of ketchup dripped from his fry and plopped onto his sandwich. "Murder is really my main concern. I can put up with pretty much anything else."

"Good. I promise not to bring any sharp objects. Although I do have a bat."

He grinned and raised his plastic glass half-full of ginger ale. We toasted to our sophomore year.

Brian was standing on his bed when I got back to the room. His stereo was playing one of the numbers from the spring musical. I flung my backpack onto my bed and jumped onto his with him, my shoes still on. I grabbed his hands and forced him to dance. His lyrics fluttered to the floor.

"What's up with you?" he said, eyes wide with bewilderment as I waltzed him across the bed. "Did you just get laid or something?"

"Does it look like I did?"

He looked at me closely and to break his stare I dipped him so low his head touched his pillow.

"Well, you haven't had this glow since that night you sexiled me to hook up with that chick from Eight," he said. He twirled on the end of my finger. I liked that he was playing along. He really wasn't a bad guy.

I jumped off his bed, making a rockstar splits.

"That was almost as good," I said. I handed him his lyrics.

"But not quite?"

"We'll see."

*

"In the movie version of our lives," Griff said, jabbing the poker into the coals and sending a flurry of sparks up the chimney, "this would be the perfect place for a montage. We start hanging out, we become fast friends. We go to movies, we crash the dining hall together, we sit on benches in the Common and watch hot girls play tennis. We talk so much in class that we're told repeatedly by Nicole to be quiet and have some respect for the people who actually want to learn something, boys. We're only roomies-to-be, but already after two weeks I consider you my best friend." He said it matter-of-factly but I looked up in surprise; I hadn't known he felt that way about me, at least not so soon. "And then one night..."

I took a deep breath. It was 4:18 in the morning and we'd arrived at the hard part.

***

"So what do you want to do Friday night?" Griff said. "Movies?" He was lying on my bed with the soles of his feet pressed against the wall, bouncing a red super ball in the rectangle of eggshell paint between two posters, catching it in my baseball mitt. It was evening.

"Sure," I said from my desk, and clicked send on a response to one of my father's emails.

"Actually, before you log off—" He caught the red ball a final time and swung his legs away from the wall. "Can I check my email real quick?"

"Your— um..." His email? But there were secrets on my computer; I never liked anyone to use it. I knew that if he sat at my desk and used this, of all programs, my act was done. My heart seized. I was afraid to say yes, but how could I say anything else? To him it was a harmless request.

He stood up, dropped the mitt on the bed. "Ashley was supposed to let me know if she's coming up."

"OK."

"Cool."

I got up from my desk and he sat down in my place. I walked over to my bed, sat down hard, put my elbows on my knees, leaned forward waiting for everything to unravel. He would click the little dropdown button on the screen name menu. He would see the other screen name in the user history. *Truman08*. He would see it and know. And then what? Would he punch me? Break my jaw, my nose—blind me? Would he not want to room together next year? Would he stop being my friend? It wasn't that I was bi, but that I had hit on him, that I had initiated our friendship based on a lie.

A lie I could've kept up. Options popped into my head. I could tell him some guy from our class had come to my room for homework purposes, had checked his email. Truman08 was not me at all, but that guy.

My stomach churned with all the fear of discovery I'd ever felt, all the close calls combined. My hands were shaking. I wanted to run to the computer and yank out the power cord before he could click that little button—the one that would unroll the secret I'd kept so carefully for so long.

I closed my eyes.

"Who is this?" Griff said. I opened my eyes and found his looking at me, the dark eyebrows above them scrunched.

I could lie, I could lie. It was that kid from class, the one who is maybe a little gay. It wasn't me at all, it was that kid.

I could lie.

"It's me," I said.

My vision blurred and I felt dizzy, nauseous. I got up from the bed and walked over to the desk, steadying myself on the way with a hand on my roommate's bureau. I leaned close to the laptop screen, as though to make sure, like a witness picking a criminal out of a line-up, and I said again, "It's me."

For a long time I could hear every atom shivering in the room. Griff's brain must've been churning as hard as mine. It's him, it's him, *it's him*, I was sure he must be thinking. But when he finally looked up at me there was no hate in his eyes, no shock or even confusion. Instead he asked if I wanted to go play pool.

"OK," I said.

The T we took to the pool place in the Fenway was crowded; it was especially awkward now being pressed against him, both our hands fighting for space on the railing. I tried to act as straight as possible, with an extra-steady voice and slow, confident movements, in hopes that I could make him doubt what he'd learned.

We played pool for two hours without saying anything more than which ball was going into which pocket. It was both reassuring and agony. Maybe rage was bubbling inside him and would soon burst forth, *Hulk*-like, and blow me across the place. The silence allowed for too much information to be sketched in with guesses and assumptions. He knew I was Truman08, but how much else did he suspect? And how much did he suspect incorrectly?

"I'm about done," he said finally, dropping his cue into a metal barrel. He offered to cover our game because my wallet was empty. "You can pay me back later," he said and pushed a few bills across the counter.

Later was a comforting word. There would be a later.

Close to midnight now, we were walking back to the dorm from the Arlington Street T station. It was the end of March, and while the temperature had been close to fifty during the day, the night was bitter cold.

I watched my breath, watched Griff walking a half step ahead of me, his arms stiff, his hands in his pockets—and I wondered, after all the silence, whether he'd really made the connection at all. Maybe he had never even gotten the Truman email. Maybe he had deleted it without reading it, thinking it was spam. Maybe he—

"Vince," he said, turning to me, spinning from his hips without taking his hands out of his pockets, "I think it's best if we get everything out in the open."

I stopped short in the middle of the sidewalk. He continued several steps before stopping and turning around. A woman passed by with a dog.

"I'm sorry," I blurted. I didn't know what else to say. My voice felt heavy with the weight of the whole thing and with the years leading up to it. I couldn't believe this was happening.

"It's OK," he said, not in a tone of forgiveness, but in one that meant he didn't think there was anything to forgive. "I didn't know you were gay. I mean, it's totally fine, I have no problem with that. I just wish you'd told me."

"I know. I never told you because I've never told anyone." I was standing directly under a streetlamp and felt exposed. We started walking again. "So you're the first to know."

"Wow." He seemed honestly surprised, maybe even intimidated by the weight of being the first. "How long have *you* known?"

"I don't know, since middle school." I kept my eyes straight ahead but in my periphery I could see he was still looking at me. "It was never a surprise. When I started to like girls I was starting to feel different about the boys, too."

"Girls? So...?"

"Yeah. I like girls and I like guys too. I guess I'm— I mean I *am*— I *am* bi." I watched the word flow as white breath into the air in front of me. I half expected it to crystallize and drop like a brick onto my toe, but it just became part of the air, released.

"I was just thinking that you were pretty into girls for a gay guy," Griff said and he laughed. "Or else you were a really good actor. So we can still go babe watching?"

"I just like watching the guys too," I said. I inhaled, deep and staccato like a person finishing a good cry. I was beginning to realize that I would come through this OK.

"Whatever floats your boat," he said. "So you never told anyone? How do you hold in something like that?"

I laughed. "Fear."

"Of what? Getting beat up?"

"Of saying, *I'm different.* And, *I'm not who you think I am.* And that feels worse, I think."

He took that in, cleared his voice. "Well you don't have to be afraid anymore. Not with me. And I don't know other little details about you—I don't even know your favorite color!—but that doesn't mean I don't know you."

"It's blue," I said. He smiled. "Thanks Griff."

"Thank you for being honest," he said.

"I *wasn't* honest though."

"You wanted to be, you just needed a little help." He put his hand on my shoulder, gave me a playful shove. When we had come to the tall iron gate of the dorm, he asked if I wanted to walk a little more.

"OK," I said.

I was glad because I wasn't ready to leave him yet. It was beginning to dawn on me, the idea that the guy I'd picked out of a crowded classroom and labeled *perfection* based on his smile, the way his jeans fit his ass, and fifteen minutes of group work was the same guy who was right now changing my life. Had I somehow known he was special? Was it fate? It seemed sillier to think it was only chance.

"It's weird that I never seem to have straight roommates...," he mused.

I felt a rush of relief. "So you still want to room next year?"

"Of course," he said. "Why wouldn't I?"

I thought surely he was the only person in the world who could be this accepting, this cool. I felt so lucky. He'd known me ten days and knew more of me than people who'd known me nineteen years. And I was OK with that. I'd always been afraid of people knowing too much, but now Griffin shared my biggest secret, my only secret—because if I'd had any others they were all rolled up in that one. It felt funny that now there was nothing I had to be afraid of him knowing. There was nothing I couldn't say. I felt completely free and completely *myself*, and the more that what had happened began to register, the more I wanted to run and stretch out my arms and leap up into the sky. Surely this exhilaration was enough to let me zoom across the face of the moon.

"Sorry if this sounds lame," he said. "But doesn't it feel weird to have the potential to fall in love with every person you meet? All your friends?"

"I don't think so," I said. "I think it's weirder to only be able to fall in love with half of the people you meet."

"Hmm." He looked a little taken aback. "Maybe. I guess it is. Like, as much as I care about my guy friends, I know there's always going to be that distance between us."

"I don't have a distance," I said—and then I was afraid he would think I couldn't separate friendship and sex. "I mean I *do*. But it's not automatic. It's about individual relationships, not just gender." It began to sound confusing even to me. "This is the first time I've ever talked about this with anyone. I don't know what I'm saying. I've never had to describe it. I have no automatic boundaries."

"Nah dude, I get it," he said. "You can love everyone. Everyone could be your soulmate. I think, if anything, you're a few steps ahead of the rest of us."

*

He was leaning back deep in the chair; he'd pulled his hood up a few minutes ago and now it framed his grin when he looked at me. "I can't believe I really said *Let's go play some pool*," he said.

"So many possible responses went through my head..."

"I told you it didn't matter, Vin."

"I didn't think about it at the time because I didn't have any experience with coming out, you know? But there are so many ways you could've handled that situation. You could've said any of the fifty things I was afraid you might say. You were a borderline saint and I didn't realize it until too late. And I don't know— How do I ever forgive myself for that?"

"I was no saint," he said. "Not even a borderline one. All I was was your friend. You should've trusted me more."

He went back to bed a little while later. I stayed up until I was sure he was asleep, then joined him.

SATURDAY

The phone ringing woke me up. I couldn't move. I was pinned. Griff was lying on my arm. I yanked myself free and fumbled with numb fingers for the receiver.

"Hello?" I croaked.

"Sorry if I woke you. It's me."

"...Mm?"

"Zane."

"Oh, Zane."

"Zane who?" Griff mumbled.

"I nee—" Zane began. "Not your boy, huh?"

"No, he's not." I looked over at Griff. His shoulder was stamped with the pale imprint of my right hand. "We aren't together, Zane."

"What are you, then?"

"Friends," I said, although that didn't feel quite right to me either.

"Social revolutionaries," Griff mumbled, and pulled the pillow that was between us up over his head.

"Whatever," Zane said. "Anyway, I need my keys. I have to open the store."

There was no question in his voice, not even the sound of a tip-toe around one. I knew now that I hadn't fired him because he hadn't gone along with being fired. Zane, while maybe not naturally as confident as he came across (he'd likely been up all night rehearsing this conversation), had an amazing ability to project it. I found this talent more attractive than if it had been natural and not a disguise. It meant there was hope for the shy.

"It's Saturday," I said, but was suddenly not quite sure of the day. It felt like a week since Griff showed up. "Right?"

"Yeah."

"So Marissa is supposed to open."

"Marissa's neighborhood has no electricity and she hasn't been able to shower. She called me yesterday and asked if I'd cover."

Griff pulled the pillow off his head and leaned close to eavesdrop—a snooping spoon. His skin wasn't quite touching mine, though his chin was hovering right near my shoulder.

"Why didn't you tell me this last night?" I said, hyperaware of the knee that just bumped my thigh.

"You would've just covered it yourself," Zane said, "and I needed you to need me to not be fired." I could picture him working through the accuracy of that sentence in the pause that followed it. "Yeah."

"Tricky," Griff said, laughing right into the phone. "He knows how to work you."

"Where are you now?" I said.

"In front of the store," Zane said. "I just finished shoveling the walk. The whole walk."

"Awwh," Griff cooed.

"And I sprinkled sand," Zane added.

"You sprinkled sand?"

"Yeah. I salted."

"All right. Come get your keys." I hung up the phone and looked at Griff. "Happy now?"

"Yeah."

Fifteen minutes later there was a knock on my front door, which meant Zane drove way too fast.

"Coming!" I pushed down the covers and sat up.

"God!" Griff groaned, yanking them back up. He'd dozed off again while waiting for Zane. "No exclamation points before noon. Wasn't that in our original roommate agreement?"

"This is my house now, pal."

I got out of bed and went out to the living room, rummaged in my coat pocket for the keys. I opened the door just a few inches against the cold. Zane was standing on the stoop, his hands in the pockets of his skinny jeans. He wore a floppy blue hat with an orange pompom. His cheeks were rosy.

"Thank you for covering for Marissa," I said. "And for shoveling." It was my apology. I held out his keys.

"Thanks for not firing me and stuff."

I shrugged and told him I overreacted—but I added quickly, "Not that it should ever happen again."

"It won't." He slid the keys onto his carabiner and went back down the steps. "Hey Vince," he said, turning around as I was about to shut the door. "Whatever you guys are, he's cute." He smiled a chapped, kind, maybe resigned smile that caught me off guard, waved once, and walked back to his car.

I closed the door and moved the curtain aside to watch him through the big picture window. Most of it was covered in frost but I could see him get into his beat-up Mustang and back out of the driveway.

I stood there with my forehead touching the glass for a minute after he'd gone, then I realized I was freezing. I adjusted the thermostat and walked on curled toes back to the bedroom, eager to get back under the covers. I could almost see my breath. Griff was facing away from me again, the way he'd slept all night.

I laid back down thinking, *I just got into bed with Griff.* The feelings that came along with that hovered in a weird space between sad and exciting. Heat crackled off him and, like a backyard mosquito light, zapped my goosebumps one by one.

"He get his keys?" he said. It startled me. He rolled over onto his back, folded his hands on his chest. A patch of curly brown hair filled the shallow groove between where his pectorals would've been if he weren't so thin. His ribs showed beneath his skin like the ripply sand at the edge of the ocean; the sheet lapped his belly like waves. If only a riptide would just pull me in and take me deeper into the bed with him, I'd never have to come out again.

"Yeah," I said. "He thinks you're cute."

He sighed. "If only girls were as into me as guys seem to be..."

I smelled the faint bitterness of his breath and felt suddenly self-conscious of my own. "You don't seem to have any trouble," I said, trying not to exhale. My voice came out monotone.

"C'mon, I have nothing *but* trouble," he said. "Anyway, he thinks you're cute too."

"What?"

"It's obvious." He rubbed his exposed forearms, pulled them under the covers and yanked the blanket up to his chin. "Is the heat off?"

"How's it obvious?"

"Well, last night when he acted all aloof about that guy, and then how he looked at you to see if you were jealous. It's obvious to me."

"He didn't care if I was jealous, though."

"He did, though, definitely."

He rolled over again and jerked the covers away from me. I pulled them back and we lay still. I watched the branches of his joshua tree sway with the gentle rise and fall of his breathing. Sunlight came through the edge of the blue checkered curtains and cast a warm yellow beam across our legs.

"You must've seen the naked guy at graduation," I said, glancing over at Griff and then looking again at the street in front of us, "the one who pulled up his robe when he was getting his diploma?"

"Shit, I forgot about that!" he said, letting go of the steering wheel long enough to clap his hands. "Yeah, I saw him. More than I wanted to!"

I laughed. "That took some balls to do that, though," I said, "to streak at graduation."

"I don't know if I'd call it a streak," he said. "But yes it did take some balls—I saw them very clearly." He stopped us at a red light and I realized I liked him driving my Jeep. "Man, Vin, it feels good to talk about this stuff with you. No one's as good at nostalgia as you are."

"Yeah."

"We'll reminisce more when you're done work."

He turned into the Golden Age lot, which looked like the surface of one of the moons in his sci-fi—full of ruts and piles, unnavigable in anything other than a moon buggy. The Jeep bounced around in the ruts and he parked us alongside a pick-up with its bed full of snow.

"Thanks for the wheels," he said.

"Sure. No problem. I trust you."

"Awh. Really?"

"I don't trust other drivers though. Be careful. People like totally forget how to drive when there's snow on the ground."

"That's true. So do you think it's going to be weird?"

"What?"

"With Zane. At work."

"It's been weirder. No. It'll be fine."

"All right. Hey," he said, "what time do I pick you up?"

I told him 8:15 but I'd call if anything changed. He told me he'd be there.

For an absent-minded moment I felt like leaning over to kiss him goodbye. That's what happened at this point in these exchanges, right? We shared a bed last night. We had cereal together this morning. It's what I did with Melanie. But Griff was drumming his fingers on the wheel and I pushed the door shut. He waved with a lift of his chin, backed away and rejoined the creeping traffic.

The walk was shoveled with sharp sides and crisp angles, the pavement sprinkled evenly with sand—the very model of perfect shoveling. Zane must've thought of each scoop as an apology. I walked to the door hoping, maybe, to find the sign turned to

CLOSED, as Zane had a habit of forgetting to flip it. But it said OPEN in bubbly yellow letters. Everything was as it should be.

The bell jingled above me. There was one customer that I could see, browsing the Vertigo trades. Zane was at the counter hunched over a crossword.

"Nice job on the walk."

"Hi, thanks," he said. "*Franny's brother*. Five letters."

"Um. *Zooey*." I stood in front of the counter with my hands in my pockets.

"Doesn't fit."

"E-y?"

"Oh. Yeah. That's right." He scrunched his nose and filled in the blocks. "You're smart."

"Slow today?"

"Not bad." He twiddled the pen between his fingers like that magic trick that makes it look like the pencil is bending. "Two people came in to pick up their pulls. A handful of browsers."

"I thought it would be slower," I said. "All the snow."

"Don't underestimate the dedication of the fanboys and fangirls."

"Haha. True. So."

"So. Where's your shirt?"

"My—?" I looked down. I was missing my Golden Age uniform. "Oh."

"Griff wearing it?" Smirking.

"No."

In the back room I took off my coat and grabbed my coat-hangered spare at the back of the closet. The t-shirt was black; on the front was the golden *O* word balloon logo from the sign, overlaid with the store's name in white hand-lettered text. I rubbed my hair in a mirror push-pinned to the wall and went back out front.

The lone customer's eyes were wandering, a sure sign he wanted some help. I obliged and he left a few minutes later with a half-dozen issues of Simon's least-favorite title.

"*Majestic* is selling well, huh?" I leaned with my back against the checkout counter; Zane was behind it. I crossed my arms and looked out at the street.

"He's a better Superman than Superman lately," he said. "As far as writing goes."

"Don't let Simon hear you talk like that. He'd do more than take your keys for that kind of blasphemy."

"Probably," Zane said, "but that would mean he'd have to be here. And you know how likely that is lately."

"Come on, I like Patti."

"She like runs his life."

"She's good for him."

Simon got married the spring before, and his wife, a local real estate kingpin we didn't know how he reeled in, seemed to be weaning him off of Golden Age. His schedule kept shrinking. Supposedly he was writing a book, a definitive history of comic books, and Patti was being very encouraging, but Zane and Marissa felt like she was stealing him away. But that meant more of Simon's responsibilities were falling to me.

"She's good for *you*," Zane said.

"You're off ten minutes ago," I reminded him.

"I'll just chill for a while," he said. "If that's OK."

"You must have more exciting places to be."

"Just doing homework."

"Hanging out with Jeremy."

"That's over," he said. "Thanks to you."

The bell jingled and a boy walked in, five or six with red mittens tethered to his sleeves, an old man trailing behind him. The boy reached immediately for the *Spawn* figures.

"Those are ugly," the man said. He looked at Zane and me and shrugged, smiled. "He says, *Let's go for a walk*, and when I've got my hat on he says, *Don't forget your money*."

"Kids are sneaky," Zane said.

"But he shoveled all the steps, so a deal's a deal."

Zane gestured to the plastic demon in the boy's hands. "If you're in the market for something less satanic," he said to the grandfather, who nodded, "we have some new *Spider-Man* figures in." He looked at the boy. "Want to see?"

The boy clutched his grandfather's leg and mumbled yes into the old man's coat. Zane came out from behind the counter and took a figure down off the hooks.

"This guy's a nasty villain," he said to the kid, describing the figure. He didn't change his voice the way most people do when they talk to kids—he spoke to the kid, not to the nearby adults, haha, via the kid. "He's got these tentacles you can wrap people up in and stuff. And he comes with slime, which is pretty cool."

The kid scrunched his face and shook his head.

"Is that... what's his name?" The grandfather was pointing to the line of figures on the top row. "I remember him..." The figure wore a metal helmet and had wings on his shoes. A blue cloud covered the front of his bright yellow shirt.

"Matt Morrow," I said. "Protector of the future."

"Ah, not Tom Morrow?"

"Tom was a few Morrows ago now. He got killed off in, I think, 1983."

"Ha! Shame. I used to read that magazine. I sold newspapers in Boston when I was a boy back in the forties." It sounded like *fotties.* "The first thing I'd do with my pay was I'd go to the drugstore and buy it. They were a dime back then—if I remember right. Which is less and less likely to be the case."

The boy had selected an action figure and he stood on his toes to push it onto the counter. The grandfather pulled out his wallet and then, as an afterthought, reached up and took the Matt Morrow figure off the hook.

"I'll get a man too so they can battle," the grandfather said, putting his down on the counter. The boy looked up at him and laughed, laughed without really opening his mouth. A spit bubble formed on his lip, popped.

"All these heroes and villains, and the kid picks *Peter Parker,*" Zane whispered to me as they were leaving the store. He stretched his arms across the counter. "In his street clothes. I don't get it. He doesn't even come with *weapons.*"

"Characters can be cool even when they're not wearing tights, you know."

"Whatever you say." He rolled his eyes. "Actually, speaking of—" He straightened up suddenly and I turned to look out the window. "Jesus," he said, "the old guy almost just fell."

"Did he?"

"So much for my sand sprinkling."

"It looked fine to me. Um. Man the counter, I'll go put some more down."

I got a container of salt from the back and brought it outside, sowing it across the slick sidewalk down to the Copy Cop, then I ran back inside shivering. Zane was checking out a customer.

When the customer left we stood at the counter looking out.

"Cold out there huh?" he said.

"Really."

He was quiet a minute and then he said, "At least you've got someone to keep you warm at night." Then he sighed.

"Zane, I don't need you picking at this. Griff and I aren't together. Come on."

"Tell me about him."

"No."

"Tell me and I'll stop harassing you."

"He's just a friend."

"Where'd you find him? Probably online, right?"

"Not online," I said, ruminating on Zane's use of the word *find* as opposed to *meet*, and how in this case it was actually kind of appropriate. "I don't even own a computer. In college. I met him in college. Freshman year. We roomed together our sophomore year."

"So he's rooming with you again?"

"For a week."

"You just being casual?"

"I keep telling you. He is straight."

"That's what they all say." He sighed. "That guy Jeremy from last night? He's straight, too." He placed air quotes around *straight.*

I felt a flare of anger at his insinuation that Griff was a closet case. There were days when I wondered about that myself (extreme tolerance, like extreme intolerance, always made a person seem a little suspect), but I didn't like anyone else thinking it. It was like how I could make fun of Superman for wearing his underwear on the outside, but when someone else who didn't love him like I loved him said the same thing, watch out. They had no right. Zane had no right.

"I don't know about Jeremy," I said, "but Griff really is straight."

"Straight and he sleeps in your bed with you?"

"I don't have a couch," I countered. "You've been to my house. What would be your suggestion? Should he have slept on the floor?"

He shrugged. "I've just never heard of a straightboy sharing a bed with a bi dude."

"If Griff was gay he'd be out. He's just that way. Sometimes I think he wishes he was."

It made me remember Griff sitting on his bed one night in our dorm room, telling me he'd seen an attractive guy in the dining hall while he was eating lunch.

"How attractive?" I said, trying to keep in check a rising thrill.

"I don't know," Griff said. "Attractive. Nice to look at. Do you think that means I might be bi?" He seemed almost excited, as though he were on the verge of discovering a new part of himself, one that would allow him to tap into unlimited potential for romance.

"Did you want to kiss him? Touch him and stuff?"

His smile faded a little. "Kiss him? Not really, no. But his skin was really clear and he had a cool haircut."

"Did he make you nervous?"

"Nervous how?"

"Like did he make you feel like you wanted to go talk to him but were afraid?"

"No..."

"Did you get a boner?"

"... No, no boner." Now he looked disappointed and I felt the same way.

Zane was eyeballing me. "Do *you* wish he was?"

"Gay?"

"Gay, bi, biologically available."

"He's my friend. I don't care what he is."

"Sure."

The bell jingled. Two high school girls came in and browsed the Indie section, giggling over *Cavalcade of Boys*, the homo version of *Archie*. One of them said to the other, "I told you." They left without buying anything.

"So who was that Jeremy guy last night?" I said. "Quid pro quo."

"OK. He's on my brother's basketball team."

"He's in high school??"

"Relax," he said, scrunching his eyebrows. "He's a senior."

It hit me that I was judging the appropriateness of the hook-up based on my own age. Zane was only twenty.

"Oh, yeah, I guess that's not a big deal," I said. "Couple years." I felt old. Zane seemed young.

"I came across his profile on *XY*. He didn't have a very descriptive pic, but there was a basketball jersey like my brother's hanging on the chair behind him. Number nine. So I went to one of Ralph's games and was like, *Yo*."

"Did his number match his inches?"

"Not even close," he said with a frown.

I laughed. "Well is he cool?"

"I guess—for a jock. I don't know. He was skittish. Too eager. Bad kisser. Told me just before he went down on me that I was quote-unquote *beautiful*. —Funny how it's always *beautiful*, isn't it? Never *cute* or *hot*."

"For newbies *beautiful* is the only word intense enough to express their feelings," I said. "They need patience. You know how hard it can be to deal with."

"Well, judging by the look on his face when you arrived last night, I don't expect to get another shot."

"Too bad," I said. "He was cute." I put my hands up over my head, shaped my lips into a surprised *O*. "*You won't tell anyone, will you?*"

"So are we laughing about this now?"

"I don't know."

He looked at the clock. "OK, Vince," he said, "I'm gonna go."

He left the counter and pulled off his Golden Age t-shirt. His white undershirt rode up and revealed his stomach and a trail of dark hair that disappeared beneath a red Gap waistband. I looked then looked away. He went into the back room, came out wearing his coat and the blue hat.

"Have a good weekend," he said.

"You too. Thanks for the company."

"Sure."

The bell jingled. Through the window I watched him go down the front walk, and when he was out of sight I felt like crying.

At 8:20 I noticed Griff standing outside the store, bent over with his eyes aligned with the hours on the glass door—the double zeros of *8:00* looked like white spectacles.

"Can't you see the sign?" I mouthed from the other side. "We're closed."

He cupped his hand around his ear. I tapped the numbers on the alarm pad and went outside. Once again there was that urge to kiss him, this time a hi-honey-how-was-your-day kiss.

"Good day?" he said.

"Kind of slow." I put the keys in my pocket. "Wow, it's chilly out, huh?"

"Slow boring or slow relaxing?"

"Zane stayed a while after his shift and kept me company."

"Dreamy."

"Yeah, yeah," I shushed. "I think he just wanted to inquire about you, actually—make sure we're not fucking or anything." I felt dizzy from saying that about Griff and me, even if it was meant to sound ridiculous.

"Ha, he *was* jealous," Griff said. "I knew he liked you. So why haven't you asked him out or whatever?"

"Why haven't I asked him out? How about I'm his boss? How about he's like five years younger than me?"

"How about he's into you and even I can tell he's cute? Here's your keys."

"Thanks." They were warm from his pocket. "I don't know. I'm not that into him. So what did you end up doing all day?"

"..." He arched an eyebrow. I wasn't sure he was going to let me off the hook about Zane. But he relented. "Had myself a little shopping trip," he said at last. We got into the car. It was warm and when I started it up the radio was playing Guster.

"Cool, you mean you spent some of your hard-inherited cash? What'd you buy?"

"A mattress, box-spring, frame." He ticked the items off on his fingers. "Sheets. Pillows. One of those foam egg-crate things?" He paused. "What's wrong?"

"Dude, you didn't really have to get me all that stuff. I was only joking about furnishing the room."

He waved dismissively. "Oh and don't worry, I got a twin-size bed so as not to cramp your comic museum."

I didn't know whether to be relieved or disappointed that he wouldn't need to share my bed anymore. "How'd you fit all that stuff in the Jeep?"

"I didn't, they're delivering the big stuff tomorrow."

"On Sunday?"

"Tomorrow's Sunday? Monday, I mean." He paused. "You don't mind me hogging your space for two more nights?"

"I slept OK last night. It'll be fine."

I knew now that I would've been disappointed. With some things it was hard to know how I felt until it was out of my hands, when pros and cons were irrelevant and all I could do was react.

On the way home we stopped at the supermarket. In the glossy, fluorescent entrance—which always felt to me like the seventh circle of hell—I grabbed a basket.

"Grab a wagon, dude," Griff said. "You're here, you might as well do it up so you don't have to come back for a while. In fact, I'll buy a wagon's worth."

"Come on. You've spent enough on me. It's going to start getting uncomfortable."

"We're sharing a bed, Vince. I'd say we're a skooch past uncomfortable already, knowi'msayin?"

"..."

"Consider it my room and board."

He took the basket from me and flung it clanking back into the stack. I begrudgingly pulled a cart from the accordioned line. Griff walked a couple steps ahead and tossed items in with seemingly no more rhyme or reason than a whimsical appreciation for the labels. Pickles, donuts, macaroni and cheese. No wonder his stomach was a wreck.

In the breakfast aisle he was saying something about pancake mix—we need more pancake mix, what kind of pancake mix— but I was barely paying attention. My focus was squarely on the woman at the other end of the aisle. Her back was to us; she was kneeling, reaching for peanut butter on the bottom shelf, but when she stood up and turned around—

"Oh god. It's her."

"Her who?"

"Melanie."

"Oh." His eyes scanned her from her knit hat to her green pleather boots. "Ooh. Not *bad*." He dropped a box of pancake mix on the powdered donuts. "Not-bad-at-all."

She was walking toward us now, looking for something on the shelves. I hadn't been seen yet but it was inevitable. She stopped and grabbed a thing of Grape-Nuts, dropped it in the basket bumping against her corduroy thigh. I was usually good at avoiding exes, had avoided her since the October night she dumped my ass in the drive-thru.

"She's coming. Fuck. *Fuck*." It was too late to turn around. I clenched the cart's plastic handlebar. She raised her eyes from her basket and met mine—a fluid, magnetic motion followed by a twitch of recognition.

"Vince!" Her lips parted into a smile. "Hi! How *are* you? I thought you'd fallen off the face of the earth or something!" She glanced at Griff, who was standing beside the cart with his fingers entwined in the plastic grid of its side.

She set her basket down on the glossy-tiled floor and opened her arms. I obliged. Her smell was familiar, like lilac—her hair whispered against the backs of my hands. Immediately I felt horny.

"I'm good," I said. I had seen this woman naked, had had my tongue on parts of her body she'd never even *seen*. I was a medieval conquistador returning to an exotic land whose soil still held my flying flag—or something. "How are you—doing?"

"I feel like I'm here all the time. Bernie is such a big eater," she said. "High metabolism." Then she lifted her finger as if to connect the plot-points of her life, and added, "He and I moved in together right after Christmas."

Without missing a beat I said, "That's great!" but I felt as though she'd pulled out my waving flag and was driving the pole through my gut. "I'm happy for you." I realized I was frowning and forced a smile. "How's he doing?"

"Oh, he's getting there, thanks," she said. "Still has a chunk of shrapnel in his thigh, but he's better. The nightmares are tapering off too, finally."

"Wow, that's, um— Oh—sorry." Her eyes were darting to Griff again. "Melanie, this is Griffin. Griff, this is Melanie, my old..."

"Ball and chain," she said, weirdly. They shook. When I saw Griff's eyes drop toward her boobs I wanted to shove him into the Froot Loops.

"You boys doing a little shopping?" Melanie said.

"Yeah. Uh." Was that a hint of coyness in her voice? Did she think we were together? I was about to say we were just friends when Griff put his arm around me.

"Vince is a big eater too," he said.

He flashed Melanie a toothy smile and rubbed the back of my hair. Melanie looked at me with you-devil-you eyes.

"I'm glad you're doing well, Vince," she said, and she seemed to mean it—I wasn't sure whether that made it easier or harder to see her go. "Stop by the gallery sometime." She put her open hand against her cheek, blocking her lips from Griff's view, and whispered to me, "I want to hear *all* about him." She smiled at Griff and in her normal voice she continued, "We're having a pop art show in June. There'll probably be some comic book–type pieces."

"That sounds interesting. Maybe I'll do that. Um. Say hi to Bernie?"

She nodded. "Nice meeting you," she said to Griff.

When she turned the corner and disappeared into the next aisle, I asked Griff why he'd done that.

"Do what?"

"Put your arm around me like that," I said. "Made her think we're a couple."

"Eh, she's got enough on her mind with Bernie's war stuff. Let her know you're taken care of."

"Oh."

"Will you really go to her art thing?"

"I don't know. Maybe."

"You should. She's fucking gorgeous." He glanced back at the corner around which she'd disappeared. "How about in the sack-a-roo?"

It was a memory I'd conjured in the shower more than once. I told him how her hair used to whip around like she was on a roller coaster.

"Nice."

"Yeah. Yeah it was."

He started walking down the aisle again, pulling the cart behind him.

"Hey, where are you going?" I said.

"Uh, we need more than pancake mix and donuts."

"Wait, we have to wait here a minute."

"Why?"

"I don't want to pass her again in every other aisle. Let her get ahead."

"Ah..." He let go of the cart, let it roll away by itself. "Then help me look for the Pantie-O's."

***

"Tell me you're kidding," I said as Griff slid his tray across the dining hall table. "Tell me those are just for decoration, for *ambiance*."

"Taco Tuesday, baby," he said with an impish grin. His hair was tied back in a short pony-tail. This was a brief experiment.

He took a seat beside me in the red vinyl booth. Beth was sitting across from us. She had burgundy hair and picked at a salad, discarding pieces of lettuce and spinach by flinging them with her fork off the plate onto the tray.

It was rush-hour in the dining hall. I liked how it looked full of students, friendly swarms of young adults I could watch from my own booth with my own friends. That was as close as I wanted to get to most of them. I preferred them as decoration to set the scene.

"What's wrong with tacos?" Beth asked. She twirled a forkful of bean sprouts smothered with enough ranch dressing to pretty well negate any nutritional value.

"They wreak havoc on his legendary delicate stomach," I told her. I turned to Griff. "Last time, last *Tuesday*, I think, what did you say when you were slamming yourself face-down on your mattress to alleviate the gas that was quote-unquote tearing you apart from the inside?"

He rubbed his face with his hands and growled. "I said, *Vince, don't let me eat tacos again.*"

"What else?"

"*Ever in the history of the universe*," he said. "But it'll be fine this time. I brought Tums." He plucked a roll from his shirt pocket.

"All right," I said, "but it's going to be *me* pounding your back to burp you and it's going to be *me* carrying you to the toilet to barf/shit your brains out."

He puffed on the end of his straw and shot its wrapper at me. It bounced off my face and landed in my pasta. I fished it out and laid it across his wrist like a soggy red bracelet.

83

"What *is* this, exactly?" Beth said with a grin. Her hands were opened toward us like we belonged on display.

We looked at each other and then at Beth.

"What's what?"

"Is there, in the Year 2000, a *name* for this? What would you *call* this? Are you some new breed of life partners? Are you lifebuddies? Nonsexual husbands?"

"I don't remember being proposed to," Griff said.

"..."

"Oh Vince my prince, you are so perfect, so spectacular in every way," Griff said in spoken-word rhythm and bit a mouthful of taco. The shell cracked and meat slathered in thick sauce plopped onto his plate. "You are my life Vince. You make me forget how much I love tacos. Oh, tacos are so yummy in my tummy yummy yummy—but not like Vince. Oh Vince my prince, you make me forget about tacos."

When I thought I could speak without laughing I asked if he was finished.

"Not yet," he said. He pressed his greasy lips to my cheek. "Taco-flavored kisses for my Vince."

*

Griff and I put away the groceries and then we made breakfast for supper—French toast with ham and bologna fried on the griddle. He had a *Rolling Stone* open on the counter and read between rounds of dipping and flipping. A few times he read me parts of articles.

Later, when the dishes were clean and the record player's needle had crawled across two Athlete albums, he padded into my bedroom and got into bed beside me. After socking his pillow a few times with his fist he laid his head carefully in the dent. There was no pillow between us tonight and he must've noticed that at the same moment I did: as though he could read my mind, he reached to the floor for the extra one and placed it in the middle of bed. I wondered whether it was something he wanted or something he thought I wanted.

"You'll never guess who called me today," he said in the dark, a touch of annoyance in his voice. He rubbed his feet together under the covers. *Zwoop zwoop zwoop.*

"Who?"

"Beth. This afternoon."

"You didn't say anything."

"Oh."

"... What'd she say?"

"She wants me to come back to Boston."

I laughed or snorted or something but in fact I suddenly felt very silly. I felt ridiculous in bed with him here, playing house with a straight guy, a straight and taken guy; living a sad, pitiful fantasy. He didn't belong here and I was a fool for thinking he did. He belonged with Beth. Of course he belonged with Beth. "Oh," I said.

"Yeah, she's back from her parents' and wants me to come get the rest of my shit."

"Oh, to— to get your shit." With a jolt I felt the opposite of the moment before: relieved and confident we would be together forever. That's how it had always been for me. I lived in tones and inflections, in glances and winks and stupid little taps. I analyzed and sought meaning from meaningless things. It was a constant tug-of-war between what I wanted and what was reality. It had made me, among other things, fickle. "Do you think she's just using that as a reason to see you?"

"I doubt it. When I told you she was final I wasn't kidding."

We lay quiet for a while. He pulled the sateen hem of the spinach-colored blanket back and forth between his fingers.

"How much stuff do you have there?" I said. "We could take my Jeep."

"And do what with it, bring it all here?"

"You could keep it in my junk room until you decide what to do with it."

"Hm. There's not a lot that's full-on mine," he said after a moment. "Computer, some DVDs and CDs, clothes. It would fit in the Jeep. All the stuff we bought together she can just have."

"You don't still have that huge-ass monitor, do you?"

"That one from college?"

"Yeah."

"Haha. No, that took a spill down some stairs senior year. It's just a laptop."

"Well then how about tomorrow? Store's closed Sundays."

"Sooner the better as far as I'm concerned."

He took off his t-shirt, dropped it to the floor, rolled over and faced the dark window. The nakedness of his shoulders made him seem even nearer than he was, and I felt the same sad and dizzy lightness of last night. Would it really be so terrible if I touched him? How could that be bad?

"I don't even know how you guys got together," I said, barely aware I'd said it out loud until he responded.

"Me and Beth?" Rolling onto his back again, he inspected me, as though I were once again unfamiliar, a stranger. "How out of the loop were you, dude?"

It made me feel sad and ashamed in equal measure. I hadn't been left out of the loop, of course. I had closed myself outside it.

"Did you like her our year?"

"I don't know. Maybe a little. Probably not yet. It was really the next year that we got closer."

"She lived in your dorm, right?"

"The little dorm, yeah. She was on the floor above me. I was sort of lacking in the best friend department at that point." He didn't say it to make me feel guilty, I could tell that by his voice. He said it, maybe, to make me feel better. Beth, as close as they'd been, was initially a substitute; she filled a gap—the gap of me. "But we didn't actually get together until my senior year, her junior. Beginning of the year. We were at a party, and when it was over we went back to her room. She had a single. We weren't drunk or anything, but I just didn't leave. I think it started as one of those casual things—"

"A friend-love-is-better-than-no-love thing?"

"Yeah, exactly. But it was just really nice, you know? I didn't expect it. I don't think she did either, but there it was."

"Wow."

"Yeah, that was my reaction too. It was out of left field. We started hanging out as more than friends, and it was still nice. It just kind of worked. But then I graduated."

"Then what?"

"I looked at apartments near Shuster but there was nothing I could afford by myself and I couldn't stand the idea of having a roommate. So I moved back to Pittsfield. We did the long-distance thing for almost a year."

"What did you do in Pittsfield?"

"I worked at this furniture store place. Then in the spring she lost her place in the dorm in the housing lottery, so she got an apartment and it wasn't long before I moved in too."

"That's when you got the blueprint job."

"Mm."

It was so much to take in, years of back-story starring a character I knew so well, yet I couldn't imagine him in any of these situations. With Beth? It seemed too weird. Beth was the little freshman who lived in our suite, two doors down, in the room with the chubby girl named Gia.

"I didn't know any of that," I said.

"Well there it is." We were quiet for a moment, and then he cleared his voice and said, "Did you miss me?"

"Yeah, I missed you. Very much." And I still missed him even though he was here, his shoulder almost touching mine. I missed him from those years that were gone and that I could never get back.

"Well," he said, "this time we'll keep in touch, OK? I'll do my part. I was as much to blame as you were."

"That's bullshit, Griff."

"No, I took the hint. Junior year, I'd call, you wouldn't want to hang out, you'd be busy-tired-working, take your pick—and eventually I just took the hint. I shouldn't have taken any hints. I should've been like, *What the fuck is up*? Maybe I would've figured out how you felt about that stupid email sooner."

"I guess."

"Better late than never, right?" He exhaled a punctuation and then asked to hear more about Melanie.

"What about her?"

"I don't know," he said, "how'd you meet her and stuff?" I didn't respond right away and he added, "Did you haul her out of a snow-ditch or something? A WWSD?"

"It wouldn't have been a WWSD with her. It's only a WWSD if they're ugly."

"Haha!"

"It was nothing that dramatic. We were on the same coffee schedule at Dunkins in the morning. I saw her every day for about a week and then asked if I could buy her coffee. We started going out."

"Nice."

"She's an insomniac," I went on, "and she'd paint while I was asleep. This'll sound cheesy but it's true. She had a little painting board set up by the window, right over there, and I used to love listening to the brush move over the paper. Watercolors. You couldn't hear it at any other time except at night, you know, when it was quiet enough. And the breeze would come through the window and blow her smell toward me; she had lilac perfume—still does. And sometimes she'd be naked while she was doing this; it would be after we'd, you know, had sex. She'd get up and paint."

"Wow," he said. "That's like the most romantic thing I've ever heard."

I felt a hollowness at the idea that those nights were in the past and not something I could still look forward to. "It was pretty nice. But now I wonder if she really had insomnia or if she was just lying awake worrying about Bernie."

He was quiet a minute. "Did you love her?"

"I don't know. I may have? If we'd had more time I may have. But you can potentially love everyone you're in a new relationship with, right? Or else why would you bother?"

"That's true."

"Of course, my qualifications for love are super low."

"They're not low," he said, "they're just wide open. You have no *Need Not Apply* signs in your windows."

"..."

"Really."

"Well regardless, it was short and sweet, and I didn't have time to notice any flaws before old Bernie came home shell-shocked. I think she felt bad, like us together was the last thing the guy needed. Maybe it was."

"You're a good man," he said, reaching over the pillow to squeeze my arm. And then after a few minutes of quiet he said, "Sorry about that."

"What?"

He kicked at the covers and warm reeking bed-air billowed over my face. "That."

"Oh god, what the fuck did you eat!" I laughed even as I gagged. It was funny the way farts are always funny.

"That bologna was maybe partially fossilized."

"You used that? I told you to use the new!"

"I didn't want to waste the old."

"Well now it's wasting you."

"*Ba-dum-bum.* Oh, oh another one. My poor ass."

"Oh god, remember how we used to make fake farts at night? Remember that? And we'd wake up half the suite?"

"Beth would come pounding at our door. *Guys, shut the hell up!* And we'd be all snug in our beds, laughing like fucking mental patients."

I put my forearm against my lips and blew. He laughed, a Pavlovian response. "See?" I said. "Still works."

"What is it that makes farts so funny?" He made a noise with his cheek. It sounded like wet clay blasting from a fire hose.

"You used to laugh so hard you'd slam yourself against your mattress and the whole room would shake. I remember it made your posters flutter."

I put the heels of my palms against my cheeks. It was thunderous. He was nearly in convulsions. He rocked back and forth, arm and leg bumping against me. Every touch of his skin against mine was like a warm spark. Everything inside me fell quiet, all my inner voices and worries and analyzations were silenced by this incredible feeling of home, of Griff beside me. It was a feeling that added up to, more than anything else, relief.

"Check this one out," he said. He sat up and slammed back down into his pillow, making the sound of his body-weight in Jell-O smacking pavement as he hit. The blankets billowed around his legs. I was laughing so hard I made no sound at all.

"That's nothing," I said when I could breathe again, doing my best to sound unimpressed. I filled my cheeks and ripped a fart through my teeth. His individual laughs merged together into a steady *eeeeee*. His eyes were squeezed shut.

"I can top that," he said. He elbowed me in the side, in the ribs. "Listen to *this*." He performed the sound of a sumo wrestler suffering from the diarrhea Griff usually got from tacos.

What if, when he wasn't looking, I folded my arms around his waist, laid my head on his shoulder? Would he care? Would he push me away?

"Dude," I said, "that's fucking child's play. Let me show you how a master does it."

"Where are you gonna find a master this late?"

"Ooooh. Harsh!"

On a cold night when we were teenagers Griff had told me I was a step ahead—that I was more advanced, more evolved, or just plain more in touch with love than he was just because I could love guys and girls equally. But it occurred to me here in clouds of mock gas—me so focused on the rough smoothness of his skin, he so unconcerned and comfortable with mine—that if one of us was a step ahead, if one of us was really a social revolutionary, it wasn't me at all.

SUNDAY

From the kitchen I could hear him still in bed, mumbling something at a volume that made me think he wanted me to understand. I'd gotten up when he was still breathing nasally and sprawled mostly on my side, feet protruding from untucked edges of blankets. I sat down at the kitchen table with a coffee and the Sunday funnies.

"Can't hear you," I said.

He came out of the bedroom with his phone against his ear. He pointed to it.

"Oh."

His tongue fell out and he grappled with what looked like an invisible noose. Then he was dragged back into the bedroom by an unseen foe. With his free hand he clutched the door jamb, clawed at it with desperate fingernails, was yanked inside.

A few minutes later he came out and opened the fridge.

"Beth?" I said.

"She can be such a bitch, but she's so damn *sweet* about it." He took out a loaf of oatmeal bread and dropped four slices into the toaster. "And she's got that smoky voice," he said. "You remember it. Like Katharine Hepburn in her youth."

He took a mug out of the cupboard, put it on the table and poured all that remained of the coffee. It went right to the brim.

He sat down and lapped it with his tongue to get rid of some before picking it up.

"She cool with us coming today?"

He nodded. "I told her mid-afternoon sometime."

"Cool. I'm looking forward to a little road trip."

"Yeah." His toast popped up and with quick fingers he plucked it out. He buttered it and dumped on a heavy layer of cinnamon sugar. "I was thinking you should ask Zane to come with us," he said.

I laughed but saw he was serious. "Zane? Why would I do that?"

"He seems fun."

"No."

"We don't *have* to, I just thought it might be interesting."

"For *you*."

He chomped into his toast and got his face poofed with a cloud of cinnamon sugar. "*Gah*. Not for you?"

"We'll need the space for your stuff."

"There's not that much," he said, wiping his cheeks with the back of his hand. "And Zane's skinny."

He went into the living room with his breakfast.

I squinted against the late-morning sunlight that reflected off hundreds of millions of crash-landed snowflakes, wondering how the fuck he talked me into this.

"Here, hold this up while I go under," Griff said, letting go of a springy branch. He dropped to his knees and then to his stomach and began dragging himself through the snow with his elbows.

"Couldn't we just *call* him?" I said. My toes were cold.

"I thought you were all anti-phone," he said. His boots were the last of him to cross through the hedge that surrounded Zane's family's yard.

"I think I could've made an exception." I followed him under, the branch scraping the back of my peacoat like an admonishing finger. Thirty feet away was the driveway, neatly plowed down to shiny black pavement. Griff thought it would be more fun to sneak in.

I stood up, wiped snow off my chest and knees.

"Which one's his?" he asked, looking up at the windows and shielding his eyes from the sun.

"Those." I pointed up at the two on the left side of the second floor. As we traipsed across the yard the breeze wisped powdery snow from the branches of a tall thick oak tree beside the house.

"All right, let's see here." He bent down and gathered a handful of snow, pressed it together. It wouldn't stick. "Dammit." I reminded him that this kind of snow doesn't make good snowballs. He looked at me blankly—"Well what *else* can we throw up there?" he said—as though our inability to find anything else would persuade the snow to just give up and turn sticky. Any other projectiles we might've found lying around the yard were buried. The whole expanse, aside from our tracks, was pristine white.

"I don't know," I said. "Your shoe?"

"Cute." He looked up. "I don't suppose you want to try climbing that tree."

"Not particularly."

"All right—looks like we resort to the old-fashioned doorbell technique, then." He sighed.

We did our best not to collapse the neat snow piles that lined the shoveled front path. I rang the doorbell; it was that kind that plays a tune instead of just ding-donging but I could never figure out what it was. After a minute Zane's brother opened the door. He was round-faced and pudgy—a freshman, he had become the basketball team's water boy for the exercise, and, according to Zane, for the social benefits that came from hanging around with upperclassman jocks. Namely, as Zane related it, *first-class pussy.*

"Hey Ralph," I said. "Zane home?"

"I guess. Hold on." He closed the door. I heard him yell.

"Let me get this straight," Griff said. "They named one of their kids Zane and the other one *Ralph*?"

"Zane's real name is Peter," I said. "Peter Perkins. He renamed himself in middle school, so the legend goes." Griff raised his eyebrows and nodded in approval. "Kind of like you, Ariel."

"Can you blame me? That fucking mermaid movie ruined my life."

The door opened again in a breath of warmth. Zane's black hair was flat on one side and sticking up on the other. "Hey guys."

"Hey."

"Get dressed," Griff said cheerfully, "we're springing you."

"You're what?"

"We're going to Boston to get Griff's stuff from his ex-girlfriend's place," I said. "We were wondering if you wanted to come for the ride or whatever."

Zane's dark eyes drifted behind me to the front yard and registered a tiny surprise, as if he was noticing the snow for the first time. There was a grain of sleep-sand in the corner of his left eye and an eyelash clung to the tip of his nose. "Now?"

I looked at Griff. "Well, yeah, you know, whenever you can be ready." I was suddenly, strangely, afraid he'd say no.

"Do I have time to jump in the shower?"

"Please do," said Griff.

"OK." Zane started to close the door but before the latch caught he yanked it back open. "Did you want to come in, or...?"

"We'll be in the car," I said. "We're parked down the street a little ways, down there."

He asked why we didn't just park in the driveway.

"We were trying to be covert and stuff," said Griff.

Griff stuck his iPod's cassette adapter into the dashboard tape deck.

"I can't believe you have one of those," I said.

"An iPod?"

"Digital music," I said, turning to look out the window, "is so impersonal. I like to hold something when I'm listening to music.

A record sleeve, at least a CD case. Something more tangible than ones and zeros."

"You're tactile like that," he said. The little white machine made clicking noises as he swirled his thumb around the button.

"When I play someone a song on the record player, it's intimate. It's romantic. If you want me to hear a song, what do you do, toss me the earbuds? And I won't even get into the issue of album art and liner notes."

"Well," he said, "you can't take your record player on a road trip, now can you?"

"..."

"I rest my case."

"That's the only thing they're good for," I conceded. "I just feel like the personality has gone out of things. Email instead of letters. Words on a screen. You can't say I'm nostalgic for the good old days, because in my good old days I learned my letters on a Speak & Spell. Something's just missing now."

"I was thinking yesterday when I was at your house by myself," he said, "that you live in kind of a quiet. A hush. With your records and your old comic books and your fireplace and your corduroy furniture. There's no pop in your house—it's all sort of like candle-light and black-and-white movies."

"A hush, huh?"

"Sort of a whisper," he said. "It feels maroon."

"Maroon to me suggests areolas."

"It's not a *visual* thing," he said impatiently. "But fine." He thought for a moment. "It isn't exactly right, but how about cranberry?"

"That's a little fruity," I said.

"*You're* a little fruity."

Zane knocked on my window. He had on a peacoat like mine over a yellow hooded sweatshirt. I got out and let him in.

"Hope I didn't take too long," he said, squeezing into the back seat.

I pushed my seat back and got in. "Griff was just explaining to me that I live in a hush."

Zane laughed. "That's not the word I would've used, but yeah, I totally know what you mean."

"What do you mean, you know what he means? Is everyone going around putting my lifestyle into catchphrases? What word *would* you have used, anyway?"

"I don't know. RetroLand?"

"RetroLand. Isn't that a ride at Disney World?"

"I still say it's more like a cranberry hush," said Griff, crossing his arms.

We stopped for gas and then for coffee and hot chocolate at the Dunkin' Donuts, and then we hit the road to the city—me piloting, Griff deejaying, Zane keeping the beat on the armrest.

Bostonians after a snowstorm reminded me of kids trying to make brussels sprouts disappear by spreading them around on the plate. Snow was pushed into huge piles in intersections, in tiny front yards and along sidewalks. Already it was turning a dismal gray.

The view while we sat in traffic stirred that strange-familiar feeling of seeing a long-lost friend—a feeling I'd been feeling a lot the past few days. I'd been back to the city a bunch of times since graduation and it had that same feeling every time— nothing major, just the feeling that I'd once called this city home and now no longer did. New buildings had been built since I'd left, old ones refaced; the skyline had changed a bit but for the most part it looked the same. A memory-lane kind of place.

Beth lived in the Fenway, down near the ballpark, on the top floor of a brownstone on Peterborough Street. Buildings like hers had a tendency to be let go on the outside and maintained only on the inside; their decrepitude was part of their charm or something. But Beth's place was old all around. The narrow staircase slanted from the wall at a vertigo-inducing angle, sagging and swaying like a rope bridge, threatening to send you over the railing into the abyss.

"Should, uh— Should we all be on these stairs at the same time?" Zane said, clutching the thick mahogany rail.

"Probably not," Griff said—but we kept walking anyway.

By the time we arrived on the fourth floor Zane and I were breathing heavy—Griff was fine, was home. Two doors faced one another on either side of the landing.

Griff pulled a ring of keys out of his pocket, raised one to the keyhole of the door labeled *4F* and left it floating there for a second. Then he put the keys back in his pocket and knocked instead, three thumps with his fist.

I heard something touch the door—the sound of someone looking through the peephole—and then it opened and there was Beth. No longer the roommate of chubby Gia, Beth was a woman now, the Ex of Griff. Although she was a year younger than us she looked grown up in the similarly indescribable way that Griff and I still looked like kids. Her auburn hair was longer than she used to wear it; she had on jeans and an olive v-neck t-shirt. Her eyes remained her most striking feature—one was blue and the other was green. It suddenly made sense to me why Griff had fallen for Beth: blue and green must've been happy colors.

She said hello to Griff, not much above a whisper, and gave him a weak smile that I found unexpectedly tender and kind. It knocked off-balance the casual contempt I was all ready to feel for her.

When Griff responded his voice was stiff, as though he were speaking in block letters. "Hey," he said. "We made it."

"I didn't really have a chance to get your stuff together," she said.

"I'm surprised you came back in the snow."

"I have work."

He shrugged. Beth stepped aside, her arm hugging the door jamb, and he slid past her into the apartment. She opened the door wider and hugged me. She smelled like cucumber-melon.

"Good to see you, Vince," she said into my ear. It was the way people who haven't seen each other in years greet at the funeral of a mutual friend.

"You too, Beth. Long time no see."

"You look good."

"Thanks. Uh, this is my friend Zane."

"The moving crew," she said, shaking his hand. He asked if she'd had any baseballs come through her window. "The park's on that side." She pointed in one direction and then corrected herself. "So no, but my neighbor might've. It'd be a hell of a hit, though. Come on in, guys."

The walls in the kitchen were painted the color of flower pots. The living room, visible through a doorway, was magenta. Lots of framed photos and a number of large black-and-white concert posters made the clashing colors work. On the wall opposite the sink was a wrought-iron shelf filled with cactuses.

Beth said, smirking, "They're the only green thing I can keep alive."

"I stopped bothering after my first three or four murders," I said. "Planticides. Now I just worry about the lawn. Keeping that green and stuff."

Zane and I leaned against the cupboards. Beth stood in the middle of the floor with her arms folded across her chest.

"No lawn for me luckily," she said. "Although a yard to read in would be nice. ...Did you find a place to park?"

"Kind of," I said, looking out the window above the sink, expecting to see cars below, but it was an alley; we were on the other side of the building. "Resident-only. That's not a problem, is it?"

"People do it all the time." She wore pink socks and tapped one foot on the linoleum floor. "Can I get you guys something to drink?" She was reaching for the refrigerator door before we answered. "Lemonade? Pepsi? Something hot? I could make coffee."

"Just some water would be good," I said, peering into the fridge. I wasn't thirsty but thought the action it provided and the time it would consume were reasons enough.

"Zane?"

"Yes please."

Beth took two glasses from the cupboard above the sink and filled them from a gurgling bottle of Poland Spring. The edge of the counter was digging into the small of my back now but I didn't move. She held out a glass and I took it and sipped, barely stifling an awkward compliment of the water's taste. We made small talk about jobs—Beth worked for some publishing company in Cambridge—and the snowstorm and Nosebag, the fat orange tomcat purring in circles around our legs.

Meanwhile Griff walked silently back and forth through the kitchen, between the living room and the bedroom, packing cardboard boxes bearing the logos of various mail-order catalogues with books and things, and a black garbage bag with towels and shoes. The bag over his shoulder made him look like a thin, sad Santa. On his every trip through, conversation between the other three of us grew even more stilted and weird as we followed him with our eyes.

"What do you do, Zane?" Beth said after Griff once again returned to the bedroom.

"Oh, I work at the comic shop with Vince," he said. "And I go to Cape Cod Comm—" There was a crash in the bedroom. "—Community."

It was the sound of a jumble of things hitting the floor. Plastic. Books. I heard Griff swear with more anger than the spill itself sounded like it deserved. I was taking a step forward when Beth excused herself and went in the bedroom. I tipped the glass to my lips, settled back against the counter.

"Good water," Zane said, his eyes shifting from me to the cat.

A moment later Beth came out of the bedroom with her arms folded across her chest and said, "He wants *you*."

***

Something was wrong, I could tell. I put my Economics book in the plastic stacker under my desk and pulled my chair over alongside Griff's bed, where he was sitting with his back against the wall, gazing out the window with a blank expression on his face. In the corner of the Public Gardens below, where the angel statute stood, bronze wings outstretched, the leaves on the trees were turning red and orange and yellow.

"Are you all right?" I said.

"Physically." Two balled-up tissues sat beside him like tumbleweeds on the bed. "She called and I finally couldn't hold it in and I was like, *Look*."

The weekend before, he had been chatting online with Ashley, his sweetheart from Roger Williams, and received a misdirected IM—one that obviously and devastatingly didn't fit the conversation they were having. Ashley brushed it off at first, said it was Griff she wanted to model her new underwear for that weekend—but then, when she put up an away message a minute later, Griff knew. Ashley had made a mistake. Clicked the wrong window. Typed and sent in the heat of a moment. It happens. Funny how often secrets are revealed when people get careless with computers.

"And what did she say?"

"That she's been seeing someone else. Just said it like that, fucking matter-of-factly."

"Oh."

"I feel so fucking pissed and orange and betrayed, man." His teeth were clenched. He squeezed his pillow. "I was going to marry that girl."

"Griffin," I said, leaning closer with my arms crossed over my knees, "you're nineteen. You weren't going to marry her."

"She was perfect. When we were going out she was perfect."

"She wasn't perfect, though. She was a sneaky, lying bitch who clearly never deserved you. You know that now." There was more I wanted to say but I held my tongue.

He pulled his legs in front of him and curled his arms around his knees. He had a sock on one foot; the other was inexplicably bare. He looked small, vulnerable. I wanted to touch him, to put my hand on his bare foot, make it warm.

"I'm sorry it hurts," I said.

"I just feel so *alone*. You know that feeling? Like you've got nobody?"

"I'm still here," I told him, and I felt the pang of having to remind him.

"That's why you're my best friend," he said, looking at me and then returning his eyes to the angel statue below, and the pang went away.

*

When I went in the bedroom he was stacking DVDs in a toaster-oven box. A few still lay scattered on the mustard-colored carpet.

"How's it going?" I said.

He smiled with his eyes closed and gestured for me to close the door. "I don't want her to see me packing."

I nodded and shut it behind me. On the floor beside him was a pile of clothes and a few cardboard tubes for, I assumed, blueprints. I sat down on the edge of the bed he'd shared with Beth. The covers were rumpled—from sleep, obviously, but still it reminded me of what had happened so naturally here between Griff and Beth. The way he slept in this bed was so different from the way he slept in mine.

I stood up.

With the box under his arm he walked his fingers across the spines of the DVDs and books on the white Ikea bookcase, every so often sliding one out and dropping it in the box. I felt bad for him for having to extract himself, item by item, from Beth's life and the home they'd shared. I'd expected Beth to have already done that.

"This one's hers, but fuck it." He flung *Independence Day* into the box.

"Anything I can help with?" I said, my hands in my pockets.

"My blue duffel bag is on the shelf in the closet," he said and pointed at the slatted folding doors. "Could you grab that?"

"Sure."

The bar that ran across the closet was filled half with Beth's clothes and half with empty wire coat-hangers. I retrieved the duffel bag and held it in front of me for a moment, and then put it down and began stuffing it willy-nilly with the pile of clothes that lay on the floor.

When I emerged from the bedroom with the bloated duffel bag over my shoulder I found Zane and Beth where I'd left them. Zane was on the floor rubbing Nosebag's cream-white belly.

"Help me carry some stuff down?" I said to him.

"Yeah." He patted Nosebag on the head—"Sorry cat"—and stood up, leaving the cat with a scowl that seemed to say, *Where do you think you're going, bitch?*

We carried down the first load of Griff's stuff—his laptop bag, the box of DVDs, the duffel of clothes.

"What's in the tubes?" Zane asked.

"Blueprints."

"He an architect?"

"Yeah. He draws a good house."

"I feel bad," Zane said. We pushed through the heavy wood-and-glass doors. "It's like he's getting a divorce."

"I guess."

"How long were they together?"

"About three years, I think."

I set the box on the hood of the Jeep and dug out my keys. We stacked the stuff on the back seat.

"Do you know why they broke up?" he said. "She seems really nice."

"She is nice," I said, wondering if Zane was again probing at Griff's sexuality. "Sometimes people need more to hold them together than just both being nice."

"Tell me about it," he said, and he gave me a loaded glance that made me look away.

When we got back to the apartment there were more boxes stacked by the door, and we brought those down too. Some of the items sticking out of the open ones were familiar—a pair of marble horse-head bookends, a framed snapshot of Adam Clayton Griff had taken at a U2 concert. These things had been in our room, had felt partly mine once upon a time.

"I hope there isn't much more than this," I told Zane as I stacked these boxes in the Jeep with the others. "Otherwise you'll have to ride on the roof."

On our last trip up we met Griff on the stairs of the third floor. He held one box—balancing on top was an aloe plant in a plastic pot the size of a big coffee mug. His vest was slung over his shoulder. His hair had been pushed back behind his ears and his cheeks were wet.

"Fucking cat," he said, sniffling faux-allergically and nodding up the stairs. He rested the box on his knee and wiped his cheeks with the back of his hand.

"This the last of it?" I said.

"Yeah."

Zane, a couple steps below Griff, held out his hands. "I can take that one," he said.

As Griff was passing the box the plant slid across the cardboard and tumbled over the banister. Zane reached out and caught the rim of the pot between his pinky and ring fingers. Dirt spilled into the stairwell abyss. He grabbed the pot with his other hand and drew it safely against his chest.

"Nice save," Griff said. "That's good luck now." He adjusted the weight of the box in his arms and started to go down the steps.

"I'm going to run up and say goodbye to Beth," I said. "I'll meet you at the car."

Griff went down with Zane, who watched Griff's feet carefully, protectively, as though afraid he would stumble. I watched them both for a moment, going down together, Zane saying "Step, step," and then I went back upstairs.

I knocked on Beth's door and went in. On the counter by the sink was a ring of anonymous keys that hadn't been there before. Beth was standing in front of a big window in the living room, looking out at the fire escape where a lawn chair was buried in snow. Circles of colored glass hung from suction cups on the window and cast purple and green shadows on the floor. She held the cat, stroked it. Orange hairs wisped from its body and looked huge and throat-clogging in the sunbeam.

"Hey Beth," I said. She turned around. Her eyes were dry but sad. Griff was my hero, it was true, but he was way too complicated to have a neat and tidy villain, if Beth could even be considered a villain at all. "Car's all loaded. I just wanted to come say goodbye."

She bent over and dropped the cat to the hardwood floor.

"It was good to see you after all this time," she said. "Would've been nicer under better circumstances."

"I know."

"We should keep in touch better," she said. "I thought we were friends. I guess I don't know what happened."

"I had some issues and stuff," I said, not knowing quite what I meant.

She apparently didn't either. She shrugged. "So he just showed up at your house? You weren't in touch at all beforehand?"

I shook my head. "He just showed up. In the morning a couple days ago."

"Well. That's a surprise."

"It was for me."

She hugged me and I put my arms around her. Griff had been the wedge that grew between us—it was probably only because she lived in his dorm, that small dorm where it was impossible to avoid anyone, that I had cut her off too.

"It's your turn with him now," she said with a level of familiarity and camaraderie that made me uncomfortable, as though we were parents talking about a child. "See if you can knock him into shape."

"He's only staying the week," I said.

"Oh—a week? He's not...?" She raised her eyebrows and closed her eyes, a knowing—and almost smarmy, I thought— enjoyment of his lack of plans. A why-am-I-not-surprised look. "Sorry, I was under the impression he was moving in with you."

"He's going to Phoenix," I said. "To help put in a hot tub." I meant it as a defense but it sounded weak, even to me. "For his cousin."

"Ah, a hot tub. Well that's great. That's ambitious. And that's assuming he goes, which he won't. Do you know what he'll do?

He'll go from your house to his mother's couch." She paused. "Did he tell you why I asked him to leave?"

"Just that it was mutual."

"Vince," she said, "come on. Break-ups are never *mutual*. What happened was he made it pretty clear he wanted to go and finally I just told him to get off his ass and do it, do *something*." She pursed her lips. "That money—the inheritance?—did he tell you about that?—that's really the worst thing that's ever happened to him. He's got it in his head that he can just live off it and not have to do anything else, but it's not enough money to get through your *life* with. So he's in stasis. He does nothing. I had to even help him find the initiative to *dump* me." Nosebag started clawing the sofa and Beth looked for a moment like she was going to stop him, but instead she turned to me again. "That's not what I want, Vince. Now that I'm graduated I can start my life, and now that he's graduated he acts like his is over. In fact, the only point in the past year where he's had any enthusiasm for anything was during the brief fling he had with the idea of going *back*."

"The post-college void doesn't scare you, Beth?"

"The what?"

I shook my head. "Well did you tell him all that?"

She sighed. "A million times. Two million."

"I don't know what I can do to help him."

"Well, I know you'll try." She shrugged. "And I think somewhere deep down he knows too. There are a lot of places he could've gone when he left here."

We walked through the kitchen to the door. The cat followed us halfway and then darted into the bedroom.

"Beth," I said, "did he ever, like, talk about me? Over the years, I mean?"

"He missed you, Vince, if that's what you're wondering." She gave me a little smile. "Take care," she said. "Write me a letter some time." She smiled again and closed the door behind me. When I heard the lock click I started back down the stairs.

Zane was nestled between boxes like a Christmas ornament in the back of the Jeep. He held the aloe plant in his lap.

"All set?" I said, examining Griff. He nodded; his cheeks were dry now.

"I was thinking," he said, "that we should drive by the old dorm. Since we're in town. I haven't been through the Back Bay way in a while."

That was something I hadn't thought about doing. I looked straight ahead for a moment thinking and didn't respond.

"Unless you don't want to," he said. "We don't have to."

"No," I said, "let's go."

We looked up at our dorm, up through the bare branches of trees that in April explode into pink and white blossoms. It was a ten-story red brick building, rectangular and almost featureless save for a strip of white granite that highlighted the windows of the fourth floor with shallow carvings of gargoyles. Our room had been almost at the top. Room 907.

"Looks the same, huh?" Griff said. He wrapped his fingers around the bars of the tall wrought-iron fence that, by decree of the Historic District Commission, could never be removed. On the front steps a boy in a knee-length green army coat sat smoking a cigarette. A boy who wasn't us.

"Seems like a long time ago," I said.

"Does it?" Griff said. "I guess sometimes. Right now I feel like I've still got the keys in my pocket." He patted his thigh, but now there were no keys there at all. He let go of the fence and walked through the open gate and up to the front stoop. He said to the smoker, "You live here?"

"Yeah?" the kid said, looking up slowly, smoke coming out his nose.

"We used to live here," Griff said, pointing at me. I came up the walk and stood beside him, feeling proud, as though living in this dorm had vested me with an authority over all its future occupants. "I'll give you twenty bucks if you sign us in so we can look around."

I laughed. "You'll what—?"

"Vin—" Griff touched the back of his hand to my chest. "Roll with me." He looked at the kid again. "Interested?"

The kid took a slow drag on his cigarette, tapped it on the edge of the stone step. Ash fell by his foot. He was wearing slippers.

"How do I know you'll pay?" he said, smooth.

I almost laughed. I wondered what Saturday matinee gangster flick this slippered kid thought he was starring in. Griff yanked out his wallet, fished out a ten. He folded it in half lengthwise and held it out between the tips of his fingers. I wondered what movie Griff thought *he* was in.

"You get the rest when we're done."

The kid examined the ten, held it up to the sun and squinted at it. Apparently convinced of its authenticity, he stood up and looked at his watch.

"You get fifteen minutes," he said, opening his coat and sliding the bill into the pocket of his jeans. "And I'm going to have to follow you around." He took a final drag on his cigarette and flicked the butt into the sand on top of the trash barrel.

"That's fine," Griff said.

"And no funny stuff," the kid said, pulling open the heavy glass door whose handle for years had been covered with my own fingerprints.

Griff mouthed it back to me, "No funny stuff," and we went in.

The grayed arches of the lobby were painted over light blue now, and the old and twinkling brass chandelier had been replaced with a boring glass bowl. Even with the improvements the dorm still looked run-down, but it had never been dirty or unwelcoming; rather, it was like my old baseball mitt—broken in, comfortable. We slapped our driver's licenses down on the front desk.

This was where I really graduated, I thought, looking around. This lobby was my stage. When I walked through here for the last time following the ceremony at the theatre, *that* had been the big event of the day. Away from the lights and the audience—it was just me and the sum total of college twisted up beautiful and sad inside me. When I left I expected never to return. This kind of thing was always happening to me. I was so intent on having endings and goodbyes, official life events recorded, that I almost always had them prematurely. There was almost always one last gasp.

"Can I sign them in," the kid in the army coat said to the girl behind the desk. She didn't respond but took our licenses and began copying our info onto a doodled-on page in a loose-leaf binder.

"I used to do this," Griff told her, as though they shared membership in a secret desksitting society.

"Fun, huh?" she said flatly. She asked the kid what room. He told her 812.

"Do you know the people in 907?" Griff asked.

The slippered kid nodded.

"That's our old room," I explained.

Griff reached across the counter and tapped the back side. "Is there an *AGD* carved here somewhere?"

The girl stopped writing and checked, mildly unamused. "No."

He moved his fingers a couple inches to the left and tapped again. "Around here?"

The girl looked and nodded. "OK. *AGD*. That you?"

Griff just smiled.

"Two girls live in 907 now," the kid said and pushed the button for the elevator. The desksitter waved Griff and me through.

"Are you an RA?" I asked him.

"No, but I get around."

The elevator door banged open and we got on. The fluorescent light inside was blinking like a strobe.

"You going to Nine?" the kid said.

My eyes met Griff's and I said yes. I didn't even think of going to Five, where I lived my freshman year, or to Three or Six, where I spent my junior and senior years. Today this building was about one room on one floor. The kid pressed the button.

"Elevator's still a piece of shit, huh?" Griff said as it chugged its way up through the guts of the building.

"Some guy and a chick got stuck in here for three hours a couple weeks ago," the kid said.

"That sucks."

"Eh, they're dating now."

The doors parted on Nine and we got off. We were in a hall, at either end of which was a door. The tiled floor was glossy still only at the edges along the wall. A bulletin board decorated with construction paper cutouts displayed the names of each student living on the floor, along with major and a short list of likes (spaghetti, sex) and dislikes (mid-terms, war).

We took a right to our side of the building, to what we'd called our suite—a cluster of five rooms and a bathroom off of a common area. The carpet was a lighter gray than I remembered but the couches were the same coarse blue. Griff and I both clocked a lot of hours draped on those cushions, when our suitemates gathered for late-night drinking games or Truth-or-Dare. Once, when the two games merged, Beth dared me to kiss Griff. He'd been willing, his eyes squeezed closed, lips puckered comically. It was me who refused. To everyone else it was just a game, even to Griff—something funny to see. But not to me.

I remembered too how we gave each other haircuts here. And that this was where we had our Secret Santa party that Christmas. Gia threw up in the corner and the weird kid Brian used to lean in that doorway when everyone else filled up the couches.

This was where we were roommates.

The door of our old room was closed. More construction paper labels written in the same handwriting as those in the hall said *Patrice* and *Stephanie*. Our guide leaned against a column in the middle of the common area, his arms crossed and the hint of a smile on his lips. Did he know he had something valuable to us, I wondered—his age, his dorm—and that all we could do was reminisce? Were we pitiful?

Griff knocked softly on the door with one knuckle.

"Come in," said a voice.

He opened the door. A girl in a pink sweatsuit was sitting at a desk typing on a laptop, the screen of which was tiled with IM windows.

"Hi," Griff said, glancing around.

Our guide said over Griff's shoulder, "Hey Steph. Some former Shusterites—they used to live in this room or something."

"We just wanted a quick look around," I said, fully embarrassed now and wanting to leave.

"Um. All right?" she said. She was baffled. Of course to her it was just a room, just a space, and her thoughts of it hadn't yet gained time's sugarcoat of nostalgia and reverence.

It was hard to say whether the desk she was sitting at was mine or Griff's because the room was set up differently. On our first day as roommates we spent hours arranging and rearranging the furniture, trying to find the perfect fit for everything. (The room was an irregular shape, not completely rectangular.) Eventually, sweaty and exhausted and nearing the beginning of the second day, we struck gold. The girls' arrangement was suitable but lacked the feng-shui appeal of ours.

"We had the desks over here," Griff said, stepping into the room and pointing to the wall against which a bed was now. Above the bed hung a poster of a model-turned-actor. "The beds opposite each other, here, here."

"We had a hard time arranging it," the girl said.

"We almost got in a fistfight that first day," Griff said, looking at me, a glimmer of nostalgia in his eyes.

"When did you live here?" the girl said. She typed something on her computer, clicked. She had multiple conversations going on; the fact that Griff and I were there in person afforded us no higher priority.

"Four, five years ago," Griff said. "Long time."

"Did the hot water suck then?" she said after typing some more. "Because it sucks now."

"I remember it being OK," Griff said, and I remembered it that way too.

He stood in front of the window with his arms crossed, no doubt looking down at the angel statue. The sight of his silhouette against the skyline brought our room rushing back to me. It shimmered over the new arrangement, over the girly cuteness, over the posters and the pink paper lantern suspended from the ceiling. It was a two-fold feeling of having never left and of having only ever been there in a dream. I could see Griff's U2 poster of the same joshua tree that was tattooed on his shoulder; a stack of my comics on the edge of my desk; the damp bathtowels hanging over armoire doors; the thirteen-inch TV, its screen fingerprinted and dusty, on the little fridge by the door. The wall Griff's outstretched hand reached for when he cannon-balled onto my mattress.

I suddenly missed it, all of it, very much, in a terrible, aching way I feared I would never really get over. I could understand getting used to someone I loved dying and not being part of my life anymore, but how could I ever adjust to the fact that a part of *me* was forever in the past? That a whole part of *my* life was over and done and now just a memory? Just photos in an album and words on a page?

I wasn't sure I could get over it, but it didn't feel like I was stuck in the past. I wasn't like those paunchy, middle-aged men sitting around a barbeque in moth-eaten high school letter jackets, recalling the glory days. There was rarely anything glorious about college, but it was *me*. And it filled every single second with ready-made *life*. At the tips of my fingers, on the other side of my door, all around me, whenever I wanted it. In college I could breathe deep and say, *This is where I belong.* Even when it was bad. And even when it was confusing, it made sense.

What hurt most was that I rushed through it, took it for granted. I was anxious to graduate, eager to mark the goodbye and move on to something else; to escape and to start again. But I'd never felt quite right afterward.

No, I wasn't stuck in my glory days. I was homesick.

When we walked out through the glass doors it was like being rejected by the dorm, a transplant that didn't take. My eyes welled up but the cold air whisked the moisture away.

"How do you feel?" I asked Griff as we passed for the last time through the old iron gates.

"Blue," he said.

"Sad?"

"No, blue. Actually more of an indigo. Like remembering." His words were so much less specific than his colors. "You have four years of memories in that building. I really just have ours."

We crossed into the street and walked down the block to the car, where Zane and the plant were guarding Griff's stuff.

"Did they let you go inside?" Zane said. The arms of the aloe sitting between his thighs waved as the Jeep settled with our added weight.

"He greased some palms and got us a tour," I said.

Griff kissed the tips of his bunched fingers, splayed them into the air. "It's the Dean charm."

We got a couple of blocks down Beacon Street and stopped for a red light. When it turned green and I drove through the intersection there was a clang under the hood, and then a *fwoop fwoop* like a sock stuck in a fan. I had an idea of what it was.

"Shit."

"That doesn't sound good," Griff said.

"It's not."

"Eh, just ignore it."

I pulled up beside a hydrant and got out, lifted the hood. One end of a broken fan belt sprang up like a cobra and then fell back upon the engine, flat and defeated. I ran my finger along the end and asked for Griff's phone.

A few minutes later we were sitting beside the hydrant waiting for a tow truck to come and haul my Jeep away to some Brighton garage.

"And so their trip took a tragic turn…" Zane narrated, kicking his heel into a clump of frozen sand.

"This is where we met, you know," Griff said to me, jabbing his thumb at the brownstone behind us.

I turned around. The windows of the brownstone had curtains and snow-covered flowerboxes. "This isn't Shuster," I said.

"Not anymore. They sold it. It's condos now."

"No shit. Really?" I stood up and walked to the front steps. Through the glass window in the door I could see the hallway (nicely wallpapered now in a dark floral pattern), at the end of which was the room where Rebellion in Lit had met.

"That's crazy," I said. "Rich people play pinochle in our classroom." I sat back down between Griff and Zane and pulled my coat down over my knees.

"Is that what rich people do?" Griff said. "Play pinochle?"

"I don't know, Griff. You'd know better than me."

He was still grinning when someone behind us said, "Car trouble?" It was the kid, our slippered guide, walking hand in hand with a girl far taller and cuter than he was.

"Apparently," Griff said.

"For another twenty bucks I can get it going for you," the kid said.

"Not unless you've got a spare fan belt hidden in that magic coat of yours," I said.

He laughed and he and his girlfriend kept walking. "We're going out for lunch," he said to us over his shoulder, raising his hand and rubbing his fingers together in the universal sign for cash.

"I'm kind of hungry myself," Zane said.

We all were hungry by the time the tow truck pulled up in front of the Jeep and a big-bellied man in a Red Sox cap climbed out. *Mason's Garage* was stenciled in white on the back of his brown jacket. A clipboard under his arm dangled a pen on the end of a shoelace.

"It's the fan belt," I told him, poking the guts of my car as he peered inside.

He pinched the broken end of the belt between his fingers. "What are these, staples?"

"It broke once before and I stapled it back together."

The guy laughed. "How many miles that get you?"

"I did it last fall, so... quite a few."

"Last fall, huh? Not bad. You're not looking for a job, are you?" He laughed again.

"No, no thanks, I sell comic books."

"Comics. Like *Superman*?" It sounded like *Soopah-man*.

"That's right."

"You can close her up." He put his foot on my bumper and rested the clipboard on his knee, jotting notes in little boxes. "Should be painless," he said. "We'll have a look at her tomorrow and get a new belt in there. If you could fill this out." He poked the form with a wide finger and walked back to his truck. Towing apparatus began to unfold off the back.

"That's not something you can get to today?" I said, scribbling my name and address on the forms.

He shook his head. "It's Sunday. Shop's closed. Pop it in neutral for me?" I did, and handed him the keys. He pressed another button on his truck; the front of the Jeep lifted off the ground as though in a sling.

"So should we come with you or what?" I said.

"There's nowhere for you to wait there. Like I said, shop's closed. Don't live around here?" He glanced down at my address on the form.

"No, the Cape."

He nodded. "I say get a room, go on a Duck Tour or something, come to the garage in the morning. It's the Washington Street stop on the B Line. Call ahead if you want, but it'll be done by noon." He ripped off the pink copy of the form and handed it to me. "Address is on there."

Griff stood beside me and poked my elbow. "I don't know how I feel about sending all my stuff off with some random dude," he whispered.

"I'm not gonna steal any of your stuff, bro, relax," the guy said. He hiked up his pants and opened the door of his truck.

"I know, of course, just... let me just cover up some things first."

He opened the door and unzipped his duffel bag, pulled out a few sweatshirts and tossed them over the more valuable and obvious of his possessions. Zane reached past Griff and grabbed the aloe plant off the seat.

"You can leave that in the car, dude," Griff said.

"It'll freeze," Zane said. And responding to our dubious smirks he added, "It's mostly water."

I folded the pink copy of the form I'd signed, stuffed it in my coat pocket and watched my Jeep get towed away down the street.

"Didn't that guy make you think of Bibbo?" Zane said, holding the plant in the crook of his arm like a football or an infant.

"Ha. Yeah, kind of," I said and then added, in what I imagined Bibbo's voice sounded like, "*Sooperman's my fav-rite.*"

"Who's Bibbo?" Griff said.

"He's a character who shows up in the *Superman* comics from time to time. Retired boxer, lottery winner, owner of a famous bar..."

"You guys are such nerds," Griff said. "Let's go get something to eat, shall we?"

We walked to a cheap bar and grill on Boylston Street and were shown to a booth by a young guy with thick glasses and too-short pants that revealed blue argyle socks. Griff slid into one side and Zane the other, leaving me to make a quick decision.

I told Zane to push over.

The dorky host splayed three menus on the table and tripped over something walking back to the little podium by the door.

"That's got to be a cover," Zane said.

"What?"

"That guy. The nerdiness. That's totally his secret identity."

"What's his superpower?" said Griff.

"I don't know, maybe a willy of steel?"

"No condom can hold him," Griff said.

The aloe sat on the table between the napkins and a bottle of ketchup. I opened my menu. Griff started to open his, left it and said he was going to the restroom. He slid out of the booth.

Zane perused his menu and without looking up, said in a goofy tone that resembled my impression of Bibbo, "Now it's like a date."

A date. My pulse quickened.

"It's not a date," I said, "it's lunch. Do you know what you're getting?" I asked it without looking at him, my face buried in the laminated menu. The light from the lamp swaying above the table reflected us both in the plastic. We didn't look bad together. But our shoulders were nearly touching, and face-to-face contact would've almost been literal. And anyway, what did it matter how we looked?

"A burger, I guess," he said. "Maybe a shake too."

"They make a good strawberry shake."

"I like chocolate," he said. "So you and Griff used to come here, huh?"

"When we got sick of the dining hall. Which was often."

"So it's a memory-lane day for you guys." He ran his finger along the serrated edge of an aloe branch. White strings from a hole in the thigh of his jeans swayed in the air from a baseboard vent like the fronds of a sea anemone. My dick tingled. I wondered if those were the jeans he was wearing at Golden Age the other night...

Griff once more filled the empty seat across from us. "Did you order yet?" he said.

Maybe she'd been waiting for him to get back, but just then a waitress appeared at the end of our table. A waitress who looked enough like Melanie—had Melanie's hair, her brown eyes—to make me do a full-on double-take. I felt my throat tighten. With the three of them here it was like I was surrounded, like I was being ganged-up on. My eyes spun like haywire compasses from the hole in Zane's jeans to Griff's blond hair to the Melanie's hips back to Zane. Zane's skin, Griff's eyes, the Melanie's hair. Zane's lips, Griff's hands, the Melanie's chest.

"Vince?"

"Oh sorry— Uh." I was amazed again at how much she looked like Melanie. "You guys can order first."

"Uh, we did."

"Oh. Ha."

She took my order and then our menus, smiled. I unwrapped the napkin from around my silverware and draped it over my thigh. I wished Zane would do the same with his napkin and cover the anemone hole. It was too much.

Griff leaned forward. "Don't you think she looks a little bit like—"

"No," I said. "I don't." He shrugged. "So what are we going to do about sleeping?"

"I'll hook us up with a hotel," Griff said, shaking open his napkin. "No worries."

In a minute the Melanie returned with two beers and a chocolate milkshake. Zane leaned forward to sip his shake from the flexible straw and when he did his foot nudged mine.

"Your food'll be right out," the Melanie said.

"Thanks."

She even walked the same as Melanie. Did Griff notice that too? Why was he looking at me like that? Or was he looking at me and Zane? Was he looking at *us*? When Zane's foot bumped mine a second time I clapped my hand over his leg, covering the anemone hole.

"For fuck's sake," I said, "can you *stop doing that*?"

The straw slipped from his lips, sunk lazily into the chocolate. He looked at me wide-eyed. Griff checked quick under the table as though something lurking down there had bitten me.

"Not do *what*?"

"You're all over me!" I said. "Give me some *space*, will you?"

"Jeez, I didn't realize I was so toxic." He slid across the seat until his shoulder hit the wall.

I sighed, embarrassed, picked at the edge of the table with my thumbnail. Our food came and I ate my turkey club in small bites.

"I'm sorry," I told him, breaking the silence, when half my sandwich was gone.

"OK," Zane said.

"She looks like Melanie and I was freaking out."

"OK," he said again.

After observing me for a few minutes more Griff wiped his mouth and tucked the napkin under his plate. "This place has always made me feel the same sienna as a nice warm fire does," he said. "I think that's why I like it." He dipped a fry in ketchup and folded it into his mouth.

Zane looked at me curiously, and then at Griff. "Sienna?" he said.

"Griffin feels in colors," I said, opening the door for them to discuss synesthesia for the rest of the meal.

We stood for a minute in the entrance of the restaurant, not wanting to leave, not knowing exactly where to go when we did. It was seven o'clock now and had been dark for almost an hour. The streetlights and the glowing traffic gave the night a bustling immediacy.

"I guess now we find a place to sleep," Griff announced, velcroing the cuffs of his jacket sleeves tight around his thin wrists.

We let the door of the restaurant close with a thump, sealing in music and heat and the Melanie, and we stepped out onto the sidewalk. A few snowflakes were falling softly, without the coordination of a flurry.

"Do you have your phone?" I asked Griff.

He unzipped his jacket and pulled it from an inside pocket. It was small, like a silver tooth. I flipped it open.

"Do I remember Simon's number?" I wondered aloud, running my thumb over the glowing keypad. I felt hyperaware of myself, careful that whatever I did or said was appropriate now in the context of my earlier outburst. A delicate balance had to be found between remaining reserved enough to convey my embarrassment but not be a total stick in the mud.

"Are you going to have him rescue us?" Zane asked.

"I'm just going to see if he'll open the store for me tomorrow."

"It's 508 585," Zane started. "Five-three-five? Here, let me." He took the phone, poked the numbers, handed it back. "I think that's right."

"It's ringing."

"Let's just start walking this way," Griff said, pointing in the direction of the library.

Simon's wife, Patti, answered on the third ring. Her voice had the gentle authority I would expect from someone guiding me through the purchase of a home. The phone was only big enough to reach from my ear to mid-cheek; I talked loud to make sure she would hear. "It's Vince, from Golden Age—"

"Hi Vince!"

"Hi Patti. Is Simon around, by any chance?"

She told me he was working on his book and went off to find him.

"Dude," Griff said, "you don't have to yell. It picks up the sound from your jaw." He tapped his right sideburn and then put his hands on his hips. "I'm not sure I want to shell out the money for a hotel," he said. "Maybe we should just go back to Beth's?"

Zane and I glanced at each other.

"Really? Is that a good idea?" I said, but then Simon was saying hello in my ear. "Simon, it's Vince."

"Hi," he said. "What's up? Enjoying the snow?"

"Is it snowing there?"

"Yeah. —Why, where are you?"

"Boston," I said, following Griff and Zane down Boylston Street now. "I'm in Boston, and my car broke down, and it won't be fixed until morning, and I'm supposed to open the store."

"I can do that for you, man," Simon said. "Not a problem."

"Great, thank you Simon."

Zane turned around and asked if I thought it would be a problem.

"I can take it all day if you want," Simon continued. "Maybe we should plan on that. I'm sure you'll be tired when you get back. What's going on in the city?"

"Oh, I was helping my friend move. I'm sure I'll be able to get there by the afternoon."

"Well either way," he said. "Don't worry about it, and don't hurry back. Do you have a place to stay? Hell, I could just come get you if you want?"

"Oh, thanks, but I have to pick up the Jeep tomorrow morning anyway. We're just going to get a hotel or something."

"So you've got company? That's good."

"I'm with my friend. And Zane is here too."

"Ah, hey, put him on for a sec before you go, would you?"

"Sure. Thanks again, Simon." I held the phone out to Zane. "Boss wants a word."

He frowned. "You said you didn't tell him."

"About the—?" I filled my cheek with my tongue. "No."

He slid the phone up under his hat. "Hey Simon. —I did, yeah, last Wednesday when it came out. —I know, it kicked ass. Kerschl is at the top of his game. —Seriously, huh?"

Comic chat.

I walked faster to catch up with Griff. "So are you sure about going back to Beth's? Won't that be—you know—a little *weird*?"

"It'll only be for a little while," he said. "We can just crash late and leave early."

"It doesn't make any difference to me, I just don't want you to be uncomfortable."

He put his hand on my shoulder. "It'll be fine."

Zane said goodbye to Simon and, like a gunslinger, flipped the phone shut, handed it back to Griff. "He wanted to know if I'd read the new *Matt Morrow*."

"So I'm covered tomorrow?"

"You're covered," Zane said. "I think he's excited. A reason to have to go in."

"I'll give Beth a call," Griff said. He wiggled his phone at us and walked under the awning of a Walgreens, sharing the space with a hobo sitting on a stacker and humming "I Am the Walrus" in a gravelly but not altogether terrible voice.

I walked over and leaned against a row of newspaper boxes near the curb. To my right and across the street, stretching high into the evening sky, was the Prudential Building, and to my left, the towering, all-glass Hancock. There was a new building between them now, shorter than both but still tall. It had a domed roof, looked like R2-D2. Zane came and stood near me.

"Is that homeless guy a man or a woman?" he asked.

The singer was saying *goo goo g'joob* in big clouds of white breath.

"Beats me," I said. The singer wasn't particularly androgynous but he looked so used and abused by life that all distinguishing features had been worn flat and characterless. "I guess since you called him a guy, you have some sense that he's male."

"Good point."

"He's not bad," I said.

"The voice? No."

I pointed up at the skyscrapers. "This used to be my view," I told him. "These buildings. When the sunset hit them it looked like they were glowing or something."

"You miss it."

"Yeah."

"The city—or college?"

A row of windows on one of the top floors of the Hancock went dark. "Both, I guess. They're sort of the same thing to me."

"I'm jealous of your college experience," he said. He set the aloe on top of a snow-covered *Phoenix* box. "I just drive to West Barnstable twice a week for classes. There's nothing life-changing about that."

"College doesn't have to be exactly like Shuster to be good."

"You seem like you were happy here though."

"It's not that I was so happy. It was just so me or something," I said. "Especially the people. Having a whole building be your living room and having all the people in it belong there, but at the same time be strangers. Comfortable strangers." I paused. Sometimes I wondered whether I thought too much about this stuff, whether I made too much of memories, put too much stock in the past at the expense of the present and the future. "Yeah, I miss it."

For a moment we stood watching snowflakes zip over the windshields of taxis speeding by.

"So he wants to stay at Beth's, huh?" Zane said. He picked up the aloe and wiped snow off the pot.

"I know, it's weird. I guess we'll humor him. I don't want to pay for a hotel either."

Griff was walking toward us now. The homeless guy glanced up at him but kept humming. "We have shelter," Griff said.

"Cool."

"It's pretty early, though," he said. "I just want to get there and sleep." He looked at the time on his phone. "Anybody want to catch a movie?"

We walked in on a movie fifteen minutes late at the Copley Mall cinemas. They showed art films ever since the new multiplex opened beside the Common my junior year. I'd always preferred the run-down Copley cinemas, with its shoebox-size theaters, over the glossy state-of-the-art multiplex.

We sat for two hours reading subtitles, enjoying the warmth like the homeless men who buy tickets in the morning and then sneak from movie to movie, avoiding for the whole day the snow or rain outside. We sat three in a row, Griff, me, Zane, all of our boots off, our feet hanging over the backs of the chairs in front of us. We sat through the closing credits, and when the lights came up we put on our boots and walked squinty-eyed out of the theater.

We left the mall and crossed Copley Square in front of the library, walked down the steps into the T station, were greeted with a blast of warm air. We bought tokens and pushed through turnstiles. A student with shaggy brown hair sat on the floor with his back against a huge subway map, strumming a guitar. Zane dropped a dollar into his guitar case. The musician nodded a thank-you.

"Supporting the arts?" Griff said.

"Supporting sexy artists," Zane said, shrugging his shoulders.

"Yeah he's not bad looking," said Griff.

The three of us stood at the edge of the platform, staring down at the third rail. A Starbucks cup rolled back and forth along the track, but when it touched the third rail it did not burst into flames, as I had expected and hoped. Finally a train rumbled to a stop. We took it to the Fenway.

"I thought I'd gotten rid of you guys," Beth said when she opened the door on our cold red faces. Her terra cotta walls glowed warmly and I seemed to float into the apartment like a cartoon character on the scent of a chocolate cake. It was just after ten o'clock. The day stretched behind me, had begun in bed with Griff eons ago. I could barely remember it.

"Thanks for letting us stay," Griff told her. Zane and I chimed in our gratitude.

"It's OK," she said, but her eyes showed that it wasn't, not totally. And of course she was right—even Zane and I knew this was weird. "I'm just getting some work done," she added. She gestured to the bedroom, where the bed was piled with short stacks of white paper. Nosebag circled on some pages and laid down. "I put some blankets on the couch, and there are pillows." She closed the door behind us, set the chain. "Make yourselves at home. I leave for work at 7:50, though, so I just need you on your way by then."

She was being awfully generous opening her home like this, and yet it seemed cold to treat Griff like a guest no different from Zane and me—as if he wouldn't know where the pillows were or what time she left for work. My opinion of her seemed to change by the minute.

"Thanks Beth," Griff said again and she replied, "It's OK." She went into her bedroom and closed the door.

We hung our coats on the hooks by the door and ventured into the kitchen. It felt like being home alone in someone else's place, and I wondered if, for Griff, it just felt like being home. Zane put the aloe on the counter beside the sink. The set of keys was still there; it seemed odd she hadn't moved them yet.

I excused myself and went into the little bathroom off the kitchen. The walls were painted green and a trio of cactuses the same color sat in a row on the window sill. I stared up at the ceiling and peed for what seemed like forever. Since I already had my dick in my hand, I thought about relieving some of the tension that threatened to make the night impossibly long. For once I didn't think too much, and just went for it.

I came quick but it felt less utilitarian than I expected. Instead my thoughts of Zane, and that anemone hole in his jeans, had made it almost romantic. But in my post-orgasm rush the small details of things stood out—sloppy painting around the baseboards, spatters of toothpaste on the mirror and on the tile backsplash. I found these things depressing. In the same way that some people are sad drunks, I tended to have sad orgasms. The idea of sleeping with both Griff and Zane, and the fact that for various reasons nothing could come of that with either of them, made me want to cry. I flushed the toilet and turned on the sink, splashed water on my face and swished some in my mouth.

When I opened the door Zane was standing there. I said "Oh!" and felt caught. We maneuvered around each other to exchange places in the bathroom.

"You took a long time," he said before shutting the door.

There were three blankets folded on the couch, which Griff explained was a pullout. He took off the cushions, stacked them on the floor and slid his hands into the bowels of the couch. It was old and the springs were heavy and stiff, and he looked like he could use some help, but Zane and I remained side by side in the doorway, watching uncomfortably as Griff navigated this home that was his and not his. Finally the mattress yawned out. Before unfolding it completely Griff stopped, let the nylon strap fall from his hand. He exhaled; it wasn't a sigh, exactly, but rather the sound of someone making peace, or trying to. When the mattress was all the way open he sat down. Along the edges ran bare metal bars.

"I'm just going to get to sleep, guys," he said. "I'm beat."

He reached for one of the throw pillows on a rocking chair beside the television and put it at the top of the mattress. He stood up enough to pull down and off his jeans and then he laid down on the bed. He unfurled a blue and white knitted afghan over himself. The metal bar ran through his fist, and he said nothing more.

"So, uh," Zane said, looking at me. We were still standing in the doorway as though we were awaiting an earthquake.

"Take the bed," I told him. "I'll sleep on the floor."

"You don't have to. There's room."

"I'd rather not go there, Zane." Quietly I lined the couch cushions up on the floor at the foot of the bed.

Zane laid down on the bed and rolled onto his side, facing away from Griff.

I folded the blanket—a throw made of sweatshirt fabric bearing an embroidered Shuster shield—in half lengthwise across the cushions like a sleeping bag and crawled in. The cushions shifted uncomfortably and the spaces between them grew more cavernous with my every attempt to get settled. My feet hung off the end. I could see Zane's feet, too, tenting his fleece blanket at the foot of the bed. I spent about fifteen terrible minutes psyching myself up and finally I told him to make room on the bed.

He scooted to the edge, grinning but trying not to. I tossed my pillow into the empty space between his and Griff's and settled into the middle of the lumpy mattress. Griff and Zane were warm and smelled like a full day.

"It's no Ritz Carlton," Zane said, "but it's nice."

Although I kept closer to Griff, could feel his back against my arm, Zane's face was still only inches from my cheek; there just wasn't room for it to be anything more. I lay on my back feigning concern for the rippled plaster ceiling. As though if I took my eyes away to meet Zane's I ran the risk of missing some important message from above.

Griff exhaled again; this time it was more of a sigh. I sighed too, or started to, and then stopped because I was afraid it would sound like I was making fun of him rather than commiserating. I was hot already under the blanket and I wished I'd taken off my jeans—with Zane there that was somehow out of the question. I kicked it to the side, freeing a leg.

A toilet flushed in the apartment next door.

"So *Matt Morrow* is good?" I whispered without taking my eyes off the ceiling.

"Yeah," Zane said.

"I haven't been keeping up with it."

"It's the *Time Knights* crossover. Glanthur somehow crash-landed in El Paso. We're not quite sure why yet."

"How about Matt?"

"Paco's missing—you know, Matt's friend? I think Glanthur is going to die and Paco is going to get his ring and become a Knight. If they find him, I mean."

"That would be cool."

"Yeah."

"Fuck this," Griff said, his voice warbling as though he was three seconds away from crying. He sat up and touched my shoulder gently, as if to soothe any offense he may have unintentionally caused Zane and me. "No— I'll be back, guys." He got out of bed and left the living room.

"What just happened?" Zane said, leaning up one elbow.

"I don't know."

Griff's blanket, left hanging over the edge of the bed, pulled itself onto the floor. I heard him open Beth's bedroom door and the kitchen lit up briefly before going dark again. There were voices, soft. I scooted to the end of the mattress, and off.

"Were we talking too loud?" Zane said.

"I don't think that's it."

"Maybe he's not ready to share a bed with more than one guy?" Zane laid back down, grinning. The springs squeaked.

I stood at the living room door for a moment until I realized both that I shouldn't be snooping and that I didn't want to know what they were talking about in there anyway.

Unnerved, I left the doorway and returned to my place beside Zane. I didn't strain my ears to try to make sense of the whispers through the wall, but my mind still swirled with theories about what could be going on. Was Griff trying to make up with her? Is that why he wanted to come back here, for a second chance? Would we have to come back tomorrow and return all his things? Would I lose him? I studied the ceiling for answers and crossed my hands over my belly to hold in the pessimistic creature who had awoken in the coils of my intestines.

"I never thought I'd see this, you know," Zane said after a few minutes, moving his hand back and forth in the small space between us. "Us in bed."

"Zane, come on."

"I know—your space. Right. I'm sorry." He crossed his arms beneath his head. His feet hung out the end of the blanket. "Does it bother you that I like you, Vince?"

"It doesn't *bother* me."

"But you'd prefer I didn't."

"..."

"Well don't think I haven't noticed how you've been giving me the cold shoulder ever since Halloween."

"I have not."

"Sure."

"We were talking in the store just the other day."

"I mean outside the store. When was the last time we hung out outside the store? We used to do that, remember? We did it all the time."

"I'm pretty sure we're not in the store right now."

"OK," he said. "But *I'm* pretty sure it wasn't *your* idea that I come along."

I sighed. "It's just... I don't know, it's been busy."

"I think you're still mad about Halloween," he said, bolder now; he was conjuring confidence the way he did, manifesting it through sheer will. "But I don't care. I don't regret it."

"Congratulations."

"Do you?"

"Go to sleep."

***

He turned his Mustang onto Old Colony Road. Marissa was in the passenger seat dressed as a zombie stewardess—her hair, dyed red, was tied up to look like a geyser of blood, and her torn black blazer sported a bloody wings pin.

"I wish I was a kid again," Zane said. "Not the suckfest that was my teens. But like seven would be good."

"Just so you can go trick-or-treating?" she said, reaching over to lower the *Fugue In D Minor*.

Zane nodded. "Yeah."

She looked back at me and shook her head. "I told you boys you'd feel more Halloweeny if you got dressed up. But nooo, you'd rather blubber over lost youth instead."

Zane's headlights sliced the fog that floated across the street and wrapped up houses full of sugar-high kids. We'd gone to a showing of the original *King Kong* that started at ten; now it was almost one.

"You need to drop me off soon," said Marissa. "I have to open tomorrow." She looked back at me again. "Unless I can get there around noon?"

"Alas," I said, "we can't disappoint the fanboys."

"God forbid," she grunted. "Well you guys feel free to continue carousing without me."

Zane pulled up in front of Marissa's house, an unassuming ranch with its porch light on and a plump scarecrow tied to the front banister. She and I got out, me to take her place in the front.

"Don't you want your CD?" I said.

"I'll get it later. There's a few more tracks on there for you to enjoy," she said. "Now don't get into any trouble." She stuffed a half a bag of peanut M&Ms into her pocket. "Oh, what the hell, it's Halloween. Just don't get arrested." She beat her fists against her chest like Kong and started walking up the leaf-strewn driveway.

I got in the car and buckled my seatbelt, watching as she waved and went in the house. Her porch lights went dark and the goofy scarecrow turned sinister in the headlights.

I pushed eject on the stereo and Marissa's mix-CD came sliding out.

"Sorry, dude," I said. "I can't take any more *Monster Mash*."

"I was thinking the same thing," Zane said. "I love Marissa, but damn, she's got lousy taste in holiday music."

"It's just that holiday music itself is in bad taste."

"Touché." He flicked off his high beams when a car passed. "So where are we headed?"

"I don't care. It just seems too early to go home. We could always go throw eggs at something."

"I have no eggs, but I do have a crate of toilet paper in the trunk."

"That works."

He chuckled. "I wouldn't mind some food, actually," he said. "McDonald's?"

"Anywhere else. I had a traumatic experience in the drive thru last week."

"Oh, that's right. Your girlfriend left you for the Hamburgler."

"Worse. Someone named Bernie."

"I don't think it's open this late, anyway. Wendy's?"

"OK."

We bought a few square burgers at the window and sat in the car at the edge of the parking lot. On the property next door a building was going up. Steel girders and bricks caught the moonlight like bones. Zane's window was open a few inches and the night air whistled through. It was warm for the first day of November.

"How many trick-or-treaters did you get?" Zane said. He was scraping the pickles off his second cheeseburger with a burnt fry. He had eaten the ones on the first.

"Zero. I kept the lights off."

"No, really? Isn't that pretty of Scroogey of you?"

"What are you, the Ghost of Halloween Past?"

"That's my cousin. I'm the Ghost of Halloween Future."

"Oh you are, are you? Fine. Next year I'll take out a loan and buy those six-inch Hershey bars."

"You'll find me at your door, you do that."

"... As a trick or a treat?"

"Both, if you want."

I felt my cheeks grow warm and I took a quick bite of my burger. "What are they building here anyway?"

"Dunno," he said. "I was telling Simon we should do some kind of Halloween promotion at the store. Have people dressed as superheroes give out candy or whatever."

"You just want an excuse to wear spandex."

"So?"

"Haha. And he didn't go for it?"

"Are you surprised?"

"I guess not."

"*Comic books are not toys, Vince*," he said. Simon's mantra. Simon's *voice*.

"That's really creepy. You sound just like him."

"I spend enough time with him," he said. "Though not as much since he married his woman. I miss him."

"He's growing up. What is he now, forty-five? Are you going to eat those pickles?"

"No, take them." He dragged the foil wrapper off his lap just enough so that I wouldn't have to pick the pickles right off his penis. I slid the pickle slices under my bread. "Probably a Blockbuster," he said, looking at the construction.

We finished our food and rolled the wrappers into balls, stuffed wrappers into empty fries boxes, stuffed boxes into paper bags. Zane went out to trash them.

He got back in the car and put the key in the ignition but didn't turn it all the way, just enough to make his cheeks glow speedometer green.

"What?" I said.

"Nothing."

"You looked like you were going to say something."

"I was, but fast food's bad."

"For what?"

"Your health, Vincent," he said. "Want to go to the beach?"

We drove across town and parked and stood on the wall of concrete that divided the beach from the street, looking out at the sea. A quarter-mile down, people were dancing around a campfire built on the sand; aside from that the beach was empty.

The bright moon illuminated nothing but the sand and the blue-black waves of Nantucket Sound.

"Let's go down," Zane said, nudging my arm. He squatted down and dropped off the wall, hitting the sand hard and falling back on his butt. "*Ooof.*"

"Are you all right?" I asked dryly, looking down.

"No."

"Did you break something?"

With a blank expression he touched his butt. "Uh oh."

"What?"

"There's a crack in my ass." He starting hobbling around like an old man and made me laugh.

I swung my legs over the edge and hopped down. The breeze blowing off the ocean had a bite, a reminder that this was November and not summertime.

We walked down to where the waves lapped the ridge of seaweed at the top of the tide's reach. I put my hands in the pocket of my hooded sweatshirt and flicked at a hangnail on my thumb.

"Do you like the beach in the summer?" he said.

"Yeah. It's a good place to people-watch."

"I think it's funny how people stake out their little squares of sand. They get all territorial."

"Like *Lord of the Flies* down there," I said.

"They're roasting Piggy, I bet," he said and I laughed again. He looked down at his feet and smoothed a half-circle in the sand with his sneaker. Shells turned up in it, bits of purple clam shell like the kind my driveway was made of. Waves rolled in, breaking at our feet in a steady thrum that made me feel like falling asleep standing up—or maybe lying down, watching for UFOs with Zane. "I always have fun with you, Vince."

"Me too."

"I was wondering." He cleared his throat. "I wanted to ask if you would want to—go out some time. With me."

My heart started to pound but I felt like laughing, too, because now everything was just a formality, a ritual, a simple dance around a fire. The topic had been broached; the hard part was done.

"We go out all the time," I said with a smirk.

"Bastard, you know what I mean."

"So what you have in mind would be like... a date, then?"

"Yes, that's what I have in mind, yes. You're a dope. I'm going to smack you. Come here."

"Can you catch me?" I slipped away from him and ran a few yards over crackling seaweed.

"Come here!"

He chased me and grabbed my arm and we stopped, neither of us sure what to do with this contact. He let go and we stood side by side, our hands in our pockets.

"Where should we go on our date?" I said. "Maybe to the beach?"

He laughed. "I guess we could go to the beach." He looked around. "Oh wow, here we are."

"You did say you were the Ghost of Halloween Future."

"That's true."

I could tell he felt relieved. How long had he been planning this? How long had I wanted it myself? And yet—and yet— maybe I was wrong about the hard part being over. Something felt off, in a way that made me realize I was trying to trick myself into believing I was going to roll with this. My mind felt full; it churned with too many other faces. But his was smiling.

"Can I..."

"What?" I said. Now he was laughing. "Why are you laughing?"

"Can I kiss you?" God, he was so cute. It made my chest hurt.

"Only if you tell me why you're laughing first."

"Because I've wanted to do this for a long time. There. Can I now?"

"Yeah."

His tongue ran over his lips, subconsciously wetting them in preparation. He stepped closer and his lips parted in a grin right before they met mine; I could feel his smile with my lips. His mouth was soft, his chin like the skin of a peach—kind of like Melanie's. He pulled his hand from his sweatshirt pocket and put it inside mine; his warm fingers closed around my hand. His thumb found my hangnail and tried to smooth it down.

"Wait," I said. "Hold on." I took a step back. My heels knocked against a driftwood log half-buried in the sand.

"I'm sorry," he said, a reflex, his eyes confused. "What's wrong? Is it too soon?"

"It's not about Melanie," I said, "I don't think."

"Do you— Should I— Should I not have done that?"

"I don't know." I felt suddenly feverish with the cold ocean air rolling across my forehead and my embarrassed-red cheeks.

"Do I have mustard breath?"

"Zane..."

"...?" He was waiting.

"I don't know, we *work* together." I said it because I had to say something and it was the first thing I thought of. "I just— It's probably not a good idea, you know?"

"Do you really think Simon would care, though? Even if he did, it's not like Golden Age is some big important career we're going to jeopardize."

He'd had salt on his lips. "It's how I feel," I told him. "I'm sorry."

I stepped on one end of the driftwood and the other end sprang up, kicking sand and broken shells high into the air.

*

A reflection from something on the street caught one of the prisms in Beth's window and three purple dots appeared on the wall and slid down to the floor.

"I'm not tired," Zane said. "And anyway, you didn't answer me. Do you wish I hadn't kissed you?"

"Whether I regret it or not doesn't matter," I said. "I think it's best for everyone if it just gets written out of our continuity."

"You can only ret-con comic books, Vince. You can't ret-con real life." For a long time we lay quiet. The voices in the bedroom droned and in a while they stopped too. After a few minutes of what I perceived as almost total silence, Zane whispered, "Here, give me your hand."

I allowed it to be lifted off my chest; he brought my arm across the gap between us and laid my hand palm-up on his belly. He traced his finger like a fortune teller over the lines of my palm. I didn't pull away or feel uncomfortable. It was remarkably without insinuation—gentle, like what a mother might do to a little kid during a thunder storm, to quiet him. After a few minutes I felt my eyelids get heavier and I started to believe for the first time all evening that I might actually fall asleep. I half expected Zane to start in on a lullaby. It was like he was trying to comfort me, or distract me. After a minute I realized that's exactly what he was doing.

In the other room, Griff and Beth were making love.

"Oh god." I yanked my hand back and sat up.

"Don't be upset, dude," Zane said. The way he said *dude* reminded me of Griff, and he was not Griff. Definitely not Griff. Because Griff was in the other room. With Beth. Fucking. "It's a *good* thing, right?"

"No, it's not."

"He would probably disagree with you on that."

He leaned up on his elbow and looked first out the window and then down at me. "It's snowing," he whispered.

"Zane, enough!"

I kicked aside the blanket and got off the mattress, dragging the blanket behind me, tripping, throwing it on the floor. I straightened my pants.

"Where are you going?"

"Bathroom."

When I was passing through the kitchen I heard Beth say, muffled, through the door, "You *what?*"

And then the bedroom door swung open and Griff nearly collided with me. He wore only boxers and they were hiked up way past his belly-button.

"Is it sex if you don't come?" he said. He squinted, a look that wanted to be accompanied by a forehead slap.

"Yes," I said as though I'd spent all evening pondering the question and finally received it from the swirls in the ceiling plaster. "She kick you out?"

"I'm kicking myself out. Sorry, but— Get your stuff." He went into the living room gasping like a person on the verge of hyperventilating.

Beth appeared at the bedroom door, tying the belt of a pale yellow robe around her waist. Behind her Nosebag jumped onto the bed, where white papers were scattered like trampled confetti.

"Vince," she said curtly to silence me before I said anything. She pushed a balled-up wad of fabric against my chest and I realized it was Griff's shirt. She relaxed noticeably as soon as I had it in my hands.

"What happened?" I said.

She was quiet for a moment, listening to Griff rooting around in the living room. "Nostalgia happened," she said finally. She went back in the bedroom and closed the door.

I stood looking at the shirt in my hands as though it were some kind of alien artifact. I heard the screech of springs and in a moment Griff and Zane were in the kitchen. Griff had his jeans on now.

"Here." I held his shirt out and he yanked it over his head and threw his arms through the sleeves.

"I'm sorry, guys," he said. His face was flushed. "This was a huge mistake."

"It's all right," I said reassuringly, happy to be that way.

Zane grabbed the aloe plant from the counter. We put on our boots and our jackets and gloves, hats, scarves, and when we were walking down the rickety staircase for the umpteenth time that day, Griff said, "What the *fuck* was I *thinking*?"

And I knew he hadn't been thinking at all, but remembering.

Ben Monopoli

MONDAY

"How was that cot, killer?" Griff said, holding out to Zane a wide wooden tray piled high with the fixings of a room-service breakfast. Steam seeped from beneath shiny metal plate-covers.

"Hard," Zane complained. "And usually I don't mind having hard things against me all night."

"TMI, dude."

Zane smiled and began sampling Griff's wares, lifting one dish cover and then another. He chose a corn muffin and a little goblet of fruit. "Your robe's very classy."

It was one of the hotel's complementary bathrobes—white and fluffy, it fell against Griff's skinny legs like a cape. "Comfy as hell, too," Griff said. "I may just gank it. Butter?"

"No thanks." Zane pulled the paper off his muffin and took a bite. Yellow crumbs tumbled onto the floral bedspread that covered his knees.

Griff turned to me with the tray. "And for you, sir?"

I uncovered a dish and found a stack of French toast underneath. I grabbed a fork. "How are you this morning?"

He put the tray on my bed and sat down with one leg curled beneath him. "All right. I was so orange last night, though. Man! But I think it was good." He took the cover off another dish; this one contained pancakes. He rolled one into a tube and dunked it in a carafe of syrup. "I mean, now I know it's really over between me and her."

The night before, I'd fallen asleep the moment my head hit the pillow on the luscious bed—mere minutes after Griff checked us into the hotel and we drew straws for the foldaway bed. I woke once at flashing-12:00 a.m. and saw Griff standing at the window in his white robe, the vertical blinds bent around him like a bad disguise. He stood there a long time looking out, then he sat on the edge of his bed with his arms folded, staring blankly into a corner. A number of times while I watched him through squinted eyelids I almost got up to sit with him, to tell him things would be OK, but I couldn't bring myself to say that, not after I'd felt so terrible about him and Beth maybe getting back together. So I just watched.

"I really know it's totally over," he went on, looking at the end of his rolled-up pancake before popping the last bite into his mouth.

"Yeah," I said, "at least now you know."

We ate our breakfasts slow, lingered on morning cartoons and talk shows. I was in the shower, the last to go, letting the hot water pound against my face, when the bathroom door opened with a *woosh* of chilly air and someone knocked on the curtain. It bulged inward in the shape of knuckles.

"Come in," I said, joking, thinking it was Griff—then afraid it was Zane. Because Zane really might've.

"You *wish*," the visitor said. Whew. "Dude, it's almost noon. We need to check out!"

"Noon? I thought we had plenty of time?"

"Time flies when you're kicking it Ritz Carlton–style. Damn, it's hot as a crotch in here."

I heard the door close behind him and I laughed all alone in the tub.

We checked out of the hotel with five minutes to spare and helped ourselves to the individually-wrapped Starlight mints on the ornate reception desk. Griff put the room on his AmEx.

Then we strode like a gang, like a band, across the plush carpet to the brass-trimmed revolving doors.

As the three of us were spinning round Zane slapped the glass. "The plant!"

"Awh, dude," Griff said from his wedge, going around again. No one had gotten off after the first revolution. "Forget about it."

"No," Zane said, "it's good luck. I'll go get it." He got off in the lobby again.

Griff and I got off too. "You don't have a key," I said after Zane.

"I'll get it back," he said, halfway to the reception desk now. "Be right back."

"What's with the plant?" Griff said to me. We sank into sleek purple armchairs in the lobby while Zane gestured to the woman at the desk.

"I don't know."

"It's my fault for telling him it was good luck," Griff said. "This chair feels good. Is this real velvet, do you think?"

"Maybe they'll sell it to you."

"Maybe they will. I'm in a spending mood."

A bellhop pushed a cart stacked with luggage in from the street. CNN was on the flatscreen TV that hung on the wall, muted but closed-captioned.

"Was there something going on outside last night?" I said.

"Outside?"

"I saw you at the window."

"Oh." He unwrapped another mint and put it in his mouth, pushed the wrapper into the front pocket of his vest. "No, I just couldn't sleep. Blue balls."

"That's what it was?"

"Yeah—blue balls."

"Why didn't you just breed the dolphin?"

"I did eventually."

"It's weird how not shooting can hurt so bad," I said.

"I remember the first time I got it, in high school, after a night of making out with this girl. Sophia Bedard, her name was.

And I thought it was food poisoning. That was the only explanation I could come up with. I thought I was dying."

"You told me about that."

"It's a Griff classic."

"I wonder if whoever coined the term *blue balls* had synesthesia."

"Haha. He probably did. Although it's more of a vicious pink for me."

Zane returned with the plant and we went through the revolving door again. I thought it was unseasonably warm outside until I noticed the heat lamps above the door.

"Enjoying your stay?" the doorman said. He wore a long blue coat and a top hat.

"Our vacation is over, but yes it was enjoyable," Griff said.

"No luggage?"

"No luggage, no—but plenty of baggage."

We took the T into Brighton and walked a few blocks more to Mason's Garage. My Jeep was parked in the front, its floor covered in white paper bearing the blurry outline of workboot prints. Griff's stuff looked undisturbed.

The woman in the office leaned forward and peered at me through thick glasses. "Heard you fixed a fan belt with staples," she said with a smile when I got out my wallet to pay.

The city stretched out behind us, fake-looking like a page in a giant pop-up book, and then shrunk away as we sped south on I-93. I took up a permanent position in the passing lane. I was eager to get home. I was always eager to get home, but even more so when I knew Griff would be getting there at the same time. It felt like I hadn't been home in weeks, and I wanted nothing more than to change my clothes and brush my teeth and drink a beer with him by the fire.

We cruised down along the South Shore, past Quincy and Weymouth. We went over the bridge and soon we were back on the flexed bicep of Massachusetts, Cape Cod. We passed snow-covered businesses and houses as the road widened and narrowed and widened. In the rearview Zane smiled when I looked back at him.

"Can you turn around," Griff said suddenly, "and go back there?"

"Back where?" I looked in my mirrors but saw only trees.

"To that Volkswagen dealership we just passed."

"OK..."

"I want to go look at the cars."

"Cars. OK."

I turned around in the lot of an antique shop. We drove up the street, and drove and drove—long enough to make me wonder if Griff had imagined the dealership.

"I was actually thinking for a while about whether to stop," Griff said sheepishly just as I was about to ask.

After five minutes we came to the dealership and I turned into the lot. Rows of cars were dusted with the remnants of hastily brushed-off snow and it was obvious from the paths snowblown around them that none had been driven since before the storm. They looked like big toys packaged in Styrofoam.

"Can you buy a car same-day?" Griff asked.

"I think so," I said. "You have to get insurance and stuff."

"You're buying a car?" Zane said, leaning forward between the seats. His arms hung chummily around the headrests, his hand lay against my left shoulder. I leaned an inch to the right.

"Maybe if there's one I like," Griff said. He gazed out the window. "I like Jettas. Maybe a Touareg—that's fun to say."

"Touareg," I said, looking out over the rows of identically-shaped profiles. "Well do you want to go talk to someone?"

"Yeah."

I parked beside a yellow Beetle with white plastic protectors on its hood and doors and the three of us went into the dealership. Two men in suits and ties were talking, one seated behind a desk, one sitting on top. They stood up when we came in.

The salesman at the desk called us *gentlemen*. He wore a blue tie. Their eyes were hungry and with a glance they seemed to haggle over who, if we were in a buying mood, would get the sale—it was an eye-to-eye version of rock-paper-scissors. The face of the man with the black tie went into a smile and the other man sank back into his chair and turned his eyes to the window.

"Great weather for looking at cars," black tie guy said, extending his hand first to Griff and then to Zane and me. "Jim Ashby, hello." He was tall and thin and his neck slouched forward at the shoulders, giving him the appearance of an upright hockey stick. "What can I help you folks with?"

"I'm looking to buy a car," Griff said.

Ashby's eyes lit up and the other salesman's mouth turned down into a little frown.

"That's convenient," he quipped, smoothing his salt-and-pepper comb-over, "because I'm looking to sell a car. We were *made* for each other."

I grinned humorlessly but Griff was all business. "Is that something I can do same-day?" he asked. "Because I'm kind of just—passing through."

Ashby told him that was no problem. "First let's see if we have anything you like," he said with a mustachioed grin, "and then we'll iron out the details."

He pulled an overcoat off a metal coat tree by the desk and led us outside. Griff walked at his side talking about turbo engines, standard versus automatic, the pros and cons of diesel.

Zane leaned close to me and whispered, "Is Griff OK?"

"I think so. Why?"

"First he pays for the hotel all by himself, now he's buying a car? Is he having some kind of post-breakup crisis?"

"He might be," I said, watching Griff talking to Ashby. "But he can afford to have one."

"Is he rich?"

I let Griff and Ashby get a little ways ahead of us, then I explained to Zane about Griff's spiteful but wealthy late grandmother.

Zane's mouth fell open a little.

"I know, right?"

"I get *socks* from my grandmother," he said.

We caught up with Griff and the salesman at a cherry-red Jetta across the lot, its hood encrusted in ice.

"This one here's the model you mentioned," Ashby said. "Leather seats. Enough goodies to give you a cavity." He rested his gloveless hand on the roof and then yanked it back from the cold, a clumsy misstep in the workings of his charm.

"I like the model," Griff said, "but it would have to be in like dark gray or black or something."

"The man wants gray," Ashby said, "the man gets gray." He smiled and for the first time it occurred to me that he was flirting with Griff. It gave me the willies. "Let's see. Ah—over here."

Glancing at the stickers on the cars' windows, he led us down the line to a charcoal gray version of the cherry-red car. He rattled off features about the airbags, the tires, the turbo, the headroom, the trunk space. Griff nodded.

"Can we test drive this?" he said, forehead pressed against the driver's window.

"Of course, certainly." Ashby rocked back and forth on his heels, either from the cold or at the prospect of a sale, I couldn't tell. "Let me run and get the keys. It'll just be a second."

Zane said he'd be right back too and jogged over to the Jeep.

"This is the perfect car for me—don't you think?" Griff said. He kicked the tire. "I've wanted a VW ever since I saw that commercial from years ago. The one where they're driving at night and they get to the party and then decide they'd rather just keep driving?"

"This isn't just a spur-of-the-moment thing, though, right?" I said as gingerly as I could. I was all for Griff spending some of his money, but fifteen minutes ago I didn't even know he was in the market for a car; I was sure he didn't either. "Not a post-breakup... crisis?"

He was peering in at the back seat, hands cupped against the window. "I've had this money for almost a year and I haven't bought anything more expensive than a fucking iPod," he said. "Yeah, it probably is spur of the moment—but fuck it."

"But you have no job. How great is your credit?"

"Who needs credit? I'll pay cash."

143

"Oh. Yeah. Sure."

"You know?"

"Yeah. Why not? Fuck it!" It felt good to say so I said it again. "Yeah! Fuck it!"

He threw up his hands and laughed. "Fuck it!"

Zane returned with the aloe plant just as Ashby came striding over, the tassels on his loafers bouncing merrily with each step. I was surprised when he handed over the keys and we were allowed to go off driving by ourselves.

We got in, me in the passenger seat, Zane in the back with the plant. We poked at the dashboard and tugged on the handles, squeezed the leather seats softly and experimentally like our first touch of a girl's breasts (Griff and me, anyway), and tapped our knuckles against the windows. Everything seemed sound. I opened the glove compartment and reached around inside. The instrument panel told numbers in red.

"God," Griff said, "it smells good, doesn't it? It smells like something I'd buy in a jar and pour on a sundae."

The Jetta drove smooth and with the steady whir of a turntable spinning recordless. White sped by in a blur and Griff had a huge smile on his face. After last night I was extra happy to see it.

"Saw it written on a so-what's-say," he sang. "How the heck does that song go? Pinka pink. Pink moon, we're on our way."

I wanted to roll down my window and reach for fireflies—the snowflakes hanging lazily in the air would suffice. We were driving along a windy street full of low cottages facing white woods when out of the corner of my eye I saw a deer step into the road.

Griff slowed down and stopped and we sat idling in the road as another deer, and then a little one, emerged from the woods and followed the first slowly across the road. The second adult turned and looked at us. And then they disappeared into the brush and trees on the other side.

"Looks like a river down through there," Griff said, straining against his seatbelt. "I want to go have a look."

"Should we leave the car?" I said.

"Just quick."

He pulled over onto the slushy shoulder and we got out. After a car went by we crossed the street and Zane and I followed Griff down a brambly slope. There was a river at the bottom, its banks crusted with ice, and the deer were standing beside it peering around with their big black eyes but not drinking.

Griff squatted down on the slope to watch them but his foot slid out from under him and he ended up on his ass. The deer flicked their ears and walked farther up the riverbank.

"Are you OK?" I said.

"Just a cold bum," he said, wiping it off.

"The baby's going out on the ice," Zane said, pointing.

"That's not a good idea," Griff said. "Let's go down a little more."

Zane was a few steps ahead of me down the slope when he lost his footing. As he went down he grabbed at a pine branch that sprang back up and clocked me in the chin. The ground rushed up behind me and slammed my back, and all the breath in my lungs turned into a big white cloud over my face.

***

Griff put his hand on my bare shoulder. "Zap!"

I squirmed, pulled up the blanket. His fingers were freezing.

"Wake up," he told me, "there are big boxes in the Dumpster." He had his jacket on, and his hat.

I sat up and rubbed my eyes until I could read the numbers on the clock on my desk: 2:07 a.m. "There are what? Why aren't you sleeping?"

"Boxes!" he said. "Let's go sledding."

"In a box? Who are you, Snoopy?"

"You rip the box apart," he told me, making a tearing motion with his hands, "and use the sheet of cardboard as a sled."

"Why do you have your jacket on?"

"I was taking a stroll on the Esplanade."

"...?"

"Got sick of studying."

"..." I swung my legs over the side of the bed. "Where are my pants?"

Out of the darkness of the room they came flying at me.

Gia, Beth's roommate, was sitting on the common area couch highlighting scribbles in a notebook. When we were locking our door she looked up and asked where we were going.

"Out," Griff said.

"Are you going to the basement?"

"No, we're going outside."

"If you go to the basement could you get me a Diet Coke?" She held out four quarters.

"All *right*." Griff took them and stuffed them in his pocket.

"And if you don't I need my quarters back."

It was cold out, but a nice cold. We swiped two cardboard boxes from the Dumpster behind the dorm and tore and stomped them into flat sheets. Then we made our way up Beacon Street, past the snow-covered angel statue in the Gardens, to Boston Common. Carrying the cardboard we climbed to the top of the hill and leaned against the base of the tall phallic monument there. The moon was big and bright and the snow was frosted with an icy glaze that reflected us like we were walking on water.

Griff spread his cardboard on the snow and sat down, folded the front edge up against his knees. He shimmied forward until gravity began to take over.

"Coming?" he said. The snow scratched at the bottom of his cardboard and soon he was racing down, hair *fwapping* the edges of his blue hat. In front of him rose the city and all its tall buildings still lit at this hour, all glowing and white like a city of the future. It seemed as though at any moment Griff's cardboard would lift off the ground and he would sail up through the night and fly into it.

"Whoo hoo hoooo!"

I dropped my cardboard on the ground and belly-flopped onto it and whipped down the hill with my fists stretched out in front of me like I was flying. The slope wasn't incredibly steep but it was long and gave you plenty of time to build momentum. Cold air pressed into my lungs and made me gasp.

"Aw yeah!" Griff cheered as I flew. He'd reached the bottom and was standing, cardboard clamped under his arm. "Watch out for the light post!"

Shit—the light post. I tried to rudder the sled with my legs but instead of steering it just spun me into a pinwheel. I crashed into Griff at the bottom and my cardboard shot out from under me, slicing through the air across the plowed footpath and crumpling against a snow bank.

"Owh, wipe-out," he said in a giggling groan as we struggled to our feet. "I told you you'd fly."

"Let's go again."

"Haha. Nah, I think once is enough for me." He was brushing snow off his legs.

"Are you *serious*?" I said, but when I turned around again he'd already taken off running back up the hill.

"See you at the top, sucker!" he called.

"Bastard." I grabbed my cardboard and chased him. The snow was icy and I kept slipping. We stood together at the top looking out.

"Funny how all that can feel like home, isn't it?" I said. "So big and yet so cozy." But I wondered if it only felt that way because I was looking at it with him.

"I'm just looking for one little place," Griff said. "One of these little houses I draw for class, just to live in with the One." He pushed up his sleeve and looked at his watch. "Speaking of which, I have a Western Civ final in five hours. And I don't even care."

"You slack with such finesse." I dropped the cardboard to the ground and stepped on it to keep it from sliding away. "Who should I go as this time?"

"The Silver Surfer," he said.

"Yeah, right."

"Hey, you asked me."

"Fine, but you better be ready to haul my broken body back to the room," I said. "Here goes."

For nearly five seconds I rode it like a surfboard before falling on my ass and skidding the rest of the way down. Griff followed me down sitting, legs out, the missionary position of sledding, and zoomed past, grinding to a halt fifteen feet away.

"That was graceful," he said. "Seriously. You could turn pro."

"I think next time I'll go on my ass."

"So you don't end up that way."

"Haha!"

We ran up the hill and sledded down, and ran up and sledded down, and each ride down made the next trip up inevitable. We were laughing, swearing, getting the wind knocked out of us, and it was perfect, because when you're twenty in the city at 3:00 a.m. with your best friend, everything is always perfect.

On one run I skidded to a stop at the bottom, my cardboard now damp and floppy, and leapt out of the way before Griff crashed into me. He sat up and dusted snow off his hat.

"Holy fucking shit, Vince."

"What?"

He pointed behind me. "Look."

I turned around and saw nothing, a nothing that made me gasp.

No dorm, no Prudential building, no Hancock, just an absence that stretched across the city. Behind us, the State House and the Financial District were still lit, but everything beyond the trees of the Public Gardens on the other side might as well have been open sea or the edge of space. In the distance we heard fire trucks wailing. We would see on the morning news that a power transformer under Copley Square had caught fire and cut electricity to most of the Back Bay.

"That's freaky," I said.

"This is as close to the apocalypse as we'll probably ever see," he said, bending down to pick up his cardboard.

"The end of the world."

"Let's go out sledding," he said, and he turned around and started running once more up the hill.

*

Griff and Zane were kneeling over me. Griff's lips were moving but all I could hear were our three deer splashing across the river. Through my fluttering eyelids I could see him peering at me. He had his hand against my cheek and when he withdrew it I saw blood on it. My blood?

"Just a tissue but it's dirty," Zane was saying.

Now Griff was touching my front teeth with his thumb, and then he had his fingers in my mouth, rubbing his index finger against my teeth, top and bottom. They were rough against my inner cheeks. It was the oddest feeling.

"I think he just bit his tongue," he said. "His teeth are all there."

Why were they talking about me like I wasn't here?

"His chin, though," Zane said.

"That's just a scrape. Don't worry about that." Griff leaned down at me, his face close enough to mine almost to give me an Eskimo kiss. His features were bent with worry, his hair messed, one side pushed behind his ear. I could see beads of sweat on his forehead, even though it was below freezing out. "You're OK, Vin," he told me, studying my eyes. "You took a pretty good knock on your chinny-chin-chin."

"Oh."

"But you're fine, right?"

"OK."

"Can you move?"

I started to sit up, could feel Zane's hands slide under my shoulders to help me.

"Sit a minute before you get up," Griff told me, and then he stood up and went down to the river. He took off his hat, but put it back on. Then he took off his jacket and laid it on the snow, and quickly wriggled out of his top layer, a long-sleeve t-shirt. After putting his jacket back on he dipped his shirt in the water, wrung it out and brought it over to me. It was cold against my face.

I love you, I wanted to say.

"Want me to carry you?" he said. I shook my head; my stomach felt a little funny but I was OK to stand. "Remember that time *you* carried *me*?" he said, and I nodded. "I'm sorry," he added, "I shouldn't have had us out chasing deer."

"It was my fault," Zane said. "I pulled the branch."

"I'm fine, guys," I said, but the words felt clumsy on my lips. I touched them and they were big. Griff's white t-shirt was pink in my hands. I raised it back to my face.

We crossed the street. Griff started the car and aimed the heater vents at me.

"You've shed blood for this car, Vince," he said, rubbing the dashboard like it was the neck of his prized pony. "Now I have no choice but to buy it."

By the time we got back to the dealership, though, he seemed less sure.

"I should do this, right?" he whispered to me. We were parked in the dealership lot. Ashby was walking out to meet us.

"Yeah. You sure about gray, though? I would've pictured you in something more colorful."

"I'm always in something more colorful," he said. "I like my vehicles neutral."

"Then do it."

"I'm gonna do it."

"Good."

We went into the dealership with Ashby—he noticed my face and his eyes bulged and his mouth dropped open but then he looked away and brought out the paperwork.

"You know what, guys," Griff said, "you can get going. You don't have to stay here for this stuff."

"You sure?"

"Yeah. Go put something on that. I'll see you at your house."

The cold air outside felt better on my forehead. I scooped some clean snow off the bumper of the yellow Beetle and pressed it to my face.

"Want to drive?" I said to Zane.

He shrugged and we swapped keys for plant. On the way home I sat with my head back and my eyes closed, listening while Zane speculated about the new creative team on *Action Comics*.

When I woke up we were parked in Zane's driveway and he was poking at my chin with a green stick. No, not a stick—it was a snapped-off branch of the aloe, gently dribbling sticky liquid into the pain.

"That's for burns," I told him, blinking myself awake.

"I don't want it to get infected or anything."

"I'll wash it when I get home."

"Do you want me to drive you? I can get Ralph to pick me up from your place."

I wanted to say yes. Waves of throbbing pain were rolling one after another across my jaw and mouth, and I wanted the company, wanted him. Just wanted him.

"I can manage by myself," I said, faking a smile that made my lips ache. "Thanks for taking care of me today."

He reached over and wiped his thumb against my chin; it came away glistening with milky liquid. We both seemed to realize at the same time how much it looked like jizz.

He cleared his voice and turned away, grinning. "I like taking care of you," he said finally, but not in a romantic or sentimental way; it was only a statement. He put his hand on my hair for a few seconds—I was sure he was going to kiss me—and then he opened the door very slowly, allowing me all the time in the world to tell him to stay.

"You should take the plant," I told him instead, holding it out with both hands as a dilapidated peace offering. I felt like E.T. "And—Zane?"

"Yeah, Vince?" A hopeful smile appeared.

"—Don't forget you're opening tomorrow."

"Oh. Yeah. I won't."

I slid over into the driver's seat and watched him slice through the headlights on his way to the door. He disappeared into a rectangle of light and then the door closed behind him.

I drove myself home. When I got there, the new mattress Griff ordered was leaning against the garage door wrapped in plastic. I balled up my fist and punched the fucking thing, as hard as I could, when I walked by.

I stood naked in front of my bathroom mirror, a double dose of aspirin dissolving in my stomach. A purple bruise had formed around the scrape on my chin and there was a painful bite on the side of my tongue—but it only made me look like how I felt.

Steam from the shower filled the empty space around me, was a cushion against it. The walls dripped. I wiped the mirror, looked again at the swatch of myself, poking with the tip of my finger at the puffy redness of the scrape. I put my clothes in the hamper and left my shirt, two days worn and now with blood around the collar, on top of it, blood-stain side up as a reminder that it needed extra attention in the wash.

I pulled back the yellow shower curtain and stood at the back of the tub. The spray burned my toes. I adjusted the temperature and stepped cautiously forward. I put my hand on the slippery soap tray jutting from the wall and leaned into the stream of water, letting it lap my face.

It stung.

After I soaped I sat down on the floor of the tub, my back against the tile, my feet flat on either side of the water spout. The water was a steady vibrating rain on my thighs and crotch and stomach. The water spout drip-drip-dripped between my feet. The stream of warm tickling water made me hard. I covered my boner with a facecloth and leaned back against the tile.

"…"

"What? Why are you staring at me?"

"What are you doing in there so long?"

"Sitting. Relaxing."

"The water's still going."

"It's warm. I was cold."

"How's your face?"

"Hurts. I'll live."

"Want some company?"

"...OK."

"Hold on."

He let the curtain fall closed and I heard his sneakers thump-thump onto the linoleum floor. His silhouette got undressed, clumsier than in those noir movies but sexy in its way. He pulled back the curtain again and stepped in, first one foot and then the other, tall and thin like a stork. Water streamed down his body and left paths through the hair on his chest and legs.

"I've never seen you naked before," I said.

"You haven't? Sure you have. You must've."

"Not the full—you know."

"Well how is it? You tell me. Mine's the only one I've seen up close."

"It's standard."

"I guess I can live with standard. Ow, it's too hot. Push over, will you?"

"Sit at the end."

"Your tub is too small."

"It's not meant to be shared. Especially by two people who aren't going to have sex."

"How do you know we're not going to have sex? We're naked and sudsy together."

"I don't think we're going to have sex."

"Well then just... just put your legs on mine—like this—so I can get out of this boiling spray."

His toes lay against my hips; my feet rested on his thighs. The water spout lay against his neck. I asked if he was comfortable.

"Not really, no," he said. "But it's fine. The water's nice. It was so cold out today. I got snow all down my shoes stomping around in the woods."

"Yeah."

"So are you sure we're not going to have sex? This is a pretty sexy situation."

"Don't worry. Just sit with me, huh?"

He nodded. Water dripped off his nose. "Why are you wearing a loincloth, by the way? Are you modest?"

"Oh, no—I had a boner. It happens in the water."

I pulled off the cloth; it had gone down.

"I've never been able to get aroused in the shower," he said, "to the chagrin of my girlfriends. Isn't that weird? Hey, I need to shift your legs for a sec." He raised my feet and bent his legs Indian-style, put my ankles down on his thighs again. "The drain was digging into my tail bone."

"Your coccyx?"

"Haha. My coccyx."

"Better now?"

"Actually, hand me that facecloth." He took it and folded it and put it under his butt. "That's better."

"I don't know why this isn't weird."

"What?"

"You sitting in the tub with me."

"It's pretty weird."

"But it doesn't feel weird."

"What's weird is that your boner went down when I got here. Don't I turn you on, Vinny? What's the deal?"

"I don't know."

Suddenly the bathroom door clicked and the curtain pulled back again. It was Melanie. She had on the Gumby t-shirt I gave her. Her brown hair fell in lively waves against her shoulders.

"Oh, sorry guys— I didn't mean to barge in."

"It's OK."

"Is there room?"

"Sure." I pulled my legs off Griff and wrapped my arms around my knees to clear the middle of the tub for her.

"Thanks. It's freezing out!"

Melanie got undressed and stepped in, sat down between us, her back against the tile wall, her smooth legs pulled up in front of her. She was directly under the water; it soaked her hair, laid it flat against her skin. She had a spray of freckles across her breasts, freckles that once upon a time I connected into shapes and words with soft strokes of my finger while she tried to guess what I was spelling. Would she mind if I touched them again? Would Bernie mind?

154

"It's a little hot," she said.

"It's OK once you get used to it."

"This shower has always run hot."

"That's like the first thing he told me when I got here," Griff said. "*Welcome to my house. And oh yeah the shower will melt your flesh off.*"

I put my toes under Melanie's bum and wiggled them. "Griff, can I have the facecloth back?"

"Vince is caring like that," Melanie said.

"Then you shouldn't have dumped him, Melanie. Remind me why did you do that again?"

"Griff—" I tried to cut in.

"Shush, Vin, I want to know. You shouldn't just dump someone after you've painted in their room. You *painted* in his *room*, Melanie."

"I told him I felt bad." She looked at me; water ran down her cheeks. "I told you I felt bad."

"Well yeah," Griff said, "but couldn't you have picked a better place to do it than a fast-food drive-thru?"

"Griff, come on. No fighting. We're naked. You can't fight naked."

The curtain pulled back again. I flinched. It was Zane. "Yeah," he said. "Fighting naked is a bad idea."

"Hey dude," said Griff.

"How did you get here?" I said.

"I don't know," he said, "the door was open."

"Oh. Well you know Melanie, right?"

"We met at the store a few times. Hi."

Melanie said hi.

"So can I get in too?" Zane said, but then he looked disappointed. "I guess there's not much room left for me."

"There's room," Melanie promised. "Griff and I will make room right here." She moved her legs. Zane stepped out of his clothes and into the tub. The hair under his belly button looked like black cotton candy. I was afraid it would melt in the water.

"Um, let's see." He stepped around our legs like we were playing a soggy game of Twister. "Well I can just sit on the side. Although that will pretty much put my junk in Melanie's face."

If I put my tongue against Zane's cotton-candy hair, I wondered, would it be sweet? Would it be sweeter if Melanie put her tongue there too?

"Griff I really need that facecloth again. Look. See? I need it."

"Wow, you do," Griff said. "Here, take it—cover that guy up. And Zane, dude, you can have my seat."

"Really?"

"Griff, you're leaving?" I covered myself with the facecloth again. "But you should stay. We can make room—"

"Nah, it's cool. I'm starting to prune up anyway. And Zane needs room."

When Griff stood up he bonked his head on the showerhead. It lurched and shot water at the ceiling.

I gasped and thumped my head against the tile, and opened my eyes. The water had gone cold. How long had I been in here?

I stood up and turned it off and pulled back the curtain. With a goosebumpy arm and blue fingers I reached for the towel. The house was silent.

Huddled in the towel I called for Griff, but there was no answer.

Every few minutes I checked for a sign of his car in the driveway. It was after eight now. I was clean, dressed, and my chin glistened with antiseptic. I ate a grilled cheese and paced.

I paced down the cellar stairs and put a load of laundry in, including my bloody shirt and the sheets and blankets Griff had bought for the new bed. While I was doing that I paced around the idea of calling Zane, of telling him I was sorry and asking him to come over.

I paced into the spare bedroom. The closet door was open and some of Griff's shirts and jeans hung on coat hangers. His backpack leaned against the wall, hanging on its aluminum frame like a scarecrow on a post.

This was my first taste of him not being here and it made me feel antsy, distracted, alone. How had I come to rely on him so quickly? Was it just a relapse? A return to my natural state? A week earlier it never would've occurred to me to have someone living in my house, let alone Griff, but now— I didn't know what I'd do when he was gone.

When there was no place left to pace I went to my room and laid on the bed. Floaters in my eyes crawled like spiders across the white ceiling. I put my hand on Griff's pillow. Touching it felt like something I could get caught at. I pulled it toward me and put my nose against it and felt some relief over how things had gone with Zane the past two days. I was embarrassed, of course, for having yelled at him during lunch for no real reason at all, and for freaking out over what had been the most innocent sofa-bed advance known to man. But anger, real or imagined or dredged up like muck from a settled lake, just made things easier. All Zane had to do was supply the catalyst and I'd take care of the chain reaction—a chain reaction of justification. I'd *had* to yell at him, right? Yes, of course. So now there was a reason to avoid him, a reason to schedule him on days I wasn't working. A reason why I was perfectly right to have turned him down. We wouldn't have worked out anyway, because Zane was the kind of person I had to yell at. The Halloween night on the beach was not a mistake, it was foresight.

I rolled back the covers and got under, smelled Griff all around me.

Griff.

***

Our dorm room door was unlocked. Surprised, I pushed it open. He was at his computer; his monster-size monitor displayed the front elevation of what looked like an office building.

"Oh—hey," I said. If I'd known the door was going to be unlocked before I tried it, I would not have gone in at all.

"Yo." He turned around and noticed Andy beside me.

"I thought you were going to BU to see what's her na— Denise?"

"Didn't work out."

"Oh." I wanted to leave, wanted to turn on my heels and run away. He wasn't supposed to be here. They weren't supposed to meet. Not yet at least. Not by accident.

"This is Andy," I said, almost pushing him toward Griff so I could hide behind him. He was stocky, had played football, provided cover.

Griff shot a confused glare at me. "Like, *Andy* Andy?"

I nodded.

He shook Andy's hand. "Delighted. Any friend of Vince's... and all that."

"I've heard a lot about you," Andy said.

Oh, I bet you have, Griff said in my head. I just bet you have heard lots about me. I'm sure he's told you everything. You must know about my relationships, about how realistic my farting sounds are. You must know about how hard I laugh at night and what kind of tattoo I want to get.

"I'm sorry," I said. "I didn't know you were going to be here."

"Nah, it's cool. Don't mind me. Or I can go chill in Beth's room if you guys were planning on—?"

"No! No, we were just going to watch a movie or something."

"You do CAD?" Andy said to Griff. He dropped his jacket on my bed and went and stood beside Griff's desk.

"I'm trying to learn it. I like drawing better," Griff told him. "This is my final project."

Andy put his hand on the back of Griff's chair. "I was thinking about changing my major to industrial design for next semester," he said. "Didn't get around to it in time, though."

"It's fun."

I looked at both of their backs, one wide, one slender, as they looked at the monitor, pointing to various menus and icons. The building rotated 360 degrees. Griff, explaining things, pressed a few keys and reduced the elevation to a floor plan.

Which of the two boys in front of me felt more familiar, I wondered. Which one was truly mine? Which one belonged to me in that special way we look for people to belong to us? Seeing them together made me realize that Andy, my boyfriend, whose body I had been inside, was the stranger here. Andy was the third wheel. Everyone else was always the third wheel when Griff was around. How could I reduce him to what he was supposed to be? Just a buddy, just a roommate, just an open-mouth chewer of pizza.

What if I couldn't?

Andy and I lay side by side on my bed watching *Batman Returns* on the little TV. Griff landscaped his building with clip-art trees and then laid down on his bed and turned the pages of a sci-fi paperback. There were things we would have to talk about. He knew it. Twice I noticed him looking at me, his dark eyebrows low and confused.

Halfway through the movie he put the book face-down on his bed and pulled open the bottom dresser drawer and got out his electric razor. The black cord uncoiled and snaked down to the carpet.

"Mind giving me a hand for a second, Vince?" he said, holding up the razor and winding the cord around his other hand.

"Now?"

"Yeah, now," he said. "It'll just take a minute." Andy looked bewildered and so Griff rubbed the back of his neck, beneath the longer hair that covered it. "I hate that hair-on-hair feeling of neck stubble, you know? Gives me the willies. *Brrrr.*"

"Want me to pause this?" Andy said as I got up.

"No, I know what happens."

I let the door close softly behind me and followed Griff into the bathroom. He plugged the razor into the outlet beneath the row of bulbs on the medicine cabinet and took his usual seat on the edge of the tub. I took the razor from him and he held up his hair.

"Why did you lead me to believe Andy was a girl?" he said, looking down at the white tile floor between his feet.

I switched the razor on; the buzz vibrated my fingers, made them numb. I touched the blade to his neck.

"I don't know." I ran the razor over his skin, lifting hairs with its vibrating blade. The hairs were soft and fine and almost invisible.

"Come on, don't pull the *I don't know*, Vince."

"..."

"Don't pull the silence either. Did you think I'd never meet him?"

"I knew you were going to meet him."

"Wait," he said, leaning up with a jerk that only by luck did not liberate a patch of hair from his scalp. "That's not even why I'm fucking confused. I already *know* you like guys too, Vince. Why lie when you finally start dating one?"

I didn't say anything, just kept trimming. I finished one side of his neck and moved the razor to the other side. He rolled the cord between his fingers.

"I mean, what's it *like*? This is a major life experience for you. Don't you want to *tell* me about it?"

"No, Griff, I don't." I rubbed my thumb over the shaved places. "I don't at all."

His neck was smooth. I blew on it once, twice. I stepped out of the tub and put the warm razor on the toilet seat and went back to our room. A moment later he came in. He got his toothbrush from the plastic basket of toiletries on his dresser, went back to the bathroom. The door clomped shut behind him.

"Did you trim him?" Andy said as I maneuvered myself into the small vacant space on the bed.

"Yeah."

"He's weird, huh?"

"..."

Griff came back into our room, stuck a marker in his book, turned off his little desk lamp, and got under his covers. The movie ended soon after, but not soon enough to save me from fearing that it was keeping him awake. I imagined him quietly seething in the dark.

Hours later I lay in bed spooning Andy, who was by that time long asleep. In the street light that came through the window between the beds I could see Griff sleeping six feet away. His eyelids fluttered; he was dreaming. I lifted my head slightly off my pillow and closed my right eye. Andy disappeared from view and Griff came into place, his forced-perspective image superimposed over where Andy had been. I hugged Andy's body, clutching him tight, and left my right eye closed until the other one followed it.

*

I woke up when the icy facecloth touched my mouth. Griff was sitting Indian-style on his side of the bed, his iPod and its earbuds tangled in his lap.

"It's cold," I said.

"That's the point." He smiled. He fished my hand out from under the covers and raised it to my face, pressed it against the facecloth, which I realized was full of snow. "Hold this here—your chin's all puffy."

"How's the car? Did you buy it OK?"

"I bought it," he said. "It's in your driveway. Feeling all right?"

"Eh." The waves of pain had downgraded to ripples but they flowed down my spine and tickled my stomach too.

"You'll heal."

"I don't know if I will."

"Vince, so dramatic."

I wiped water off my chin with the edge of the cloth. "Your stuff is still in the Jeep."

"I brought it in."

"The mattress—"

"I put it in the garage. We'll set it up tomorrow."

"Laundry—"

"In the dryer already. Dude, relax. I've taken care of everything." He wound the earbuds around his iPod and reached across me and put it on the night table. "Push over, I'll be in in a minute."

"OK." Did he have any idea what those words meant to me? What I wanted them to mean?

He left the room and I listened to him rummage around for half an hour in the boxes of things he'd put in the spare bedroom. Then the water ran in the bathroom, his toothbrush clicked against the sink, the toilet flushed. I felt the air change when he came into the room. It felt more comfortable somehow, like I could relax, the feeling I'd been waiting for all evening, the simple feeling of Griff. It took me out of myself, out of the pickle juices of my own mind, and gave me something else to focus on. The blankets lifted off me as he got under. They settled around us both. He did not put the pillow between us tonight.

"You still awake?"

"Yeah."

He didn't say anything for a moment, and in the dark I felt him fidget uneasily. "Was that a stupid thing I did today?"

"What?"

"Buying a car like that."

"I don't think it was stupid. You should have a car. It's a good thing to have. It was a responsible choice."

"It was a lot of money. It put a big dent in my money."

"Not compared to what you have."

"Twenty-five grand is a lot no matter what. I could've lived for a year on that. Two if I was careful."

I moved my hand to straighten the hem of the blanket that was tickling my chin; when I pulled it back under the covers my fingers touched against his bicep. I didn't move them away.

"But live and do what?" I said. "Stay in the house and eat store-brand cereal for the rest of your life?"

He sighed, smoothed his hair.

"You had your fingers in my mouth," I said.

"My fingers? Oh. I wanted to make sure you didn't knock out any of your teeth. We would've had to look for it. They can put those back in, you know."

"It felt funny."

"They're just fingers, Vince." He exhaled. "Funny the things you'll do when you're panicked, I guess."

"Yeah."

"What a rough couple of days, huh?"

"You seemed OK."

"Most of the time it was fake. Most of the last couple of hours I've felt like sobbing."

"Yeah. Me too."

"We're such a couple of sensitive pussies," he said. He turned his head to me, flashed a quick smile. "Aren't we?"

"I'm half gay. What's your excuse?"

He laughed, then sighed. "It's just that for a long time there I really thought Beth was the One. I thought I'd found the One. I was going to marry her. And then, I don't even know. It became more and more obvious that she wasn't—and if I had any doubt, last night cleared that up. I mean, we were kissing and then we were fucking and I was like, What the hell am I *doing*? I don't know what I was thinking, going in our room, going to the apartment even. I didn't want to get back with her, I'm just—I don't know—trying to be comfortable. And on top of it all I realized on the drive home—I mean, to here—that I'm not a step closer than I've ever been to finding the One." He turned again to look at me. "You know, Vince? Not one fucking step."

"You'll find your other half," I told him. "They say it always happens when you least expect it or something."

"I keep telling myself that. And sometimes I wonder if— Or— I don't know. It's very complicated." He sniffed hard and swallowed. "How was your ride back with Zane?"

"OK." My fingers encircled his bicep now. In the space between his arm and his ribs he was soft and humid, like a mitten warmed by breath. And he wasn't pulling away.

Now, I knew, was the time to lean over and kiss him—just one kiss, just once. I'd always felt that one kiss was all it would take to get him to feel for me what I felt for him. One kiss would demonstrate it, would wake him up like Sleeping Beauty to the happiness we could have together. He would feel on my lips everything he meant to me—and why would he not reciprocate? Because I was a guy? Only because I was a guy? How could something like that possibly spoil what we could have together? I was Vince, his Vince. Vince, his prince. This touch, my hand circling his arm, the tickle of my knuckles in his armpit, might be all it would take. Or maybe a hug tomorrow. Or a sympathetic glance next week. Or one kiss right now.

I was bi and my heart was off-limits to no one, at least not for any reason like what they had between their legs or whether their chests were flat or round. And maybe because of that I never really could believe or understand that Griff, or anyone else, could be deterred from falling in love by such a trivial thing as gender. The idea of not being wired to love certain people had never made any sense to me, and did not make sense to me now. If I could just show him. If he would give me one chance. I would show him he could love me. Just one kiss. That's all. One kiss, please God, and if I'm wrong I promise I'll call it a day.

"Zane was really worried about you when you got hurt," he said.

"But so were you."

"If you had seen his face, you'd be a lot more willing to give him a chance."

"Griff, you make it sound like I've ever once said I want to be with him."

"Don't you? He obviously adores you, Vince."

"What do you mean, don't I? Why should I— It's not even— Just shut up. He's just a kid."

"He's not a kid. He's a man. You're making excuses. And you're overthinking. You overthink, Vince. You never just *do*."

"And you underthink. You wouldn't've half-fucked Beth if you'd thought a little bit beforehand."

"That's harsh. You should be *glad* I underthink. I wouldn't be here if I didn't. And then where would we be?"

It was on my tongue to say that we'd be better off, that's where we'd be, but of course I didn't mean that, and I was glad it hadn't slipped out.

He rolled over and his arm pulled away from my fingers. I wasn't sure he ever even realized they were there.

"I miss college," he said, and went to sleep.

TUESDAY

I put a spare set of house keys on the kitchen table and left for work without waking him up. The morning was cloudy and cold and on the ground was a dusting of new snow. Griff's new Jetta was parked in my driveway, its charcoal paint shimmering through the snow. The license plate had a lighthouse on it.

The mattress was no longer against the garage—when I lifted open the door I found it inside. The plastic wrap covering it crinkled in the cold breeze.

The exertion of lifting the door reawakened the pain in my mouth. I spent most of the morning at Golden Age alternately rubbing my temples and adding letters to the crossword Zane had started days before. Simon had supplied a few answers too. I circled the counter, arranged the action figures in order of preference for character, Windexed the display case. When Marissa arrived at four to relieve me I could've kissed her, had her lipstick been a more appetizing shade of blue.

"Hey loverboy," she murmured. She tossed onto the counter an army-green messenger bag bedecked in buttons, went to the back and returned a minute later wearing her Golden Age shirt. Underneath it was a black long-sleeve t-shirt that went down to her knuckles. Her thumbs came through holes in the sleeves.

"I heard your electricity finally came back on," I said.

She nodded, peering at me first through a curtain of dark square bangs that hung against her eyes, and then through purple horn-rimmed glasses. The lenses were plain glass—she didn't have or need a prescription. "You get in a fight?" she said. She leaned with her arms folded across the counter, her long sleeves ending handless.

"Oh, this." I touched my chin. "Just a little accident. We were tracking deer in the woods. Although yes, I guess I did."

"Stitches?" She raised the purple glasses and looked more closely.

"It's just a good scrape." I'd experimented with Band-Aids of various sizes but decided that even the smallest looked creepier than the wound itself. "I'll probably have a scar though."

"Scars are memories made of flesh," she said. "What about the fight?"

"Eh."

"Sore subject? —Haha."

I smiled. "Sore subject."

She shrugged.

"Did you write your column yet?" I said.

She shook her head. "I still need to choose the letters." Marissa dispensed relationship advice in her college lit club's weekly zine, *The Salty Marlin*. (I'd never known her to be in a relationship herself, beyond the fake one she was in with Zane when his parents' attention needed deflecting.) She pulled a stack of printed emails from the main pocket of her bag. "Here we go. You can help me pick out a sob story worse than yours."

I laughed. I had a little crush on Marissa for the way she was both warm and off-putting, a combination that seemed unique to her. It was just a playground crush, the kind that might induce me to throw a snowball at her, make sure she knew it was me, then run away. When Simon introduced us, out in the parking lot where she was sitting on the guard-rail smoking a cigarette, she asked me how old Siegel and Shuster both were when they first published Superman. I was off by two years but that had been enough to impress her.

"I have to do two columns this week, actually," she said, "since I'll be away for WonderCon in a few weeks."

"I'm still jealous you're going to that. I keep saying *next year*. —What kind of letters do you have?"

"Let's find out." She skimmed one of the emails. "Blah, blah, blah—three-way." She crumpled it up and dropped it in the wastebasket behind the counter.

"You get a lot of three-way letters?"

"Oh jeez yeah. From straight guys who want to know how to get their girlfriends to agree to it. From straight girls who want to know if they should do it for their man. From homos who want to know if it'll wreck their relationships." She rolled her eyes. "Apparently it's the ultimate I-need-advice question. Should I do it, should I not. They can check the back issues. It's been covered."

"My sob story involves something like that, actually," I said.

"A three-way?"

"Not in the traditional sense."

"Zane told me you've got a houseboy." She said it matter-of-factly. It was pretty hard to shock Marissa.

"A roommate," I corrected. "There's no nude vacuuming involved. Griff is straight."

Now she raised her eyebrows. "A straightboy. Must be some three-way then. Who's the third?"

"Actually it's more like a four-way," I said. "There's the ex-girlfriend I don't think I was done being with yet when she dumped me. I saw her the other day for the first time since, and that was—" I sighed and continued. "There's the straight best friend, who in college I was crazy in love with, who was and seemingly still is my fucking ideal *everything*, who has come waltzing not only back into my life but into my *bed*. And then there's the spiky-haired guy I've been smitten with since the first time I laid eyes on him, when he was standing behind this very register selling me a new copy of *Crisis on Infinite Earths*, who is now my employee and four-fifths my age to boot."

She stopped shuffling the letters. "Predicament much?"

"It's like they just keep piling on. I had this dream last night where I'm in the tub, right? And suddenly Griff is in there with me, just sitting there bare-ass, talking, the water running. And then Melanie is getting in too, and it's the three of us. And then Zane's there and he's like, *Can I get in too?*"

"That's bizarre." She scrunched her eyebrows, turning this over in her advice columnist's brain. A customer came in and began pawing through the new arrivals. Marissa reached under the counter and boosted the volume on the store's audio system. The Ramones started singing a little louder, loud enough to cover us. "So you had an orgy dream?"

"No, that's the thing. It wasn't sexual. Well, not really."

"Did it freak you out?"

"In the dream?"

She nodded.

"No, in the dream it all seemed natural enough. The conflict was just that not everyone could fit in the tub."

"And Zane was there too..." It was a statement, not question; like a fortune teller, she was ruminating.

I sighed. "Yes."

"That's kind of a surprise. I assumed you didn't like him like that."

"Because of the Halloween thing?" The customer came up to the counter with a few comics and a credit card. When he left I asked again, "Because I said no when he asked me out?"

"He told me you did," she said, pushing her glasses up on her nose. "He was pretty disappointed. I told him it was for the best, though."

"You think it was?" I felt kind of vindicated that the relationship guru agreed with me.

"Well it's like you said. What if things didn't work out? You both love the store. It would get messy."

"It could."

"Zane *is* delicious, though." A dreamy rouge rose in her cheeks and she suddenly looked more girly than usual.

"Oh boy. Not you too. I should've seen it before."

She shrugged. "Why do you think I agree to be his beard? It lets me pretend. He's the only guy I've ever seen who'll come out of a tattoo parlor after getting inked and pierced and then help an old lady cross the street. But like sincerely."

That made Zane seem like something I didn't want to lose. If she was trying to convince me to leave the Zane situation alone, she wasn't doing a very good job. Was it supposed to be reverse psychology or something, or did she really just suck at relationship advice?

"Don't worry, you did the right thing." She patted my hand, her rings thumping my knuckles. "I read letters about heartbreak every day. It's better to avoid the situations where it seems destined, you know?" She picked up the letters, stacked them into a neat pile against the counter. "Plus," she said, "there's plenty of spiky-haired, quarter-Japanese, comic book–loving, do-gooder gay boys on Cape Cod, right?"

"..."

"Right?"

I drove home trying to decide whether Marissa had meant that last part sarcastically. When I got there I found Zane's car in my driveway, parked behind Griff's. I parked beside the Jetta, annoyed that they were hanging out without me. I tried to remember whether I'd told Zane anything about Griff that he might be telling Griff now.

The garage door was open and the mattress was not inside. I pulled the door shut and went in the house. Habit made my hand reach for the switch even though the lights were already on.

"I'm home," I called, suspicious, getting out of my coat.

Zane's peacoat was hanging over the back of the blue chair; his boots stood side by side by the door. Griff jogged into the living room. In his hand was a wrench.

"Hey dude," he said. "We're doing some construction."

"Zane's here?" I mouthed.

He nodded. He came closer; he smelled of apple Dum Dums pop. "Son of a bitch from the high school fucking outed him. He came here looking for you. I told him he could chill."

"The high school? Who?"

He raised his hands over his head. "Stick 'em up."

"That guy? Awh, fuck." I wondered how much of this was my fault for stumbling in on Zane and Jeremy, for scaring the kid off. There were ways I could've handled that situation better, I was sure.

I followed Griff into the spare bedroom. The new mattress and box-spring were leaning against the wall by the window. Zane was sitting on the floor in the middle of the bed frame, twisting a nut onto a bolt.

"What happened?" I said.

He looked up at me. His spikey hair seemed drooped like the hair on a sad cartoon character. I knew he had been dreading this day. His parents were hard to feel out, were old-school, conservative. He'd always feared the worst.

"Can I give you the NC-17 version?"

"By all means."

"Well, the little motherfucking *cocksucker* apparently decided to do some preemptive-strike public relations," he said in a tone of forced calm. "Blabbed around to the basketball team that Ralph the water boy's brother tried to blow him. Which is especially ironic given that *he* was the one who was fucking desperate to get his mouth around *my* dick."

"Do your parents know?"

He nodded. "My mom, at least. Fucker blabs it at school, brother comes home pissed that he's now associated with a rumored fag, tells mother, mother asks homo son if it's true."

"What did homo son say?"

"I said yes."

"What did she say?"

"Ready for this? You might want to sit down." He patted the desk. "She said, *No you're not*, with the same fucking matter-of-factness she would if I was insisting I was from Pluto or something. *No you're not.* And then she started to cry and said I was just confused and that they would get me help, that there are people I can talk to." He put a wrench around the nut and turned it. "This is the twenty-first century, you know? This is fucking *Massachusetts*. We have gay marriage. We live an hour from Provincetown, and she's this fucking clueless? Well bullshit. I take it from the governor, from the president, from the pope. I will *not*," he said, with a weary emphasis on *not* that broke my heart, "take it from my family too." He noticed his teeth were clenched and he rubbed his jaw. "You look like shit," he said, pointing at my face with the wrench.

Because there was really nothing to say about anything, the three of us finished assembling Griff's bed in a weary silence that grew more comfortable as we built this thing. We connected the headboard and footboard to the sides and laid the box-spring on the frame and the mattress on top of that. And when it was done, it was a bed. Zane kicked a leg of it the way Griff had kicked the tires of the Jetta.

"Not bad, huh?" Griff said. He laid down and crossed his arms behind his head, kicked his heels against the mattress. "Yeah, this'll do me a couple nights. Then I'll have a place for when I visit." He began gathering up the tools. "Thanks guys."

"Sure."

"No problem."

"Anyone hungry now?" he said, his arms full of tools and plastic wrap as he left the room. "I could boil up some spaghetti?"

Griff called all pasta spaghetti. He cooked a pound of rigatoni and the three of us balanced plates on our laps and watched *Evil Dead* in the living room. They sat in the two chairs and I turned the ottoman on its side and sat on the floor against the cushion. When the movie was over Zane brought his plate to the sink and went in the bathroom. Griff stood up with his plate and picked mine up off the floor.

I told him thanks and pressed the stop button on the VCR with my toe. The television turned to static.

"Are you surprised he came here?" Griff said. He sat down again with the plates in his hand.

"Sort of."

"He probably figured you could relate?"

"I guess. What I can't relate to is how his mother could say all that bullshit, though."

"Yeah. Incredible."

"And that's not even close to the worst of what I've heard. Sometimes I honestly feel like I want to line up every single person who's ever made life difficult for a gay kid and shoot them one by one in the face."

Griff laughed.

"I'm serious, Griff. And it scares the shit out of me, you know? Because I really feel like I could do it. That's how angry it makes me. It makes me a monster."

"Vince, you're no monster. You're just angry. And yeah, you have good reason. People fucking suck a lot of the time. The people who don't sort of have to clean it up. So get out your mop. WWSD?"

He brought the dishes to the sink. Zane came out of the bathroom drying his hands on his pants and pulled his coat from the back of the chair.

"I guess I'll get going," he said. "Thanks for the food and the solace and stuff."

From the kitchen Griff shot me a look.

"Um—" I stood up. "You can—stay here tonight if you want to give your parents some space. If you need more solace. You're welcome to stay."

He hesitated. "I should probably go," he said at last, doing up the first button of his coat.

"Stay," Griff said. "Vince buys solace in bulk. It fills his garage, his closets, his cupboards. Do the guy a favor and take some off his hands, huh? Have the new bed. I'm gonna go hit the sack myself."

Zane looked at me, shrugged, nodded.

Griff switched off the kitchen light and shuffled away down the hall like an old man. "Vin, I think the sheets for it are still in the dryer."

"Thanks for the company, Griffin," Zane said after him.

Griff replied without turning around, "Don't let the heteros keep you down. We're not all bad."

He went into our bedroom and closed the door.

I smirked, as though I was just now getting a joke. For some reason I'd expected that Griff meant for Zane to share my bed, given that he'd just put together his own. I relaxed a little.

"You sure it's cool for me to stay?" Zane said.

"Sure. It's probably better to let things cool down at home before you go back."

"Probably." He put his coat down on the chair.

"So are you just heading to bed, or do you want to chill for a while?"

"I can chill," he said. "Do you have any hot cocoa?"

I smirked. "I think I can scrounge some up, yeah."

In the kitchen I filled the kettle, put it on the stove, got a pair of mugs out of the cupboard. It was, in a way, what I anticipated doing last Friday when I woke up to find all that snow. I was only getting around to it now.

"Do you still have that Mogwai record I gave you for your birthday?" Zane said. He was standing in the living room with his arms folded on the half-wall.

"Of course, yeah. It's in the bin. Put it on."

I watched the kettle simmer, blasting it with imaginary heat vision to speed up the process. I wanted the hot chocolate done ASAP—something to do with my hands. Zane found the record and now was fumbling with the turntable.

"How come it's not playing?" he said.

"Did you turn the power on?"

"The green light is on. I don't know. Come look."

I spotted the problem immediately. "Dude, you need to put the needle down!"

"Oops. I'm not going to have to rub sticks together or chant or anything too, am I?"

"No, ass-face," I smirked. I lowered the needle—it sketched against the vinyl.

"Good, cheese-cock. Now how do I pick a song?"

"You don't pick one. You're supposed to listen straight through." He looked perplexed. "Here," I told him, "this is a good one." I lifted the needle and moved it into the record, let it fall into one of the middle grooves.

"You have the grooves memorized?"

I shrugged. He smiled.

The kettle began to whistle just as the first ambient notes of music wafted from the speakers, as though the appliances in my house were part of an orchestra. I took it off the burner, filled the mugs and mixed in some packets of Swiss Miss.

"Wish I had some marshmallows," I said.

"Give me a dollop of Fluff, if you have it," he said.

"Good idea." I plopped in a spoonful, and as it began to melt I remembered back to when I'd worried about marshmallows making it seem too much like a date, and felt that fear renewed. "So she said you're not gay, huh?" I handed him a mug and sat down in the blue chair.

"Yeah. Can you *believe* that?" He held his mug close to his lips but didn't drink. "As if I was mistaken or only doing this for shits and giggles. Because *wheee!* this is all so fucking fun I can barely stand it."

There was a worn-out anger in his eyes that scared me. He must've had it so much more difficult than I did. There was no life for him to escape into; the best he could do was lie. Whenever I felt different, it was only until the next pretty girl walked down the street. Then I was just an average guy like everyone else.

"I don't think I've ever been so angry at someone I loved," he said. "Man. But I don't know what I was expecting. I guess I just hoped that like despite the clues to the contrary I'd be lucky, you know? That I would be the kid whose dad comes to him and says, I love you and I'll love anyone you bring home, boy or girl."

"I doubt many people have it that easy."

"How long did it take your parents to deal?" He crossed his legs on the ottoman. His skinny jeans ended in red socks.

"A while. Although the way I came out didn't help."

"Didn't they catch you making out with a guy or something?"

"My first boyfriend, just after sophomore year of college. In the pool."

Andy and I had camped out in my backyard that night. It seemed to me now slightly ridiculous that college students would camp out in a tent in the backyard, but it was easy to forget what it was like when privacy was hard to come by. Living in my own house spoiled me quick.

"We got the idea that it would be great to go skinny dipping in the middle of the night," I continued. "So we went in our underwear and then let them sink to the bottom." I said it with the same sort of horrified pride with which I thought about my childhood stunts, like standing with one foot on the seat of my bike, the other leg kicked out in the air behind me as I raced down the street. I couldn't help but admire my recklessness, but kids could be so stupid. "Anyway, we got frisky. Andy was sitting on the edge with his feet in the water, and I was in the pool with my head, you know, between his legs. My mom had gotten up to let the dog out—"

"Wait—*that's* how you were outed? You got caught *blowing* him?"

"Hey." Suddenly my cheeks felt hot enough to steam.

"Why'd I think you were only making out?"

"Usually I gloss over the details. But I figure now you can relate."

"Why, because you caught me getting... blown?"

"I guess."

"That doesn't count. When *I* walk in on *you* getting a beej, I'll be able to relate." He used the mug to cover his smile. "So what happened?"

"She screamed." It was the same choked gasp she would've made if a burglar had sprung from the shadows in our own dark living room.

"No shit." He was enjoying this. "So what did you do?"

"We ran bare-ass back to the tent. Farley was running around, trying to catch us, thinking it was some kind of game, and somehow he weaseled his way into the tent with us. I zipped up the door anyway as fast as I could, trying to make like a barrier between us and my mom, who in hindsight I'm sure just ran back into the house. So we're in there, wet and naked, with a huge German Shepherd."

"Oh my god."

"I'm trying to push him out, and of course this had to happen in early summer—prime shedding time—and in about ten seconds I look like a fucking *werewolf*. It was disgusting."

"Wow. That is one hell of a coming-out story. Your poor mother!"

"I know, seriously."

"But to be fair, she probably would've screamed the same way if she'd walked in on you eating pussy, don't you think?"

"I don't know. Figures I've never gotten caught doing that."

He smiled again. I liked that he never had any issues about my other interests.

"Obviously it would've been less traumatic if I'd told them outright. Plus, they can always pray for the fifty-fifty chance I'll end up with a girl." I laughed and then felt myself instinctively pull back a little. This was feeling too natural, too nice.

"That's true."

"They're uneasy about it," I said, adjusting my tone from *friend* to *mentor*, where it felt more comfortable and somehow appropriate, "but they didn't disown me, and yours won't either."

"That doesn't feel like a lot of comfort."

"No, probably not."

We sat for a while, sipping our hot chocolates and listening to Mogwai. The long arm of the wind-up clock on the mantle traveled slowly around its face, and every so often the front yard lit up in the headlights of a passing car. When the music was replaced by the soft static thump of the finished record, Zane slid his legs off the ottoman and told me he needed to get to sleep.

"Your sheets are still in the dryer," I said. "I'll go get them."

I went down cellar and pulled the blue plaid comforter and yellow flannel sheets from the dryer. They were freezing. I gathered them up into a ball that wouldn't drag and carried them upstairs.

Zane came into the room behind me. "I borrowed some mouthwash."

"OK. Griff said he bought an egg-crate. Should be around somewhere. You can check the closet."

He slid open the closet door. "Oh hi Griff," he said, peeking inside. "Just kidding."

He pulled out the rolled-up and shrink-wrapped pink foam, pushed his fingers through the plastic—they popped through one by one. We smoothed the egg-crate over the mattress, which smelled vaguely like the new Jetta, and fitted the sheet over it.

"These sheets are cold," he said.

"I know. Sorry. The dryer vents to the outside."

"Yeah. They'll warm up fast."

He looked at me and smirked and I smirked and looked down.

When the fitted sheet was finally secure we shook the flat sheet over the bed and let it settle like a parachute around the egg-crate. We looked at each other from opposite ends of the bed. He had hat-hair and bedroom eyes, and maybe because he looked so tired and sad, he looked mine. I found myself leaning over and then crawling over the headboard; he was doing the same from the other end. Our mouths met in the middle. We kissed, softly at first and then in a frenzy. It was hard and hurt my injured lips.

In a lull that offered us the chance to say something, to acknowledge what was happening, neither of us did and we began undressing instead. He pulled my t-shirt over my head and I fumbled with his fly. His skin was soft and smooth like porcelain. When we were naked we entwined, pushing hard against each other in tangles of sheets. The egg-crate curled up off the mattress and wrapped around us.

Laying my head on his thigh I took him in my mouth and listened to him gasp. After a minute I came up and kissed him and held him, my fingers tight on the small of his back, pulling him against me as though he might come through on the other side. Against his neck I whispered a request and wrapped my legs across the backs of his thighs.

"You want me to?" he said.

"Just be easy."

"I can do that. Condoms?"

"Medicine cabinet."

He jumped off the bed and sprang naked out of the room. The bathroom door smacked the wall as he barged in. The loud bang was like a splash of cold water, a record needle screeching across vinyl in the middle of a romantic song, the slap of a teacher's ruler on a daydreaming student's desk. It made me realize that we were being noisy, that Griff could probably hear us, that Griff was in fact mere feet away, that Griff was in my bed.

Griff.

I sat up, my heart pounding. I couldn't find my boxers and instead grabbed my shirt and held it over my dick. Just as I noticed my underwear hanging on one of Griff's blueprint tubes, Zane jumped over the threshold as though he'd come out of the sky. Instantly the smile disappeared from his face.

"... What are you doing?" The hand clutching the condoms and a little clear bottle of lube fell to his side.

"I can't do this." I got off the bed, still holding the shirt against me. "I'm sorry, I want to but I can't." I started to reach for my boxers.

He threw the condoms and lube down on the bed. The lube bounced off the rumpled egg-crate and disappeared through the crack between the bed and the wall. "What do you mean you can't do it? You look capable enough." He glanced down at the erection I was trying to conceal.

"There's so many things wrong with this. For starters, Griff's right there." I pointed at the wall.

"He fucked Beth when *you* were nextdoor." He looked at me expectantly but I didn't know what else to say. "You don't know how many times I've dreamed of this, Vince. And I don't mean just with my dick, I mean in *here*." He thumped his bare chest with his hand. "It was as blissful as I always thought it would be, you and me. I mean, until you decided to slam on the brakes so you could go sleep happily with your straight boyfriend instead."

"Why do you keep *doing* this?" I squeezed my underwear until my fingers cramped. "Why can't you just let it go?"

"Because *you* can't let it go, Vince. If you weren't interested, hey, fine. If you only wanted to date chicks because it's easier, that's your choice. But I don't get why you insist on jerking me around like this."

"You think I don't—" I was shouting, and I lowered my voice. "You think I don't want to lay with you here for hours and days and have it be blissful? But what about after that? Things, man, things are not as simple as some fucking dream, and things don't end up that easy, and I'm sorry if you can't accept that. There are boundaries. I'm your boss. You're not even old enough to drink."

He cringed. "I may be a little younger than you but you're the one who's totally fucking immature." His eyes were welling up. He gathered his clothes off the floor and left the room, came back. "It's him, isn't it? Has it always been him, even before he even came here?"

"..."

"Are you *that* hung up on a straight guy?"

"..."

"He doesn't love you!"

"He does."

"Not the way you love him. And you know what? He never will. *Straight* means he never will. So deal with it."

"Fuck you."

He flinched, and in that same moment seemed to realize he was naked. He looked down at his belly, at his penis. He turned around and left.

I started to follow him but the doorway felt barred with some kind of force field. After a minute I heard the front door open, close, and then the grinding engine of his car fading away.

***

"Get my keys," I said, thrusting my hip toward Andy. "Front pocket." Griff's left arm was around my shoulder; his body hung between Beth and me like a scarecrow.

"Oh, he's drooling," Beth said.

A strand of spit hung from Griff's lips, clear and fine like fishing line. I let go of his arm and wiped the back of my hand across his lips.

"That's gross," said Andy. He yanked the loop of keys from my pocket and unlocked the door of room 907.

It was 3:00 a.m. on the first Saturday since our return from winter break. We'd gone with Beth to a welcome-back party in Kenny Grimshaw's room on Seven. Kenny's room was half-empty—his roommate had transferred—and he crammed the empty space full of people, alcohol, music—full of college.

Andy pushed open the door and Beth and I hauled Griff into the room, his feet dragging over the splintering threshold. I noticed he was only wearing his socks.

"Fuck. I forgot his shoes."

"No shoes?" Griff gurgled.

"I'll go get them," Beth said, her teeth clenched under Griff's weight.

We got Griff over to his bed and let him collapse into it. I lifted his legs the rest of the way onto the mattress. He put his arm around his pillow, buried his face in the jersey sheets.

"Jeez, he's heavier than he looks," Beth said, massaging her shoulder.

"Hey, I offered to carry him," Andy said, holding up his hands.

"I know. Now what kind of shoes does he have?"

"Those black Converse ones," I said.

"OK. I'll be back." She glanced at Griff before leaving.

"He's not going to roll off, is he?" I said, sitting down on my bed.

"He's not going to roll off." Andy sat down beside me. He had a Veryfine container full of Jack Daniels in his hand. "So what was going on with the Architect tonight? He's not usually a big drinker, is he?"

"Who knows." Normally I was protective of Griff but I'd emptied a juice bottle more than once too and what did it matter, anyway? Everything about Griff was hanging out tonight, for everyone to see.

"He get his heart broken again?" Andy said.

"He spent the entire break online chatting with Tricia Johnson from the second floor. Couldn't wait to get back to school so he could hang out with her in person." I pressed my cheek against Andy's shoulder. He offered me the Veryfine container and I shook my head. "It was all he talked about. *Vince, I think she and I are really gonna hit it off—this could be the big one.* Tonight he just kept knocking them back every time she sucked face with that guy Steve."

"Poor Griffin," he said. "The perpetually broken-hearted Architect. Will he ever find his soulmate?" He put the container on the floor and laid back on the bed, overshooting the edge so his head knocked against the wall. He laughed and rubbed his skull. "Ow. I had too many too. —What if you're his soulmate?"

It was like a spark. "Me? Griffin isn't into guys."

"No, you're right. But guess what?" He sat up and pressed his lips against my neck. "*I* am."

"Are you?"

"One in particular, in fact. Hey—" His voice turned sneaky, conspiratorial, sexy. "Want to do it with him in the room?"

"What?"

"Yeah. Yeah, it'll be hot. Let's do it while we watch him sleep." He wiggled his eyebrows.

"You're drunker than I thought."

"It'll be so hot, Vince."

"No."

"You know you want to."

"Come on."

"Then let's go to my room."

"I can't, Andy. I need to keep an eye on him."

He put his lips on my ear and whispered and whined, sad and deprived like a horny Oliver Twist. "But I *need sex.*"

"You *need* to go to *bed.*" I pinched his shoulder. "Come on, get up. Can you make it back to your dorm?"

"I'm not that drunk, Vince, for fuck's sake."

I stood up and opened the door, left my hand on the brass knob. "I'll IM you tomorrow," I told him, and I kissed his bristly black hair as he went through.

"I'm going to go jerk off to you," he said.

I closed the door and rested my head against the molding, listening for the sound of the suite door closing behind him.

I'd wanted to—what Andy had suggested first. And I would've, too, if not for Beth's imminent return. I was sure I would've, because I knew it was the closest I would ever get. I could've closed one eye and done the trick with the forced perspective...

The suite door thumped again and there was a knock on mine. I opened it and Beth held out Griff's shoes.

"Andy leaving?" she said.

"Yeah, he's drunk."

"How's our patient doing?" She peeked in.

"He'll be fine." I took the shoes and tossed them on the floor beside the little fridge. "Thanks for your help."

"No problem. He's such a romantic, isn't he? It was like he was in a movie or something, watching Tricia making out with Steve. Almost cute in a screwed-up way." She smiled and the light from the common area reflected in her different-colored eyes. "Anyway, if you need anything, you know where I live."

I nodded, told her goodnight, closed the door.

I sat down at my desk and put my face in my hands. I read people's away messages for a while and clicked random icons, highlighting, unhighlighting. After a while Griff groaned and sat up.

"What time is it?"

"After four."

"Fuck, really?"

He ran his hand through his hair and then panic flashed across his face and he sprang off the bed, pushing past me as he made for the door. He whipped it open and it smacked the wall. He barged through the common area into the bathroom. Luckily it was empty. I followed him there. Griff was the kind of guy who would clean up some random girl's puke at a party; I didn't think he should have to throw up alone. He lifted the toilet seat and fell to his knees in front of it, just in time.

"Come on, man," I told him. "In the toilet, not on the floor. There you go. OK."

When he was done he sat staring into the bowl. Then he rocked back on his knees, raised his face to the ceiling, his eyes full of regret.

"Better?"

He nodded and smiled weakly and leaned forward to throw up again. He clutched the rim of the toilet, speckled with pubic hairs and splotches of yellow grime, clutched it with both hands, his head disappearing into the bowl. Gags and whimpers echoed off the porcelain.

"Dude, don't drown, come on." I put my hand on his back, rubbed fast in circles.

He leaned back on his heels again. He looked pissed off. He would've called it orange. Puking was like getting violated by your own body.

"Let's see if we can find you something." I dug around in the medicine cabinet, through curled-up tubes of toothpaste and two gnarly toothbrushes and found a bottle of blue Listerine with an eighth of an inch left in the bottom. I unscrewed the cap and handed it to him. He took it, swished half-heartedly, spat in the toilet, flushed.

"Thanks," he said, squinting now. He closed the lid and put his hands on it to stand up, and only then noticed the yellow-olive puddle on the floor where he'd missed the toilet.

Instead of reaching for toilet paper he rubbed his knee into it, smearing it around with his jeans until it was all but gone and the floor merely glistened in the ugly fluorescent light.

He stood up and looked at his open hands, rinsed them under the tap. He threw a palmful of water at his face. Then he loped back to our room, dragging a wet hand along the wall, leaving a shiny trail on the eggshell paint.

While I closed and locked our door he unbuttoned his jeans and pulled them down and off, not seeming to notice or care that his boxers went down with his pants. I felt a moment of embarrassed surprise and looked away, but his t-shirt, as usual, was far too big for him and covered everything. He got into his bed and yanked up the covers.

I turned off the light and kicked off my shoes. With my back against the wall I sat on my bed and watched him sleep. Minutes multiplied into an hour, at least. When the smell of his vomit-soaked jeans finally got to me I got up to pick them up. But here, hanging out from beneath his plaid comforter, was Griff's socked foot; here was his calf and the soft, hairless nook at the back of his knee; past these, his arm and his long thin architect's fingers. He was lying on his side, facing the wall. His skin glowed blue in the light that came off the street.

I stood beside his bed for a long time and then bent down. From his jeans I pulled his boxers, untwisted them, opened them, held them to my face, felt the cotton against my lips. I unzipped my jeans, pushed them and my underwear down to my knees and knelt on the floor beside his bed. I lifted the covers and could see the small of his back, his ass, blue in the light, fine hairs sprinkled across it.

I leaned forward, carefully, carefully, pressed my lips to the small of his back where his spine met his pelvis, held them against his skin, shivering, my eyes closed. My breath came in quick gasps, like crying. I laid my cheek on the mattress, opened my lips, breathed his skin, smelled warm musk. I was caught in a raging tug-of-war between being drawn to him, between wanting to lay my face there, the curve of his ass matching perfectly the shape of my throat, and fall asleep with my head on his back. At last I was against him and it was everything, everything I could do to keep away.

I came into his boxers.

My whole body throbbing, I pulled my head away from his back, aware now that this was as sexy as a hot stove. Details of things flooded me as I opened my eyes and wiped my penis with his boxers. A zit on his hip, the smell of vomit, sirens on the street below. I sat staring at his back, at the soft ridges of his spine, in disbelief. My eyes welled up.

I pulled up my pants, wrapped his wet boxers into his jeans and then opened his armoire door, careful not to let it squeak, and stuffed his soiled clothes into his laundry bag, all the way to the bottom. My hands were shaking. I sat down on my bed and then got up and went in the bathroom. I sat on the edge of the tub in the place where I cut his hair. I put my elbows on my knees and my wet face in my hands, and in the space between my fingers I looked at my feet and measured them against the square white tiles of the floor.

*

I sat in my underwear on the edge of the bed I'd been sharing with Griff. His pillow was bunched against the headboard, more like some kind of hat than a pillow, and his head lay on the mattress.

I inhaled a quivering gasp, the kind that precedes a sob. He groaned and opened his eyes.

"S'the matter?"

I made some kind of gesture at the wall.

"Where'd Zane go?"

Some tears fell out of my eyes. I closed them and pressed them with my thumbs.

"What's wrong?"

"I think I'm in love with him." It felt funny to say, but was familiar too, like saying my own full name out loud. *Vince Joshua Dandro. I love Zane.*

Griff rubbed his eyes and sat up, the blankets gathering at his waist. "Isn't that a good thing?" he said gently. "Does he not feel the same? I could've sworn he liked you."

"He does." I wiped my face.

" ?"

"I don't know," I said.

He slid over and tried to put his arm around me but I blocked it with my elbow, pushed him back by the shoulder, got out of bed.

***

One random Tuesday six weeks after the welcome back party, I was at my computer chatting with Andy when Griff burst into our room waving an envelope. He tossed his backpack onto his bed and sat on my desk. Pens and pencils clinked in a Shuster mug. He pulled a folded sheet of paper through a jagged tear in the envelope.

"Oh, what's this?" he said, grinning. "It seems to be a housing lottery letter." The paper was folded in thirds; he opened it slowly flap by flap and took a moment to examine it as if for the first time. "Well my goodness me. It says here that yours truly has drawn...," he turned into a game show host now, "lucky number thirteen, baby!" Jumping off the desk, he took off his U2 baseball cap and zinged it across the room. "Can you fucking *believe* it, Vince? How many thousands of people at Shuster, and I get to pick thirteenth for room selection for next year! Thirteenth!"

I didn't know where to look; I watched his hat slip down between his armoire and the wall. "Congratulations," I said. Andy sent an instant message asking if I was still there. I ignored it.

"Did you get your letter? There wasn't one for you in the mailbox."

"I got it." It was tucked beneath a stack of books on my desk.

"Well?"

"Nine forty-seven."

He raised his letter like a winning Megabucks ticket. "Beat you! We get to use my lucky thirteen. We can get any room we want, Vinny boy. Well practically." He flopped onto his bed. "Which one should we get? How about one that has its own bathroom? Then when I have to wallow in my own puke I can do it in private."

"I've actually been meaning to talk to you about—rooms."

"Do you know a good one?" He sat up.

"I'm, uh," I started quietly, and then continued more quietly, "I'm gonna try for a single for next year, I think."

His smile flatlined. Doctors, nurses ran in with machines. "A single?" His face looked pale. "Wow. I mean, I guess. You don't want to live with me again?"

"I think I want to try living by myself." It felt like kicking him in the teeth. *Bam*. It felt like slipping on a pair of brass knuckles and beating the shit out of him.

"Oh." For a moment he pulled at a piece of rubber on the sole of his All-Stars. I opened my eyes wide and breathed in. *This will be the last of it*, I told myself. *Do it quick like a Band-Aid.* If I could just get through this, this would be the last.

"Can you even *get* a single with 947?" he asked finally.

"I'm going to take my chances."

"Because I'll have already picked by then. I mean, we could maybe work out something with Housing later if you need a back-up. Or maybe before, some kind of safeguard. Just in case."

"Griff. It's OK."

"Just in case."

"I need to give it a shot."

*

He scrambled out from under the covers and grabbed my wrist, hard, when I was no more than a few steps away from the bed.

"No," he said, teeth clenched. "You're going to talk to me. I'm not taking any fucking hints this time, Vince. Don't give me the cold shoulder. You're good at it. You've done it before. You're quick and you're fucking slippery and you're doing it again with Zane, aren't you?" I tried to yank myself free of him but he had my arm with two hands now and dragged me backward. The backs of my legs hit the side of the bed and he pulled me down onto my back, and suddenly he was sitting on my stomach. His feet clamped down on my thighs. His architect's fingers clenched my wrists, one by my side, the other up near my head. My hands felt prickly. I couldn't breathe. I tried to squirm and the flannel comforter burned against my ear. "But as hard as you push, Vin, from now on, I'm going to fucking pull even harder."

"Griff—! Get *off* me!"

He leaned down, bringing his face very close to mine. His hair touched my cheeks and all I could see of anything was Griff's face. Story of my fucking life. "No," he said. "No, Vince."

"Griffin! Fuck!"

I yanked my left hand out from under his and got my arm around his neck, had him in a headlock, spun him and flipped him off me. He hit the mattress on his side and the whole bed lurched on its castors, opening up a big space between the headboard and the wall. He wound up to come at me again and in moving to block him I whacked his nose good with the side of my hand.

Instantly we stopped.

He put his fingers to his nose, looked at them, touched his nose again, looked again.

"That was fucking unnecessary, Vince."

"I'm sorry, I didn't mean—"

"Save it. Just—just save it." He was breathing heavy and held his nose with one hand, rubbed his shoulder with the other. "Ow, *fuck*." He laid down on his back; I laid down beside him. "I was hoping to wrestle you metaphorically, but whatever." He put his disheveled hair behind his ears, stared up at the ceiling. "Tell me what happened with Zane and I'll forgive you."

If he had let me go I would've felt very alone. I knew that. There was a reason I'd come to my room in the first place. What I needed, what I had always wanted in Griff, was someone who wouldn't let me get away with my own bullshit.

I sat up then and he did too; we sat Indian-style, facing one another in the low light. I told him about the Halloween night on the beach, about how Zane had rubbed aloe on me after the pine-branch thing, and about what had just happened in the spare bedroom. All those things and everything in between. It came out in long streaming sentences as though I'd been rehearsing it for months.

"I feel like I fall in love with every fucking person I meet," I told him. "I can't handle anyone else and I don't want to deal with anyone else. Especially when I know they're all just going to end up ripping my heart out. It's too fucking overwhelming. I only want *one*."

He didn't say anything until I was finished, and when I was finished he told me, "Come here."

I could never describe what it felt like to hug Griff. Not because I couldn't find the words, but because I never remembered them. I could describe the grooves on the surface of a record, the feel of a leather steering wheel against my palms, the cold, grainy snow—all that was vivid. But the density of his muscles, the shape of his shoulder blades, the smell of his neck, the feel of his hair against my cheek all eluded the grasp of my memory. Always as soon as it was over, after every hello and every goodbye and every congratulations, it was like it never happened. I was left, blinking, a time traveler with missing moments. Sometimes I thought it was better that way. Certainly easier. In the morning I would not remember a thing.

Ben Monopoli

WEDNESDAY

Like a beacon of guilt, the spot on my hand that had clobbered Griff's nose was sending out signals of awareness to my brain. It didn't hurt, but it pulsed just enough to remind me. I sat down in the brown chair with a bowl of Cocoa Krispies to watch the news before work. The weatherman forecasted—correctly, it would turn out—that the next few days would be warmer and warned of flooding as snow melted into streets and through roofs. The icicles hanging on the other side of my picture window released crystal beads in a steady *plink plink plink* timed to the sensation in my hand.

Griff walked into the kitchen pulling on a yellow t-shirt with a Shuster shield on the front.

"'Morning," he said, folding his arms across the half-wall like a bartender ready to take my order or hear my troubles. "How ya doing?"

"Eh." I rubbed the side of my hand against the cushion.

"Heard anything from Zane?"

"No."

"Do you know where he went when he left?"

"No."

"Mm." He went to the fridge and took out the orange juice. He pinched the carton shut and shook it. "You working today?"

"Yeah." With my tongue I pushed a chewed mass of cereal into my cheek and squeezed chocolatey milk through my teeth like tobacco juice. "Looks like the weather's warming up."

He took a glass from the cupboard and filled it. "You should call in sick."

"To who, myself?" I changed the channel. I liked my news to come from multiple sources.

"Whoever. We should go have an adventure."

"We had an adventure a couple days ago, didn't we?"

"That wasn't an adventure," he said, "that was a predicament. Just the two of us this time. Get Clarissa to cover for you."

"Marissa," I corrected. "I would, but today's new arrival day. We have to put out the new stuff. It's the biggest day."

"Oh, OK." He frowned. "Then maybe tonight after work we can do something? Or tomorrow? I only have two more days on my reservation, you know. We've had kind of a rough couple days and I was hoping we could have some time to chill. You know, before I hit the road. Just the two of us."

"I know." Why did he have to remind me he was leaving? It seemed cruel of him. Why did he even *have* to be leaving?

I put my bowl in the sink and went to brush my teeth. In the spare bedroom the new bed lay empty and violated, a three-by-six–foot crime scene. There should've been chalk outlines on the carpet, police tape across the door; the unused condoms belonged in an evidence bag.

I closed the door.

Simon was at the counter perusing a binder of spring solicitations. His Golden Age t-shirt was stretched over a belly grown not from beer but from a seemingly endless intake of Sprite, a can of which sat sweating by his elbow. He wore thick round glasses and his grayless brown hair was slicked back. He was not an unattractive man, but years of being surrounded by geekdom had left a lot of it imposed on him, adding traits—the glasses, the gut—I suspected were not completely natural but rather just part of the job. Like farmer's tan or plumber's butt.

"Hey Vince," he said cheerfully when I came through the door. He took a swig of Sprite. "*Ahhh.*"

"You're here early," I said.

"Wanted to get a jump on the day—Patti's got something up her sleeve for this afternoon." He turned the page and jotted something with pencil on a sheet of lined paper. "How was your Boston trip?"

"Dramatic," I said, folding my coat over my arm. To most other people I would've just said it was fine, but with Simon I could tell the truth without fear of being pressed for more information. It wasn't that Simon wasn't interested—he took in what you gave him—but he wasn't the prying type. Maybe comic-book cliffhangers had taught him to wait patiently for future developments. "But my car's fixed, so that's good."

"Good, good. Nice to see you and Zane hanging out too. Seemed like you two hadn't been clicking lately."

"Really? Nah, we're fine."

He nodded. "Just my overactive imagination, then."

"Deliveries come yet?"

He tapped his watch anxiously. "Not yet. Makes me nervous."

"They'll be here. You always get nervous."

I went to hang up my coat and then turned on the computer behind the counter. Standing beside Simon, I read over the order he'd written out. "Might want to boost the *Majestic* by a dozen or so copies," I told him gently. "We've been selling out."

"Ugh." He made a hole in the paper trying to erase it so he just crossed it out. "He's a Superman rip-off, you know."

"Who isn't?"

"Good point." He laughed and took a swig of Sprite. "This enough?"

"That should do. So what's up Patti's sleeve?"

"Nan*tuck*et," he said.

"She's still on the Nantucket thing, huh?"

"She's a firecracker," he said, shaking his head. A rosy glow came over his face, a glow of happiness and also relief—the relief of a never-married forty-five–year-old comic shop–owner finally making the catch of his life. "Her dream house is on the market, apparently."

"You go look at it?"

"Not yet," he said. "Probably today if the ferry times work out." He took another sip of Sprite. "She's trying to get me to move there, you know. I think she whispers it to me in my sleep. *Nantucket, Nantucket.* I'm not sure I'm an island man."

"I'll help you reverse the curse," I said, and then whispered, "Harwich, Harwich."

He laughed. "Hey, I couldn't find the pull lists. Do you know if Marissa printed them out? Oh—deliveries are here!"

He went to let the man in.

Not long after I returned with our lunch and Simon and I were chowing ham-and-cheese subs at the counter, Patti burst into the store looking like she should have bubble-lettered exclamation points bouncing over her head. Her hair was wild and brown and she wore a red leather jacket that sat nicely against her wide hips.

"*Si*mon!" she chirped. Her lips matched her jacket. Red red red. I found her intimidating in the way a sixth-grade boy might feel about a voluptuous teacher who leaned close to explain long division. Over her shoulder she held by a finger a coat-hangered blue shirt in a clear plastic bag.

"Hi toots," he said. He wiped mustard off the corner of his mouth with a napkin and leaned over the counter to kiss her.

"Hi Vince," she said. I smiled. "It's like spring out there! Wow!"

"What brings you to Golden Age, ma'am?" Simon said.

"The ferry is running and we have an appointment," she said with a wink.

"But Patti, you know it's my day to work," he said. It was playful but I knew Simon well enough to know there were few places he'd rather be than Golden Age. He looked at her sadly and pushed out his lips, which had a silly sheen of red from the kiss. I hadn't had a lot of opportunities to see these two interact and I was enjoying every second of it. It was so strange, so full of apparent conflicts, and yet I couldn't imagine either of them with anyone else.

"Pish posh," she said, squeezing Simon's pursed lips. "Vince is a big boy. He can handle the store. —Can't you, Vince?"

"Of course, yeah," I said. Simon glared at me from behind his thick glasses. "I mean, I guess I could. If I absolutely *have* to."

Patti looked at Simon and drew a circle in the air with a red-nailed finger. "Let me look at you."

He came out from behind the counter and obediently rotated. The black shirt stretched over his belly made him look like a moon orbiting Patti.

"It's just as I feared," she said, smirking at me. "You can't wear your comic book t-shirt to a real estate showing." Unlike the rest of us, Simon wore his store shirt all the time. His closet must've been full of them, a superhero's wardrobe. "We need to look serious!"

After hanging the coat hanger on one of the arms of the action figure display, she grabbed the waist of Simon's t-shirt— he raised his arms and—*swoop!*—she yanked it up over his head and off. In my surprise I choked on a chunk of cheese. It shot from my mouth and clung to the hair above Simon's right nipple for a second before tumbling down the face of his stomach and splatting on the floor. Patti brushed his chest with her hand before pushing the dry-cleaned shirt against him.

"Here you go, lover."

Simon took the shirt from the bag and looked at me with an expression that was—to my surprise—not embarrassment, not shame, but total satisfaction. He put his arms through the sleeves and started doing up the buttons.

Patti's specialty in the real estate world was fixer-uppers. I imagined her walking through a rundown house, hands clasped together in practiced delight. "A fresh coat of paint and this place will be *darling*," she would say. And I couldn't help but wonder whether she'd seen the same qualities in Simon that she might praise about a house with an outdated kitchen or a leaky roof.

When Simon was dressed and tucked, Patti tugged at his sides to straighten him and gave him a once-over. She nodded in approval.

"That'll do. Now grab your jacket and I'll bring the car around. Nice seeing you, Vince!"

When she'd left Simon pulled the shirt out of his pants a little—just a little—to give it some slack and took a last swig of Sprite. He tossed the empty can over the counter and landed it squarely in the trash.

"I love that woman, but this house better be amazing," he said. "Now, don't forget to bring the empty boxes out back and finish the pulls. Big-Ears McKenzie will probably be in on his lunch hour, so have his ready first. And check to make sure we have enough blank subscriber forms. And the new *Comic Shop News*—make sure those are out."

"I know, I've got it, Simon, don't worry. Did you want the rest of your sandwich?"

"Nah." He stepped away and then turned back and grabbed it off the wrapper.

"Don't spill on your shirt."

"Famous last words," he said. He raised his hand in a wave without turning around, and then he was gone.

I spent the rest of the afternoon setting aside comics in white paper bags for the regular customers who only wanted to pop into the store to pick them up. On each bag I wrote a customer's name.

It was funny to look through the comics on the shelves—they seemed frozen in time. Most of the issues at the top of each stack were ones I'd put there myself a week ago, two weeks ago, before Griff came, before any of this. That was how it was— there were some weeks, even months, where nothing happened, where I was the same person doing the same ordinary things. And then there were weeks that changed everything.

At around three I helped a kid who'd obviously come down from upstairs pick out some comics to kill a post-Novocain afternoon with. His mouth was stuffed with gauze with red tendrils of blood creeping to the edges.

"I know how you feel," I told him, pointing to the scrape on my chin. It made me think of Zane dabbing aloe into it. Apparently even Simon had noticed the weirdness between Zane and me, and he almost never worked with us together. Had it been that obvious? That strained? I decided to call Zane when I got home. To apologize for last night. To ask him to go out for pizza, as friends, as whatever. I would call him, I promised myself.

I promised myself a lot of things.

I closed the store and stuffed the keys in my pocket. My stomach was rumbling—I hoped Griff was at home making something for supper. But he wasn't. He was in the Golden Age lot, leaning against the side of his Jetta with his arms folded. Beneath his vest and hooded sweatshirt he wore a gray t-shirt that said *Elsewhen* in blue letters. I remembered the night he got that shirt. It was the only one he had that actually fit.

"Well hello," I said.

He stood up straight and put his hands in his pockets. "I was in the neighborhood."

"You should've come in."

"It's OK, I haven't been here long. Hey, I need you to follow me in your car somewhere."

"Why? Where to?"

He grinned and opened his door. "Just follow me?"

I did, and it didn't take me long to figure out where we were headed, given the general direction and Griff's limited knowledge of town. I thought of losing him down a side street or banging a U-turn after he'd gone around a bend, but I couldn't do that to him. Whatever was going to happen at his not-so-secret destination, he was excited about it. I would have to suffer through my own surprise party. I would have to trust him.

He pulled up in front of Zane's house near where we went through the hedge and I parked behind him, my heart racing. *Just leave, leave,* I told myself with even more urgency now that we were here. *Just step on the gas and lay down a mile of rubber behind you and leave.* I put my hand on the stick to knock it back into drive, but just then he got out of his car. He opened the back door and brought out a black plastic bag, a second bag, and—my god—a big bundle of green rock-climbing rope.

"What is *that* for?" I said before I'd even rolled down my window enough for him to hear.

He walked up to the Jeep and pushed one of the bags through the window. "Put this on."

I opened the bag and saw blue and red spandex and the top left corner of what I knew to be a very familiar *S*.

"Griff, what are you doing to me?"

"You were an ass to him last night." From the other bag he pulled a waist harness typically used for scaling mountains and repelling into icy crevasses. He held it up, buckles clinking and glinting in the streetlight. "It'll take a superhero to get him back."

It was ridiculous, what he was going to have me do, if at that point I had any real idea—and yet, looking at him, I did trust him. I did trust that everything would be OK if I did what he told me.

After struggling for a few minutes in a space even smaller than a phone booth, I emerged from the Jeep in full regalia: tights, cape, red underwear on the outside. I didn't feel ridiculous at all. Actually, I felt strong. I felt fucking great.

Griff had ducked through the bushes and while I was changing he managed to get one end of the green rope to go over the big oak branch above Zane's second-story window. It took tying his shoe to the end of the rope and flinging it up like a grappling hook, but he'd succeeded. I crept through the bushes, careful not to snag my cape on any branches.

"Well holy shit, it actually fits," he said with genuine gladness. He was holding the other end of the rope that snaked down from the tree and twitched in the breeze. His vest was on the ground and the sleeves of his hooded sweatshirt were pushed up to his elbows. He reached out and pinched my cape.

"It's a little tight on my balls," I said, plucking at the red underpants.

"Little tight on the nipples, too, looks like."

"Shut up, it's cold out."

"I'd give anything for a camera right now."

"I'm surprised you didn't bring one."

"The one thing I didn't think of."

There were no outside lights on to illuminate our exploits, but Zane's bedroom window was glowing. So were other windows. People were definitely home. Awake. Ready to catch us. I remembered the night in the swimming pool, when my mother was suddenly there in the backyard, her hands clenching the pool fence. Zane's mother could come through the door at any moment. At least this time I was obviously wearing underwear.

"Earth to Vince," Griff said, snapping his fingers up at me. He was kneeling and jiggled the waist harness impatiently at my feet. "Come on, step into this." I stepped through the loops and pulled the harness up around my red trunks.

"You should've gotten a red one so it would blend in," I said.

"Haha! Blend in! You're singing a different tune now that you've got the suit on, aren't you?" Touching the cape again, he said, "Well it *is* pretty cool." He hooked a beener onto the loop at the end of the rope. "The guy at the sporting goods store tied the knots, and he *seemed* to know what he was doing, so they should hold. He showed me how to do this. I hope I remember."

"Yeah, I hope you remember too, dude." In the snow lay a second harness. "What's that one for?"

"Duh. So you can *rescue* him." He picked it up and clipped it to mine. Carabiners swung from it, jingling. "That'll be fun getting into. The rest is up to you."

"If he gets in at all."

"Good point. But don't worry about that just yet—you'll figure out something to say. Just tell him what you told me last night."

He picked up the other end of the green rope and pulled it with him across the yard, tossed it over the hedge and left for a second a Griff-shaped hole in the hedge. Through a first-floor window I could see a low-lit dining room table and chairs, and a doorway beyond them. A shadow moved past.

"OK," Griff called after a minute. He must've been standing on my bumper or something because I could just see his head over the top of the hedge. "You're all connected and I'm going to start backing up to hoist you up. Ready?"

I gave him a thumbs-up. I could hear the Jeep's motor rev and then loops in the rope began to straighten out across the snow. I reached up and gave the rope a tug to check this bit of engineering when suddenly my red underwear squeezed my hips even tighter and my sneakers, draped with red flaps to represent boots, lifted out of the snow. I rose inch by inch, very slowly, until my feet were ten or twelve feet off the ground, and then my progress slowed and stopped. Standing on the bumper again, Griff peered over the top of the hedge to check my progress. When I gave him another thumbs-up he started laughing, just a smirk at first, then louder, then practically hysterical. His head disappeared; he was probably doubling over. I knew he didn't think this was ridiculous, but rather that it was awesome. Beyond awesome. When he got himself under control his face appeared again; he was wiping his eyes with his sleeve.

"Yuck it up," I told him.

"Sorry. If you could just see yourself."

"Yeah, yeah."

"So another ten feet or so?"

"OK."

The Jeep revved and I began to rise again.

I clutched the rope in front of me to keep from tipping backward. For a moment I could see into Zane's bedroom—it was cluttered with posters and towers of white comics boxes like a scaled-down version of Golden Age—and then it was lost again to blue siding as the rope slipped along the branch. I reached out and touched the side of the house. Then once again I soared skyward. The window sill, encrusted in ice, passed my eye-line again and I could see into the room. It was dim, lit with moving blue pictures of the television. I couldn't see Zane.

I tapped on the glass with my finger. The harness was crushing my balls and I was sure I was wearing it wrong, that it was inside-out or upside-down or something. Griff lifted me up a few more feet so that I was directly in front of the window. I was almost looking down into the room—there was a pair of jeans lying on the brown carpet—when Zane came into the room. He had on flannel pajama pants and a red t-shirt that said *Everybody loves an Asian boy*. He saw me and dropped his Doritos. My heart started pounding.

The rope was turning me gently and I rotated away from him so that I was now facing the front yard and the neighbors' houses across the street. I looked down at Griff, who no longer had to stand on the bumper to see me, at the small cars in the driveway, at the flat expanse of snow below. Suddenly a foot or two of slack appeared in the rope as it slipped farther along the branch and I fell that distance with a nut-crushing jerk. The branch *spronged* like a diving board and dumped down snow and stripped bark. Snow dropped down the back of my neck into my suit. I went rigid and clenched my teeth.

Behind me the window opened, crunching ice on the sill. It sprinkled to the ground. I kicked my legs, trying to turn myself around, my cape swooshing back and forth with the effort. There was a tug on the back of my neck, pulling open wide the collar of my suit, and even more snow went down my back. I gasped. The collar was let go with a cold snap.

Then a hand on my harness as Zane gave me a twirl, and I faced him.

"OK," I said, "I deserve that." A clump of snow shifted between my shoulder blades and made an icy trail along the small of my back. "*Ah.*—Oh my god."

"What are you doing, Vince?" There was a hint of a smile in the corners of his mouth, but a severity in his eyes made me feel like this was all for nothing.

"Can I come in?"

"I really don't know if I want you to."

"Please? This thing really hurts."

He looked down at the ground, then at me. "All right."

I tried lifting my feet up onto the sill. He grabbed my ankles and pulled my red-booted legs up into the room. When I was sitting, half inside, half out, Griff called up to hold on so he could give me some slack. The Jeep drove forward a few feet and the rope behind me got loose. I ducked under the top of the double-hung window and slipped inside. It was easier than I feared but clumsier than I hoped.

I pushed the window closed on the rope and unclipped myself; the knot fell to the carpet. The bedroom was lit only by the television and a flickering red candle on the bureau. The aloe plant was sitting beside it, as if keeping warm.

"This is amazing," Zane said, but it sounded like a concession. He idly poked the knob on his dresser drawer. "I don't know what else you want me to say."

"You don't have to say anything." I sat down on the foot of his bed and my cape pulled tight under me, choking me. I tugged it away.

"You hurt me, Vince," he said. "You can't pull some trick with ropes and expect me to be your friend again, you know."

"Yeah, I know."

"Then what are you doing?" He looked sad. I felt like something to be pitied. "What's this all for?"

"I guess to apologize."

He nodded, pursed his lips. He tugged out the drawer a couple inches then pushed it back in. "Did Griff put you up to this?"

"He puts me up to everything."

"I was right, huh? You really are in love with him."

"It's more complicated than that. He's straight."

"I don't know if he is."

"He is."

"Well I don't know if you understand that he is."

"What do you mean?"

"What is *gay* and *straight* to someone like you, Vince? Do those words even make any sense to you? You can't relate to them. You're always going to be waiting for your chance. For him to fall for you."

"..."

"And in the meantime, all there is is consolation prizes. I don't want to be a consolation prize, Vince. Not even yours."

202

"Zane, come on, you're not a—" If I finished the thought would I just be deluding myself and lying to him? "You're not a consolation prize. I'm just stupid."

He didn't say anything for what must've been a full minute; we just stood looking at each other. He let his hand fall away from the drawer. I knew he was at the crossroads of a decision and I wondered what he was thinking. Finally his face softened and he looked up. His eyes were moving over my costume as though he were really noticing it for the first time. He laughed, a quick short burst, and bottled it again. He sat down next to me on the bed.

"I'm sorry for last night," I said.

"Yeah. Me too."

"I know I was an incredible jerk. He's just really thrown me for a loop."

"Quite the loop."

"Zane— I wish there was something I could say. Some magic words that in a comic would be big and yellow and would make everything OK between us. But I know there isn't."

He looked at me, almost through me. "No," he said, "there isn't. But I can tell you really wish there was. And maybe that buys you a night."

"One night?"

"And we'll go from there." He looked at my harness and at the rope coiled on the floor. "So where do we start it?"

"Through that window."

"Then this is mine?" He touched the extra harness hanging from my waist.

"That was the idea. If you're interested."

I held out my hand; he didn't take it. Instead he put his on my *S*. His fingernails were trimmed low, looked like they hurt. He kissed me. I smiled against his lips.

"What?" he said, pulling back.

"Nothing... I just wasn't even expecting to be let in, let alone this."

"I couldn't say no to 'Superman,' could I?"

"No, I guess you couldn't. I guess I couldn't either." I thought of Griff shoving the plastic bag through my window. Then I looked at Zane. His long, dark sideburns matched the color of his soft eyes.

He cleared his throat. "I need some clothes," he said. "Because unlike Lois Lane, I'm not going flying in my pajamas." He squeezed my knee and stood up.

"When did she fly in her pajamas?"

"In the first movie. When Superman takes her flying in her nightgown."

"That wasn't a nightgown, it was a dress."

"No. That was a *dress*? That sheer blue thing?" He kicked down his pajama pants—his boxers were white with purple stars; I suddenly realized I knew what he looked like underneath them—and he picked up the jeans that lay on the floor.

"She wore it out afterward with Clark," I said, "remember?"

"Yeah, but I thought she was still in a starry-eyed love-daze from flying and forgot to change clothes."

"Well she was in a daze, but it was a dress." He still looked skeptical, so I added, "It was the Seventies."

He smiled. "In that case, RetroLand, I'll take your word for it."

He pulled on his jeans, stepped into a pair of Chucks, grabbed his yellow hooded sweatshirt from the back of his desk chair. "Now help me get this harness on," he said.

I unclipped the extra harness from mine and held it open for him. He stepped through the loops with one hand on my shoulder for balance and hiked the harness up around his waist. I fed the rope through both of our carabiners.

"I don't know if this was made to work this way," I said, holding his harness with one hand and pulling on the rope as hard as I could with the other. It seemed secure but of course I couldn't simulate our combined weight with just my hands. We hobbled to the window like contestants in a potato-sack race and opened it. "We may be killed."

"The snow'll cushion our fall," he said, looking down.

"It's pretty packed down."

"Then I'll cushion you."

"I don't know, you're pretty skinny."

"I'm not skinny, I'm small-boned."

Griff was leaning against the Jeep, looking off down the street. I waved and caught his eye. "Ready?" he yelled.

"Almost," I called. "OK," I said, turning to Zane, "any ideas on how we should do this?"

"It sure as hell isn't going to be graceful."

Griff was at the door of the Jeep waiting for my signal.

"I think if we sit on the window sill first..."

We each slung one leg over the sill, then the other. It was barely big enough for two people. Rope coiled across our laps and raised into the air as Griff backed up the Jeep.

"Get ready to push off," I said.

"How are we going to close the window?"

"Oh. Good question," I said, and then I and Zane after me slipped off the icy ledge into mid-air. We swung suspended, entwined, smacking the side of the house like a wrecking ball. Zane held his crotch and winced and then was laughing.

We lurched down a couple of inches and then began a steady descent. The Jeep inched back along the curb.

Suddenly the front lights blazed on like interrogation lamps.

"Shit," Zane and I murmured in unison.

A moment later the door opened and Zane's father stormed out in sweatpants and slippers. His eyes followed the rope stretching across the yard and landed, finally, on us.

"Um, hi Dad."

"Oh dear god," he groaned and put both hands over his face. "Irene, Ralph, stay in the house. Irene—"

"Why, what was that— *Peter!*" his mother yelled. "What are you doing? Get down from there!"

"Mom, I'm safe. Look who I'm with!" He wrapped his arms and legs around me and my cape.

"You're such a homo, Zane," Ralph said.

"Go close your brother's window," their father said, pushing Ralph back inside the house.

Zane's mother looked after Ralph and she seemed to be deciding based on his language that this stunt was not only dangerous but had something to do with *gay*, as well.

"Peter, this— This is *wrong*, Peter!" she shouted. "What do you think you're *doing*? You! Vince!" She pointed at me. "Are you a homosexual too?"

"No, um, I'm bi."

She wandered off the steps with her hands spread stiffly at her side like an action figure. His dad sat down on the stoop and crossed his arms over his knees.

"Wh-what does *that* mean?" she said.

I didn't know what kind of answer she was looking for—by the expression on her face it didn't seem the question was rhetorical. How could I sum up myself while I was hanging with her son fifteen feet above the ground, the yard and house revolving around me? "It means I can fall in love with both men and women?"

"Love!" She looked down and shook her head as though she'd just been fed a spoonful of suspicious broth.

As soon as our feet touched the snow, Griff came running, in a more dramatic fashion than it probably warranted, through the hedge over to us, the hood of his sweatshirt flapping behind him like a cape. Zane's eyes darted to the rope, to Griff, who was rapidly unbuckling us.

"Peter, you're not going with them. If you go with them..." She looked speechless. When she finally found her voice again, it came out as a whisper. "I'm your mother. You're not like those people."

"What people? These people? A comic book nerd? An architect who's not even gay?"

"You know who I mean, Peter."

"Mom, I'm just trying to be happy. That's all anyone ever does, isn't it?"

Zane yanked the buckle on his harness and it dropped to his feet. Griff was unhooking mine, untying the rope with quick fingers.

"But this isn't happiness," she said, holding her open hands out in front of her, as though in them sat a crystal ball showing her Zane's whole life. "This isn't *love*."

"You guys bounce out of here," Griff said, handing Zane the keys to my Jeep. "I'll take care of the props."

"Thank you, Griffin," said Zane, and he took off across the yard.

"Peter, don't run away. You're just *confused*," his mother said, putting her hands on her knees as though she were going to lean forward and puke into the snow. "You're not gay! They've *brainwashed* you!"

Zane stopped short a few feet from the hedge. "Brainwashed? Mom, come on. Do you really think I'm that weak? That easy to manipulate? That *naïve*? I'm stronger than you'd ever believe. I'm as strong as him." He pointed at me and I didn't know whether he meant me or the comic book character I was dressed as. And then, just when I thought he would explode, because I thought he had every right to, the anger fell off his face like a mask and he smiled, the kind of smile that sticks in your mind forever. "Someday you'll see that and be proud of me, Mom," he said, and then he disappeared through the hedge.

"Peter!" she called again.

"That's enough, Irene," his father said tiredly. He stood up, put his arm around her shoulders and steered her back inside the house.

I stood watching the door close behind them.

"Go," Griff said, nudging my arm. "He's waiting. Don't forget to take the rope off the car, you'll be dragging the whole neighborhood behind you."

"How can I just—"

"Don't worry about them. They'll come around. Now go. I'll drive around for a couple hours so you can have the house." He winked.

"You don't have to do that."

"It's OK, I have some thinking to do anyway."

I walked through the yard. The night was clear, and in the sky a billion witnesses to our escapades sparkled. I could hear the

Jeep's motor running. My cape snagged in the bushes and tore off as I went through. I immediately felt silly without it, and I went back for it, and then got in the car with Zane and drove home.

With the night he gave me we went to my bed and finished what we'd started the night before. It hurt a little but it was smooth and warm and he told me I was beautiful. Afterward we were sweaty and chilly. When I pulled the blankets back up over us, the air they brought with them smelled like Griff. I breathed it in and felt like crying so I rubbed my face against my pillow, to be silly. We lay face to face, sharing the pillow. A strip of hallway light came in from under the door and lit the room in an underwater glow.

Zane brushed his thumb across my forehead, as he might've if my hair had been long enough to fall into my eyes.

I laid my hand in the soft groove above his hip and let my fingers open and close on his bum. "I'm sorry about your parents," I told him. "I don't know why people have to be like that."

"They're just worried for me," he said. "They think I'm destined for unhappiness. I'm not. Tonight made me happy."

I kissed him. "Good."

Below each of his collar bones was a row of three dark shapes, each about the size of a dime. They looked like a bit like pips on a military uniform.

"I like your tattoos," I said.

"My superhero symbol tattoos."

"They're cool."

He took my hand from where it lay on his hip and pressed my fingers against the tattoo closest to his right shoulder. "The S symbol," he said. "You know about Superman. He's very strong, but he's lonely—but he loves everyone and belongs to everyone." From there he moved my finger to the next tattoo. "Batman's bat signal." He moved it again. "Wonder Woman's W."

"And over here?"

"This is the Flash's lightning bolt," he said, putting his hand on mine again, moving it across his chest as though he were teaching me Braille. "And Green Lantern's symbol. And the Martian Manhunter's globe or whatever it is."

"I always assumed it was a Trivial Pursuit piece. Or a pizza."

He laughed. "Because those make more sense than a globe?"

"Well, he's Martian, who knows what they value."

He laughed again. "Well that's the tour of my tattoos."

"I like them."

What they really reminded me of was Griff's joshua tree. Although Zane was naked and snuggled against me, the bed still smelled like Griff and it was hard to think of anything else.

I woke up later and my mouth was desert-dry, my lips raw from Zane's stubble. (That was a drawback to sleeping with guys— girls were so much softer.) My stomach felt empty too and I realized I'd never gotten around to eating supper. I pulled back the covers and rooted around in the costume tangled on the floor until I found my boxers, and then pulled on the shirt part of the costume too. I started to tiptoe out of the room, but thought of something and stopped. From the bureau I grabbed a photo of me on a whale-watching boat and put it on my pillow in case Zane woke up, so he'd know I was coming back.

The kitchen light was on and Griff was sitting at the table with a beer, his interstate road atlas spread out in front of him. The sight of it stung me. He belonged at that table.

"Hey, Mr. Dandro," he said, snickering. "Finally have to come up for air?"

"Screw you." I could tell I was blushing under the yellow ceiling light. I grabbed a bag of Goldfish crackers and poured a glass of water and sat down with him. His t-shirt had a hole in the shoulder that suggestively revealed a patch of skin. Beside him was a legal pad scrawled with the names of cities and with numbers written small.

"This would be a lot easier if you had the Internet, you know," he said, thumbing the eraser head. He slipped the legal pad between the pages of the atlas and closed it. "I guess the Internet doesn't exist in your cranberry hush?"

"I avoid computers when possible."

He smirked. "No more Truman angst, I hope."

I shrugged.

"So did you have fun with Zane?"

"Yeah..."

He looked at me, pressing the pencil against his lower lip. "How much?"

"Home run."

"So you mean you—?" Suppressing a smile, he formed two fingers into an *O* and pushed another one through it.

"Yeah."

"Who was the—?" He held up the *O*.

"Me."

"Huh."

"What?"

"Nothing. Sorry. What's that like?"

"It's just sex."

"Must be pretty—um. Intense?"

"Yeah. It can be." I wanted to show him. I wanted it to be him.

"Hmm. Well I'm not sure you look like a person who just rounded the bases with someone he cares about."

I gulped some water and ran my finger around the lip of the glass. I felt so full of tension that the low *oooo* from the glass might've actually been coming from my vibrating skin.

"Should I not have put you up to it?" he added.

"You didn't put me up to it, you just drove me there. I wanted to go up. I wanted to do everything I did. It's just— I don't know. I wish it was clicking better than it is. I feel like it can, but I don't know what I have to do to make it— Or *feel* to make it." I took a sip of water and dragged a finger through the wet ring on the table. "Just my typical shit."

"Maybe it's time to let that go."

"What makes you so sure I want to be with him?"

"Um. Last night you told me you loved him. I'd say that was my main clue."

"But beyond that. Is it something I show? What makes you know? How do you know for sure when someone's in love with you?"

"Because I'm your lifebuddy, that's how. I know everything about you."

My lifebuddy.

He got up from the table and pulled a bag of chips from the cupboard. "And we still need to have our adventure," he said. "Tomorrow's my last day. I need some us time. A couple of hours. It's important."

I wondered what he had planned that would only take a couple of hours. A couple of hours seemed like a short time, or a long time. What I needed from him would only take a minute, a moment. We could do it right now. I could show him right now. And then he'd never want to leave.

"I can try to have Marissa cover my afternoon shift tomorrow," I told him, and he nodded.

Let me kiss you, Griff. Just once. Let me touch you. Let me undress you and take you to bed and show you how it can be to be in it together, not just side by side but through and through. Let me do these things and I *know* you'll realize this can work. I know you will.

"So," he said, "you better be getting back to your man."

"Oh. Yeah." I got up, put the glass in the sink and the crackers away. "Oh— Hey Griff?"

"Hm?"

"How'd you know it would work? With Zane, I mean. The ropes and everything. The suit."

"Oh. Well I figured you and Zane are a lot alike—and that's what I would've done on you."

"..."

"Sweet dreams, Vin."

I turned and started up the hall, thunder clapping in my chest. I didn't have to look back to know how he looked, what he was doing—tipping the beer bottle to his lips, brushing back the hair he used to hide behind but which now seemed more to frame his face, looking at his maps.

He'd be gone by the weekend. I didn't have much time.

THURSDAY

"Again," Zane said, his lips against my shoulder. "Snooze it again."

"I can't." I reached for the other button, the smaller one, pressed it. "I snoozed it three times already." I unwound myself from Zane and got out of bed, yanked the covers back up to his chin. I rubbed him hard through the blankets, the way you rub someone who's just fallen through the ice. He grumbled and rolled over.

The door of the spare bedroom was open and the floor was cluttered with piles of clothes and the boxes of Griff's stuff. His backpack stood empty, waiting to be filled. I looked farther in. He was sleeping, his arm hanging over the bed as though he was making sure the floor was still there. He seemed so far away now. The existence of another bed made sharing one impossible.

Later, Griff rinsed the cereal bowl I'd left on the counter and filled it again with Cocoa Krispies. "...Just lounge around until you call me, I guess," he said when I asked what he was up to this morning. "I need to finish figuring out my route, too."

"Why don't you come with me?"

"To work?"

"Yeah, why not? We can hang out, I can show you the place in the daylight. Then I'll get Marissa to take my afternoon."

As he'd said, his week was nearly up and I wanted to pack more into it. The best way to make time slow down was to do a lot of things, be a lot of places, so at the buzzer you can look back and wonder how you managed to cram everything in. I wanted to have every second and all the possibilities they afforded.

"We need to leave soon, though," I told him. "I have to get Zane home. He has a class at ten."

Griff was about to pour milk on the cereal but stopped just as the first drops sloshed out. "Cool. I'll skip breakfast."

Zane, wearing a towel, emerged from the bathroom and walked down the hall to my room slowly, as though he knew my eyes were locked to the cotton stretched tight against his ass.

"My turn," Griff said. "I'll be quick." He knocked back the last of his juice and slid the glass to the edge of the sink. It hit the stainless steel lip, teetered, did not fall in.

From the back seat of the Jetta I leaned forward into the front as we were driving Zane home. They were talking about classes and dorms, grades and professors, the trials and tribulations of college life.

"You're so lucky you're graduated and done with this crap," Zane said.

Griff looked in the rearview mirror and caught my eye and delivered an expression of shocked bewilderment. "What are you talking about?" he said to Zane, stabbing his finger into Zane's knee. "You're so lucky you're *not.*"

"Why? It sucks."

Griff looked back at me again. "Sucks? Sucks? That's blasphemy! Vince, what have you been telling this guy? College is a fucking paradise. It's a fucking golden age. I'd give up everything I have to go back."

From behind the counter and through the window I could see Griff leave the Dunkin' Donuts and cross the street. He came in—jingle—with a chocolate donut hanging from his lips and dropped a pink and orange bag on the counter.

"Breakfast," he mumbled. "You call Marissa yet?"

I grabbed a chocolate-covered donut. "Doing it now."

I rummaged in the drawers for the address book, found it and flipped to her info. "She'll probably be glad to do it," I told him as I dialed, "to make up for her snow day. But of course this is Marissa so she'll need to put up a stink first, just for effect."

She answered. "OK," she said, groggily and with the expected dramatic reluctance after I'd made the offer, "but I can't get there until like noon."

I told her I'd see her then.

"We good?" Griff said when I hung up. His fingers crept into the bag and he looked away as he withdrew another donut.

"She's coming but she needs three more hours of beauty rest." I finished the last bite of donut and licked chocolate flakes off my lips.

"You don't have an extra one of those GA shirts lying around, do you?" he said, pointing to the logo on my chest.

"Probably. Want one?"

"Eh, sure, why not." He pushed the last bite of donut into his mouth.

I brought him into the back and found him a new shirt under a box of bags and boards. He ripped it out of the plastic and pulled it on over his hooded sweatshirt. It was creased and tight over the sweatshirt; the hood, trapped beneath, gave him a hunchback.

"Looking good?" he said, rubbing his hands down his chest and over his hips.

"It's sort of *Michelin Man* chic."

"Haha. Nice. I'll just go stand on the street and let the poon roll in."

I heard the bell jingle and went out front. When Griff joined me a minute later he was minus the sweatshirt. "So what do we do now?" he said. "Just wait?"

"I don't know. Whatever. Straighten up the trades if you want. People paw through stuff and get it all out of order."

I brought him to the island of paperbacks, each one a story arc collected from a half-dozen or so monthly comics. I ran my hand against the books, sliding them back so their spines met.

"We used to have a yard sale like every summer when I was little," he said. "And people would come browse, hemming and hawing over like the quality and value of our whatever, our items. And I remember being so offended if they didn't buy anything. Like nothing we had was worthwhile or something. *Oh this is junk.* Which I guess it was, but still."

"I felt like that here at first. Like what do you mean you're not buying this issue? Are you a dumb-ass?"

He laughed. "You dig it, don't you?"

"The store?"

"Mm."

"I do."

"How come?" He asked it not interrogatingly, but with curiosity. Pulling out a book and pushing it into its proper alphabetical place a few spaces over, he said, "What is it about this place that does it for you?"

"I guess I like having something to escape into. There's so much continuity to learn in comics. It's a good hobby."

But it was more than a hobby. The world of comics was a refuge, a safe house. I thought of the slim, gay teenage boy perpetually in black clothes and eye-liner who came into the store almost every Wednesday morning, definitely during school hours, and headed for the shelf of new arrivals. His name was Abe; he was the kind of cute that made me feel like I missed something by not coming out until college.

"Hey, Vince," he would say somberly, sliding an *X-Men* across the counter. I'd take it and ring him up. If it was raining out, or snowing, he'd want a bag; otherwise no. Usually he'd ask about some other title he hadn't been able to find on the shelves, and if we were sold out, or if it had been delayed, I'd feel bad.

I knew why I liked being among comic book characters, and it wasn't about a hobby. The X-Men are mutants, freaks—hated, hunted, cast out—but on the other hand, practically gods. Kids like Abe, digging out his wallet, pushing three dollars across the

THE CRANBERRY HUSH

counter with skinny fingers and nails of chipped black polish, might be called a freak every day at school—on the days they could tolerate going—but in secret, in disguise, who knew what wonders they could create with waves of ice, what havoc they could wreak with their unbelievable strength.

"A lot of the queer kids like *X-Men*," I explained to Griff.

"Not you?"

"Sure, but for me it's always been Superman."

"I don't think of Superman as being angsty, though."

"That's the problem. Most people don't. But really he's pure angst. He has a Fortress of Solitude, you know? What do you think he does there, throw parties? No. He broods."

"Good point."

"But that's not what I really like about him, though."

"What do you like about him?" He smiled. He'd probably heard this a million times. A billion.

"You know, in the first movie, the scene in Lois Lane's apartment? Right after Superman has taken her flying? He's dressed up as Clark Kent now and he loves her and he wants to tell her his secret, he wants to share this giant secret. He takes off his glasses, straightens up, becomes an entirely different person—becomes, I don't know, beautiful. *Lois*, he says, *there's something I have to tell you.*"

"That part is good."

I nodded. "I can always feel how much he wants to tell her, you know? How *desperate* he is to. This powerful man who can lift continents and shoot laser beams from his eyes. But then he gets scared. I can see the fear in his eyes, and I can feel that too." It was the same fear I had when Griff sat down at my computer that night, when he clicked that little drop-down menu and learned that Truman and Vince were one and the same. "He puts his glasses back on—I know his heart is pounding—and his voice gets squeaky again. He calls the whole thing off and he feels both relieved and disappointed about not actually crossing that line he's made for himself, you know? He's the most powerful man in the world but he's perpetually in the closet."

"He just needs a good buddy to help him come out," Griff said, and with a smile he moved another book to the right place.

I was ringing up a customer when Marissa arrived. According to the angle of the beam of sunlight coming through the glass door, it was a little after noon.

"Yo," she said.

"Thanks for doing this," I told her, sliding a credit card through the machine.

"No thanks necessary. I will extract payment at a later date." She went to the back and I heard her say, "You new?"

And then Griff: "New to you. I'm Griff. Vince's friend."

"Ah, the ambiguously straight roommate. I've heard about you. I'm Marissa."

"I've heard about you too," Griff said. "Vince says you're angsty."

"He projects."

The customer left the store with her bag and a puzzled expression. Marissa came out pulling her hair out of the neck of her Golden Age t-shirt, bedazzled with blue sequins on the sleeves. Griff followed her.

"You guys met, I heard?" I said.

"We're practically engaged," she said. Griff put his hand over his mouth to be silly but his surprise looked genuine. "OK boys, you can scoot out on whatever little *Tour de Vince* you have planned."

In the back room Griff and I exchanged our t-shirts for coat and vest.

"Thanks again Marissa."

"Yeah, yeah." She smiled and waved us away.

Melting snow ran in little streams across the sidewalk Zane had shoveled so carefully last weekend, washing his sprinkled sand into the grass and the parking lot.

"She's interesting," Griff said as we climbed into the Jetta. He started it up. Cold air blew from the vents.

"I think she likes to make a strong first impression," I said, cranking up the heat. "But she's cool."

"I couldn't tell whether she wanted to make out with me or stomp on my toe."

"Exactly!"

He was idling at the edge of the lot. Traffic rushed by in both directions. "OK, Vinny, where to?"

"You mean you don't have some big plan?" I pushed my gloves into the compartment in the door.

"The *adventure* was my idea. I'm not expected to come up with all the details too, am I?"

"The destination is hardly a detail."

"It's the *journey*, my friend."

"Well, let me think. ... We could... Hmm."

"What?"

"..."

"Any ideas?"

"No, I don't fucking know!"

Even in college we never knew what to do. We used to sit around in our room, increasingly whiny and antsy as it became more and more evident that we were going to end up staying in for the night, watching movies or playing Trivial Pursuit in the common area with Gia. But those nights often ended up being the most fun. So it worked out.

"Just drive," I told him. "See where the road takes us."

"OK." He pulled out of the lot and a little way down the street we stopped at a red light. Sun glinted off the shiny hood. "It's fucking bright," he said, lowering his visor. "I may crash us."

"Please no. I don't want any more wounds."

"Looks better, by the way," he said, jabbing his finger at my chin.

He put us on Route 6 and we headed northeast up the crook of the Massachusetts elbow.

***

From my desk I watched the door of room 907 open and Griff quietly enter, but I didn't say anything and neither did he. He dropped his backpack onto his bed and sat down. He took off his sneakers and peeled off his socks, wincing in disgust as they unrolled down his clammy shins. They looked like he'd stepped in a puddle.

"So fucking hot out," he said after sitting there a minute with his socks in his hand. "I hate being sweaty. I'd prefer anything to dampness. Frostbite, fine—but dampness..."

"Yeah." I looked back at my computer, resting my chin in my hand, my palm slick with sweat. The windows were open but it was doing jack-shit.

He walked barefoot to his computer, laughed at some forwarded email joke he didn't share with me, poked around in his desk for a little while, and then asked me if I'd forgotten about the concert.

"The concert?"

"The Elsewhen show tonight." That was all he said. He didn't precede it with a *duh* and he didn't shake me by the shoulders or playfully slap me across the face for forgetting.

"I guess I must've, yeah."

"Oh."

We bought the tickets months ago—eons in college time— stood in line for them out in the cold the morning of the welcome-back party. Now it was the last week of the semester. Classes were either over or winding down, and the same could've been said of our friendship. Room selection was three weeks ago. Griff, with his lucky number 13, took a single on the third floor of the little, less-nice dorm down the street, because there was no one else he wanted to live with. The remaining singles were long gone by the time my 947 rolled around, as I knew they would be. I took a double by myself and by that point Griff didn't ask about trying to work something out with Housing.

"Well do you want to go?" He was fanning his flushed face with the tickets.

"I don't know. I guess you can have my ticket. Take whoever you want."

He stopped fanning. "Why do you have to be like that?"

"Like what?"

He sighed. "Fine, I'll take whoever I want." He put one ticket in the front pocket of his t-shirt, dark in the pits and sagging like too much skin over his thin chest, and threw the other one at me. It did a few curly loops in the air and came to rest against my shoe.

There was a silence between us that even punk rock filling the arena at a chest-pounding volume could not penetrate. Our tickets were general admission for the floor. We were twenty feet from the stage, on the edges of what was fast becoming a mosh pit. People kept stepping on my toes, bumping my shoulders, pressing against me. People in soaking wet shirts, in no shirts, in bone-white bras and bare flesh. Usually the idea of a crushing orgy of half-naked young men and women would be sexy, but not here and not now. I received an elbow in the ribs and I shoved the guy I assumed it belonged to. I expected him to retaliate; maybe even wanted him to—I was almost craving a fight. Instead he gave me a crazy-eyed grin and then shoved the guy standing next to him. Mosh dominoes.

I used the claustrophobia and the reeking strangers and my ringing ears to stoke a rage inside me. And when it was burning nice and hot I turned my eyes to Griff, who was hopping up and down beside me like a fucking pogo stick.

Was he *happy* in this place? Was he at home in this tight, smelly cacophony? Was this *him*? It was not me. We would never be compatible and we could never be together. There. Done. Finished. After all that, he wasn't even someone I wanted to be with! We were too different. Way too different. It was easier then, easier to know that fate and biology were the least of our problems. When all was said and done, I could barely even *stand* the guy.

Right?

The frontman of Elsewhen, shirtless with sleeve tattoos and wearing cut-off Dickies, stopped screaming into his microphone long enough to do a back-flip off a speaker.

Griff, his face flushed in the swirling colored lights, his hair damp, was mouthing something at me. Though he was only inches away, I couldn't hear him. I gave up after his second shout and returned my eyes to the stage. He cupped his fingers around my ear and screamed, "Are you having fun?" It was in the middle of the fourth or fifth song of the set. And after he'd said it, maybe a half-second later, the legs of some crowd-surfer went over us. I saw a black leather belt with metal studs. The crowd-surfer's black boot met the back of Griff's head. I heard the *thump* even over the music; maybe I felt it myself. His fingers tore away from my ear as he started to go down. I yelled but it made no sound. Not even I could hear it.

I had heard of people being trampled to death in crowds without anyone around them noticing, not until the crowd dispersed and a crushed body was discovered among the litter and footprints. I started to panic.

But Griff didn't go all the way down. He was supported by the tightness of the crowd—there was no empty space to slump into. I got my hands under his wet armpits and hoisted him to his feet. His hair had fallen down in front of his eyes and I couldn't immediately tell that they were open, but fluttering and dazed. He started to sink back down. No one noticed. I knew no amount of yelling or flailing was going to clear anyone away.

I kneeled down, taking a deep breath first as though I were going under water, and leaned against his legs so that he tipped forward over my shoulder. Then I stood up, locked my arm around the backs of his thighs and fought my way forward. His black Converse stuck out in front of us and mercilessly crunched against shoulders, chests and faces, parting us a path through the crowd. I felt his fingers squeeze my waist and then clutch my belt but he made no other movement.

The crowd thinned at the outskirts of the pit. I carried him to the back of the floor, waiting there a moment because I thought I would need to catch my breath. His shoelaces swung in front of me; colored lights played over his jeans. I adjusted my grip on his legs and then I carried him to the landing at the top of the first set of stairs, past rows of people standing on seats, just scenery—it was just me and Griff in this arena. He felt light. Maybe I just didn't want to ever put him down. I carried him up to the second landing and then out into the empty corridor that encircled the arena. I brought him to a soda machine and knelt down and, in a series of jerky movements, slid him off my shoulder and leaned him against it. The side of the machine dimpled. He promptly threw up in his lap.

I bought him an Elsewhen t-shirt, gray with blue letters, in a size that would actually fit him, and helped him change.

*

Griff turned down the Elsewhen and tapped the red dial behind the steering wheel. "Jetta needs gas," he said.

"You still have almost half a tank."

"It takes diesel," he said. "You can't find it everywhere so you have to get it where you find it."

"Ah."

We pulled into a Tedeschi's with a gas station and I watched him in the side mirror as he unscrewed the tank cap and filled his new car. He drummed his fingers on the charcoal roof.

I liked watching people pump gas. It felt almost intimate, a thing they didn't think about being observed at. Like watching someone brush their teeth—they get lost in themselves. He looked across the salt-white street, put his hair behind his ear, rubbed his nose between his forefinger and thumb. What was he thinking about, I wondered. About Beth? About packing up his new car and driving to Phoenix? About what highways he would take, what giant roadside balls of yarn and chocolate cows he would pose for photos with on the way?

When the nozzle clunked full he walked across the lot to the convenience store, pulling his wallet from his back pocket as he went. I leaned back on the headrest. I was glad I'd taken the afternoon off. For all the time he'd been at my house, we hadn't had much time alone together. It was easy—it was just starting to be easy.

But Phoenix loomed.

He got back in the car, emptied some change into the cupholder between the bucket seats. He tossed into my lap a package of Hostess Snoballs—pink, coconutty, almost alive the way a sea sponge is alive. I tore open the cellophane wrapper and held one out to him.

"Come to daddy," he said, coaxing it off the cardboard onto his palm. He pried off the coconut-and-marshmallow shell and ate the chocolate cupcake hidden underneath. He held the marshmallow, jiggling and quivering, in his open hand. "Isn't it almost arousing? It's practically begging me to fuck it."

"I knew you weren't completely straight," I said, biting into the other Snoball. "You're one of those cocosexuals, aren't you?"

"You caught me. Should we go have an awkward game of pool now?"

I laughed. He folded the marshmallow shell in half and crammed its entirety into his mouth. Pink strands of coconut poked out between his lips as he attempted to chew.

In Orleans we parked in the snow-packed lot of a little pub called Soundings. The walls inside were lined with old photos of fishermen, some in frames but most tacked up with push-pins; the bar was lined with old fishermen perched like gargoyles on wooden stools. All old men on the Cape looked like fishermen to me—they looked crusty, weathered, even if all they'd ever done was own a goldfish. Maybe it was the salt air.

A stereo behind the bar played Neil Young. Our waitress, a wide woman with gray-streaked hair pulled back in a ponytail, whose name-tag said Lois, brought beers to our booth while we looked at the menu. It was written out longhand and the prices were marked on little white stickers.

Griff took a swig of beer, swished it through his teeth like mouthwash, swallowed, licked foam from his lips. "Talked to my cousin Dave yesterday," he said.

"Oh yeah?" I rotated my glass slowly counter-clockwise on a napkin. "He buy his hot-tub yet?"

"Yeah, it was delivered."

"Cool."

"One of those ones with all the spouts and seats for like twenty people."

"I have a kiddie pool," I said, looking across at him, not even sure what I meant by it.

"A what?"

"You know, those plastic kiddie pools." I looked down at my glass. "It has pictures of starfish."

"And you use this for what?"

"Came with the house. Last summer I'd fill it up and sit out there and read."

"But it's not deep, right?"

"About like this." I held my hands a few inches apart.

Lois brought our burgers and then disappeared to find us a bottle of ketchup.

"Anyway," he said, banging the bottle against his palm, "the trip'll give me something to do, you know? I figure I can get out there pretty cheap."

One of the old guys at the bar put his hand on the shoulder of the guy sitting next to him. "Barney?" he said.

"It's something to do, all right," I said, returning my eyes from Barney to my plate. I ate a fry. It was good, had some kind of seasoning on it. Spicy.

"You know what?" Griff said, leaning forward a little, brushing his sleeve against a pickle. "You should come with me! What do you think? You can keep me company on the way out there and I'll buy you a plane ticket home. We could take our time, see the country. It'd be like that summer road trip we took in college." There was a glimmer in his eyes that made me want to say yes. I would've liked nothing more.

"But I have the store."

"Oh—right. Yeah."

He put the burger to his lips and was about to take a bite when there was a thud at the bar. The man named Barney had fallen backward, was lying on his back on the floor with one leg over the toppled stool.

Griff spun around. I got up fast without first sliding out of the booth—the edge of the table slammed my crotch. The ketchup bottle tipped over and rolled into Griff's lap. He absent-mindedly placed it back on the table.

The other men at the bar were scrambling into a group surrounding the one on the floor. One busied himself with uprighting the stool. The few other people in the pub were standing, some moving toward the bar, sneaking to it, almost, in a way that made clear they were only there to watch and wanted nothing to do with any blood.

"Is he OK?" I said to Griff.

"I think—don't you know CPR?"

"In health class!"

One of the old fishermen was kneeling with his hand on the guy's chest. He held his cheek over the guy's mouth, waited for a moment without moving. Griff and I got up and stood on the edge of what had become a semicircle around the sick man. The bartender was on the phone asking for an ambulance. When it seemed it was up to me alone to help the guy, Lois pushed through the circle and told everyone to step back. People parted and Griff and I were given a scenic view neither of us really wanted. Lois started pumping the man's chest, shapeless beneath his green plaid shirt, then breathing into his thin-lipped mouth. She did this for five minutes, maybe ten. Griff stood at my side, his arms folded, his fingers anxiously drumming on his elbow. I began to hear the distant but oh so reassuring wail of sirens.

But then, just like that, the old fisherman died.

His transition from living to dead was amazingly obvious maybe because it didn't happen everywhere at once. His lips were still alive even as his eyes were dead, and then his nose. It was like a curtain being pulled from his forehead down to the bottom of his white-stubbled chin.

"Barney," growled the guy kneeling beside him. He had a thick, phlegmy voice I suspected a good throat-clearing could do nothing to smooth. "Come on." He took Barney's liver-spotted hand and squeezed it white, whiter.

Lois kept doing CPR, now with her eyes mostly closed, until the paramedics came through the door. The man kneeling beside the old guy looked from Lois to these new men, the rescuers, with hesitation, with skepticism, as though unsure whether these strangers could help his friend better than their familiar waitress could.

"Let them do it, Stu," Lois said, and she stood up to let the paramedics take over. She smoothed her apron. Her chest heaving, she looked at Griff and me and said, glancing at the men on the floor, "Barney and Stu. Been friends since before television."

"You did good," Griff said as she pushed past us.

"He's dead, honey," she said without turning around. She went through a white swinging door in the back of the pub and that was the last we saw of her.

We went back to our booth and poked at our cold lunches and watched the paramedics bring the old fisherman's body out of the pub on an orange stretcher. There were diagnoses being bandied about by the patrons—heart attack, stroke. The ambulance pulled out of the parking lot with its lights off.

"Your food's on the house, folks," the bartender said, wiping his forehead with the back of his hand. Stu returned to his stool and laid his head on his arms folded across the bar. The bartender filled a glass and pushed it against the man's elbow, but he didn't seem to notice.

"A kiddie pool, huh?" Griff said, reaching for his vest.

"I used to sit in it and read."

"That sounds nice."

He left Lois a forty-three dollar tip. It was everything he had in his wallet.

***

Five days after the Elsewhen show and one day after my ears finally stopped ringing, I sat down on the bed—my bed, at least until my RA arrived to check me out. It was empty now, bare green fireproof vinyl. The room looked strange split down the middle this way. It wasn't bare the way it had been when we arrived last September. Griff hadn't packed yet and his stuff was still there—his posters (always the items that left the most noticeable absence) still hung off-kilter on the walls. Only I was missing from it now, as though I'd been cut out with a scalpel.

I felt the feeling of leaving, of *leaving*. That low sadness, that weight in my chest. That feeling that if I could only just fully hyperventilate it would relieve some of the ache. I took my keys off my keychain and squeezed them until my knuckles turned white.

The RA knocked once, came in, apologized for being late.

"That's OK," I told her.

With quick glances—this exercise was a formality—she examined my furniture to make sure I hadn't wrecked anything. I filled out a mail-forwarding card and then locked the door for the last time. She held a little yellow envelope squeezed open like a frog's mouth and I dropped my keys inside.

"You're free now," she told me, tucking my key envelope and the forms into a manila folder.

"We'll see."

She gave me a funny look. We left my suite and she continued down the hall to the next one. "Have a good summer," she said before opening the other door.

"You too."

I pressed the button for the elevator, feeling caught between wanting it to come fast and wanting it to get stuck so I'd be forced stay a little longer. I felt caught between everything. Part of me wanted to hide and hole up for the summer in some dusty, forgotten corner of the dorm. Another part couldn't get away from here—away from Griff—fast enough. I thought I'd almost made it—I was almost to my parents' car. He'd been out all morning. I thought I could sneak away without seeing him. And then the elevator door opened and he stepped toward me. Griff.

"Oh, hey," he said. He had on shorts and a white long-sleeve t-shirt rolled up to his elbows.

"Hey." It felt almost impossible to say anything at all to him now. How had things degenerated so quickly? We'd talked the night before; it was chilly, but we'd talked.

"I saw your parents outside," he said, but it sounded like a question.

"Yeah. I'm leaving."

"*Leaving* leaving?" When I nodded he added, "I thought your check-out wasn't until this afternoon?"

I looked right into his eyes and told him that my parents happened to come early.

"And you're all checked out and everything already?" The elevator door closed behind him. I reached past him and pushed the button again.

"Yeah."

"You should've called me. I would've come back and helped move your stuff."

"It's OK."

"..."

"..."

"Huh." He looked at his hands, pushed his sleeves up again. "Then this is it."

I nodded.

"So I'll see you around?"

He started to step closer, I thought, to hug me—but then he put out his hand instead. It was warm, dry. I left it moist.

"I'll be around," I said.

"If your freshman is annoying, or smells, or anything, you're welcome to sleep on my floor any time."

I nodded again. "Thanks."

The elevator door opened for the second time. I started to get on, but for a short eternity I froze with one foot in the elevator and one foot in the hall, knowing I should apologize, should explain myself, should say goodbye, should say all that and more. But I didn't. I didn't. I stepped all the way on. I jabbed the door-close button again and again with my thumb—not even the lobby button, the door-close button.

He glared at me through the narrowing gap. "You were just going to leave, weren't you? Your parents weren't early. You weren't even going to say goodbye."

His eyes looked bigger than usual. They were the last part of him I saw. The door clanged shut and the elevator hung unmoving in the shaft. At any moment either of us could push the button and the doors would spring open again and we'd have a second chance, a second chance for all the things I knew should be said and done. My finger hovered in front of the button. And then there was a thump on the door and on the other side Griff said, softly but as clear as if he'd whispered it in my ear, "Fuck you, Vince."

I descended.

The next time I saw him in person was on graduation day.

*

We drove up the Cape Cod coast, taking the long way when we could, the scenic routes on little roads, but even as the new Jetta ambled along it seemed Griff had some destination in mind for us. Maybe he had all along.

He drove to the tip of Provincetown, where the road ended at the mouth of an unplowed beach parking lot, between snowy dunes that rose high on both sides of the little gray car. We idled there for a minute, exhaust forming a cloud in the windless trench.

I looked out the window. It seemed we were encased in white, a misty blank place between two worlds. "I guess this is as far as we can go."

"Feel like taking a walk?" he said.

"Um... OK, sure."

He turned off the car and got out; I grabbed my gloves and got out too.

"What do you think's on the other side of this dune?"

"I don't know," I said. "Beach?"

"Let's check it out. I want to see some waves."

We scrambled on all fours up the steep snow and sand slope of the dune. Little clumps of snow rolled past us, growing into snowballs on their way down to the road. Wind rushed across the top of the dune, blowing off wisps of snow like steam, making the dune look at once very hot and very cold.

"Now how far can we go?" Griff said from the top of the dune, his arms spread for balance like a tightrope walker. Down and across the beach was the ocean, white and frothy at first, and then, farther out, a misty black.

"That lighthouse down there?" I said, pointing to the small building on the end of the peninsula, three-quarters of a mile away. Long Point. The tip of North America, reaching out as a finger into the gray Atlantic.

"Let's do it."

We slid down the other side of the dune and were on the beach. After smacking snow off our clothes we walked along the crest of the waves, stepping over clumps of frozen seaweed and balls of icy sand. The wind had swept most of the snow off the beach; it lay in razor-sharp drifts along the dunes, bristles of yellowed beach grass sticking out like ancient hair.

Griff walked with his hands in his vest pockets, his hair slapping his cheeks. The lighthouse was fixed in front of us far down the beach.

"Do you think those old guys, Barney and Stu, do you think they were together?" he said, raising his voice to compete with the crashing waves.

"Depends on what you mean by together. I think probably they were just old friends."

"Lifebuddies?" he said with a smile.

"Maybe."

"I wonder how they met."

"Probably some freak thing that almost didn't happen," I said. "I bet they crashed their boats into each other or something."

He laughed and wiped snow off his knees. "It used to bother me how precarious the start of our friendship was," he said. "Like how if anything had been different it never would've happened. You know? If I hadn't transferred to Shuster. If we hadn't been in that same lit class..."

"Yeah, but nothing happens without a million pieces falling into place beforehand."

"I guess." He kicked a stone and watched it splash into the waves ahead of us, leaving a circle of white bubbles on the surface for a second before the wave rolled over on itself. "But even then, none of the pieces would've mattered if you were straight. If you didn't think I was cute in that class we had—if you hadn't been *capable* of thinking that—we never would've become friends."

"All I did was ask you to room, Griff. If I was straight I still may have. There was nobody else."

"You wouldn't have," he said with perfect certainty and shook his head. Of course I knew it was true too. He kicked a piece of driftwood and then stepped over it and we kept walking. "You didn't know me at all. If you hadn't had a crush on me, one stranger would've been as good as another."

"So it was just luck? Me, I mean. So I could meet you?" It was hard to walk in the sand and I pushed myself to keep up with him, to stay at his side. He seemed now both vulnerable and powerful, as though I could knock him over with the slightest shove if only I could catch up to him. He looked up at the lighthouse again and his face was determined.

"I just mean, I know how sometimes you like get overwhelmed by being the way you are, Vince. But look at what we both owe it. I'm thankful for it, even if you're not."

Now we had come to the lighthouse. It towered above us and cut the wind like a big rock in a big stream. It wasn't the kind of lighthouse anyone lived in; rather it was a beacon made up to look like one, really just a rotating spotlight in fancy packaging. Icicles stuck out from it horizontally, defying gravity thanks to the strong ocean breeze. In the distance on our left, across the bay, the Pilgrim's Monument rose into the sky, lights flashing on its turreted top.

For a long time we stood shoulder to shoulder watching the waves.

"It's getting late," I said finally, in a voice that earlier would've been overpowered by the wind, but here in the shelter of the lighthouse was only quiet.

"Yeah." He turned away but then turned back quickly. "Hey Vince—"

Griff grabbed the collar of my coat and pulled me up and toward him, my heels lifting out of the sand. I felt him recoil, almost imperceptibly, when his lips met the stubble surrounding my own. White breath from his nose warmed my face, the warmest warmth I ever felt. He tasted like the pub's spicy fries. It lasted sixteen seconds.

The first second was the best one of my life. I wasn't surprised that this was happening—it's hard to be surprised by something you've imagined for so long. The moment, the one chance I'd longed for, had arrived. I hadn't had to kiss him at all. All along I'd only had to wait for him to kiss me.

The second, I felt his tongue push against my tongue, his nose move against my nose. He wanted this. I pulled off my glove and put my hand on his cheek, felt his stubble, felt his jaw, touched his ear and held the back of his neck, his hair thick in my palm.

The third second lasted forever and then was gone. It held within it a whole lifetime I knew now would actually come true for us. All I ever had to do was wait.

But the eleventh second, Griff opened his eyes.

The thirteenth, I lowered my hand.

The sixteenth, I realized that none of this would ever happen. That the lifetime I imagined was never meant to be. No kiss could change that.

We parted and he was looking at me, his eyes green with flecks of brown, quiet and sleepy like midnight, the weariness of midnight. He stepped back and looked at the sand. He licked his lips, laughed once, one single huff, and shook his head.

"My life would be so much easier if I wanted to do that again," he said. He hit the side of his thigh with his fist. "You know that? Why the *fuck* can't I just want to do that again?"

"Mine would be so much easier if I didn't." I felt my eyes well up and this time I made no effort to keep them from overflowing.

He turned and looked out at the black waves. The clouds on the horizon were turning pink. "Do you know that's really why I came to see you, Vince? To do that?"

I didn't understand. What had just happened was something I'd imagined for years—imagined and dreamed about and even cried for. Something I wanted back when it was a joke to everyone else. Something I'd wanted so badly it ended us. I always thought that all I needed was one kiss to get Griff to love me— Never in a million years did I think he'd be the one to kiss me.

When I didn't respond he turned back and looked at me, as though he thought I might've sneaked away.

"When things flamed out with Beth and I was looking for a place to go, when I felt so scared and out of sorts, all I could think about was how comfortable and good I used to feel with you that year, you know? And how everyone said we were lifebuddies. And how I knew you loved me."

"You knew—?"

"Of course, Vince. Of course I knew. That's part of why I was so confused about why you stopped being my friend. How could you love me and just cast me aside like that?"

"Because one-sided love hurts, Griff."

"You never stopped to think that I loved you too!" These words were like a lightning bolt to my heart, resuscitating all my hopes. But then he added, in a low voice as though it had been his great failure, "But just not in the same way."

"Oh."

"But I started to wonder if it *could* be the same way. If I could just somehow feel something *more*. If I could just— I don't know."

"…"

"I don't know, Vince. *Be* with you!" There was a kind of hurt in his eyes I hadn't ever seen before, but it was brief, and went away. A tear made a cold line down my cheek. He put his hand on my shoulder. "Dating was so easy before I met you, you know that? I had a blank slate. No expectations. I wanted to marry every girl I met. But the way you know me, the way we get along— What I've been looking for is a girl who can meet the standard of Vince. But I need to start dealing with the idea that I won't find one. That my," he paused, "shit, that my other half is a *dude*. That my soulmate is not going to be the woman of my dreams, but is my best friend. And the distance between those two things is the distance I'll unfortunately always have."

I squatted down, rested my butt on the backs of my heels, ran my fingers through the stiff gray sand. "I don't know why you're telling me this." My lips felt cold now without his against them.

"Because I'm *sorry*, Vince. OK? I'm sorry that I can't be everything you want me to be for you. It *kills* me that I can't. And it kills me too because I feel like I'm *missing out* on you, on this ready-made happiness that's just standing there waiting for me. If one tiny switch inside me had flipped the other way twenty-five years ago, I'd be home, with you, and we'd be happy—and everything would be fine." He lifted his foot, rested it on my thigh for a second and let it slide off, leaving a smeared waffle imprint of sand on my jeans. "Vince, do you know how *lucky* you are? You have no boundaries. No limits on who you can be with and love."

"I do have limits. I can't be with *you*, Griffin. Your limits are mine."

"I know." He said it hard, harsh. "But we've tried it now. We've tried it. I love you but when I kiss you I feel nothing."

"How is that *possible*?"

"It just is, Vince. It's just the way I'm wired. You need to believe it."

"I never have. Griff— I always thought that if only I could kiss you or something, everything would fall into place for you."

"That's what I was hoping too."

"OK."

"It didn't happen."

"... OK. I know."

"So you need to quit pining for me. And I need to quit *trying* to pine for you. But I know something now: I'm done agonizing about finding this soulmate I've been looking so hard for, because you know what? It's found, Vince. It's *you*."

"Me. And what does that mean for us?"

He was quiet for a little while, watching the waves. Maybe those were tears on his cheeks; maybe it was just the salt air stinging his eyes. "It means we have some adventures ahead of us. It means the post-college void is a lot less scary."

"OK."

"It means everyone else can get a second look now that we don't have to worry about finding the One anymore."

I stood up, wiped his footprint off my leg. "And you're OK with that? With everyone else only ever being second place? With marrying someone who only gets the silver medal?"

"Yeah," he said. "Yeah, I am. Actually it sounds really nice. It sounds really easy. It's so much less pressure. Silver can be pretty great," he added. "Silver is a happy color."

And with that, he reached out and touched the flaking white paint on the side of the lighthouse, smiled, and started walking in the direction of the car.

As we walked back along the beach the lighthouse light came on behind us, making the sound of a meteor entering the atmosphere. Ahead of us our two long shadows stretched across the sand, intermingling, but never quite becoming one.

We said very little on our drive back from Provincetown, but it was a different, easier silence than a lot of the silences we'd shared in the past. It was there not because we were avoiding something, but rather because we'd said everything there was to say.

He drove slow and looked around, taking in the sites of Cape Cod as they passed by, the clam shacks and mini-golf places, sometimes with a little smile on his face. He looked unburdened now.

Still my lips felt different where his had been and I knew they probably always would. Every so often, when he wasn't looking, I'd touch them, experimentally, with my fingers, reminding myself of the feel of his mouth against mine, reminding myself that I was now and would forever be a person Griffin Dean had kissed—had *wanted* to kiss, had cared enough about to kiss. It had not done the things I'd always expected such a kiss would do. It hadn't changed Griff. But it changed me. It brought with it an end, as well as the knowledge that I was not pitiful; I was not some silly fag pining for an oblivious straightboy all these years. It had been mutual all along. Different, yes, but mutual. That knowledge felt like a gift. Like a deep breath to end years of gasping.

"I'm sure going to be doing a lot of driving in the next week or so," he said.

"Yeah." I didn't like to imagine him on the road again. I wanted time to see what could become of this new us. "You are."

"I need to get my shit packed tonight."

"I'll help you."

"We'll get drunk."

"Deal."

AND FRIDAY

Morning light shined in through the gap in my bedroom curtains and around me the edges of the bed loomed empty and cold. I pulled my arms and legs together in the middle under the sheets and blankets and squeezed my eyes shut tight against the growing sunlight, listening to the sounds of Griff moving around my house—savoring them. Every once in a while the front door would open and close.

I should be up, I knew, should be helping him pack his car, but I couldn't quite get myself out of bed.

I'd barely slept. All through the night I'd been debating in my mind, weighing pros and cons of something I'd felt in the air for days, maybe from the first glimpse of his snowy silhouette coming up my street. I wanted to ask him to stay. To live here. Now that I knew about the silver medal, about the happy color, I thought being roommates again would work. I knew he'd say yes, too, would jump at the chance to stay. And that's what kept me from asking. If we ever lived together again it needed to be the best option for both of us, not just a defensive huddle against the post-college void. It wasn't quite time. I knew there were still things he needed to do.

So instead I imagined into the future, to when the time was right, to when the post-college void was conquered. I imagined him affixing a small satellite dish to the sand-colored siding of my house while I watched from the starfish-spotted kiddie pool in the back yard. *Is this straight?* he would ask, and then with a smirk he would ask what I knew about being straight.

I imagined him painting his bedroom and the paint spilling over into the hall and the living room until my entire house was brightened and made new. The living room would be painted the exhilaration of the year's first snow, the kitchen the color of high-fiving an old friend.

I imagined him at last unleashing his inheritance and buying Golden Age from Simon when Patti finally convinced him to move to Nantucket. I imagined Griff and me as partners there. *There's enough superheroes in here already*, he would say. *We need some spaceships!*

I imagined him, five summers later, leaving my house to start a family in a nearby house of his own, with the beautiful sister of our young customer Abe.

I imagined him at my wedding, proudly toasting me and my beloved. Afterward he would jump in a pile of snow in his tux and emerge with a snowball, which he'd bite into and chew. I imagined him pressing his cold lips against my cheek. *Slushy-flavored kisses for my Vince*, he would say. I would laugh and wipe it away and tell him he couldn't do that anymore, I was a married man now. *I can always do that*, he would tell me. And of course he'd be right.

I imagined far forward, past weddings and births and anniversaries and funerals. Past failure and success, past happiness and pain, past all the colors of a lifetime, of two lifetimes. I imagined Griff and me as old men, our arthritic fingers hooked through the green links of a fence, watching youthful, middle-aged women play tennis.

All of that would come in time, all of those things, just like how I imagined them. But now—now there was a knock on my bedroom door, and Griff was there.

"Vince?" The door squeaked open a few inches and he peered in. "You awake?"

"Yup." I leaned up on my elbow. "Just daydreaming."

He opened the door the rest of the way and leaned in, one hand still on the knob. "I'm about ready to hit the road." He jerked a thumb behind him.

"Like now?"

"Car's running."

"OK. Let me put some clothes on."

It was cold out, sunny but cold. I blew into my hands and rubbed them together, clamped them under my armpits. Beneath my shoes the purple shells of my driveway crunched amid ice and snow. Griff closed the passenger-side door after stowing his backpack on the front seat. In the back were the boxes of stuff we liberated from Beth's. Exhaust poured from the humming car like breath.

"It's freezing out," I said. "Where's your jacket?"

"Bah. Too bulky for driving. It's in there somewhere." He came around, dragging his hand across the hood. "Can you believe I'm really doing this?"

"Sure I can."

He had a glad smile. "I've wanted to drive cross-country ever since we did that little road trip during college. Almost did it a few times. Now here I am."

"Now here you are. Actually doing it."

More serious now, he said, "I'm glad I came, Vince."

"Me too."

I grabbed him and hugged him, hard, because I could. There was something about him, some part of him now, that was mine. I could let him be mine, because there was a part of him, however wishful, that wanted it that way too.

"Oh, I almost forgot." He reached back and pulled a key from his pocket. "Here's this back."

"Keep it," I said, pushing his hand away. "I like to know you have it, for if you ever need it. I expect you to need it."

"But you might want to give it to Zane."

"I can make another one for Zane."

He nodded, smiled, put the key back in his pocket. "So then I'm off."

"You're off. Do you know where you're headed?"

"I have a pretty good idea, yeah."

"You'll figure it out," I told him. "Write me?"

"Of course."

"Maybe I'll start saving up for a computer. So we can do email."

"Haha! Vince! You're evolving."

"Shut up."

"You shut up." He pulled open the door and stood with one leg in the car. He was looking at my house.

"Hey Griff?" When he looked over I straightened up a little, looked down at my hands; it felt like I should've been holding a pair of folded glasses—a disguise I no longer needed. "There's something I want to tell you."

"Sure."

"When you kissed me? It was the best I've ever had."

He blushed a little and looked down at the car seat.

"And I'll never forget it."

He nodded, pursed his lips. "You don't have to forget it. You also don't have to wonder anymore. Neither do I."

I knew now that at the lighthouse we went as far as we could ever go, Griff and me. Like a pendulum, we'd been to both extremes, from years of nothing to sixteen seconds of everything. And now we were coming back to the middle, at last finding the place where we hung without force.

He got in the car and closed the door. The window went down. "I used up the last of the milk this morning."

"I'll get more."

He winked. The window went up.

He backed out of my driveway onto the narrow street, waved at me, and drove away.

I stood watching the empty street for a while, until I became aware that it had been too long, and then I went and sat down on the porch.

And in my arms and my chest I could still feel Griff against me.

Could still feel his arms, which were thinner than I'd expected they would feel; could still feel his shoulder blades, which were sharper—he was in fact skinnier than I always imagined him. In reality he smelled like deodorant and Johnson's baby shampoo and jeans that needed a wash. In real life his cheeks were rough, his hair soft. That's what he felt like—that's what he was. The final hug lasted. I could remember. And maybe remembering was letting go.

I sat for a while longer until something in the yard caught my eye, something that had been buried by the storm and now was emerging. It was blue and shiny—my Shuster mug. I walked over and picked it up, then went back in the house to call Zane.

EPILOGUE
Five Months Later

Zane smelled good, warm and like sleep, and when at last I pulled myself out of bed, I stood beside it for a minute, watching him sleep in the silver morning light. Watching him sleep was like watching Griff pump gasoline, like watching Melanie brush her teeth.

Often when I was with Zane I thought of Melanie, of her painting in my room, of her lilac smell and the freckles across her chest. I thought of Andy too, of the way he laughed that night in the tent, wrapping his sleeping bag around his dripping body to keep Farley away. And of course I thought of Griff, of those mornings last winter when I woke up with him beside me, his joshua tree moving with his breath. I have learned, though, that memories aren't things that have to pile up and overwhelm you. They're just colors, like Griff's colors, that shade all the new things you feel.

Zane opened his eyes, closed them again. I pulled on a t-shirt and stepped into some flip-flops.

According to the radio it was supposed to hit ninety today. The sun was bright already—it streamed into the kitchen and lit up the hall and it sparkled against the shiny aluminum frame of a backpack that lay on my living room floor.

When I saw it I gasped and I turned on my heels, nearly tripping out of my flip-flops, and went to the spare bedroom, which I discovered was no longer spare, and which I knew then would not be spare again for years to come. Griff was on the bed he'd bought during the winter, on top of the covers, face-down and fully clothed, as though he'd come out of the sky and crash-landed here.

"What!" I exclaimed.

He rolled over, rubbed his eyes, groaned, shaded them from the golden sunlight that flooded through the window. Then he grinned. "I would've called first," he said, "if you had a phone."

"I have a phone," I said, and tackled him.

SPECIAL THANKS

To Chris, my love, for being my gold. To Maggie Locher for her endless encouragement and for letting me ramble to her about Vince and Griff for the past million years. To Tom Hardej for his editorial prowess and for slaying the dragon that was this book's synopsis. To Heather Allison, of course. To Aaron Tieger for his support. To my brother Jake for his graphic design advice. To all my awesome readers for all their wonderful messages. And most of all to my parents for, among other things, sending me to Emerson, where all the magic happened.

ABOUT THE AUTHOR

Ben Monopoli lives in Boston with his husband, Chris.